PERISH

in the

PALM

a Sunny Meadows Mystery

by
Kari Lee Townsend

This is a work of fiction. Names, characters, places, brands, media, and incidents are either the product of the author's imagination or are used fictitiously, and any resemblance to actual persons, living or dead, business establishments, events, or locales is entirely coincidental.

For more information, please direct your correspondence to:
The Story Vault
c/o Marketing Department
364 Patteson Drive, #228
Morgantown, WV 26505

Perish in the Palm
Copyright © 2015 by Kari Lee Townsend
All rights reserved.

www.karileetownsend.com/

ISBN-13: 978-1512081947
ISBN-10: 1512081949

Cover Design by Kelly Crimi
Interior Book Design by Bob Houston eBook Formatting

Published by The Story Vault
Website: www.thestoryvault.com

DEDICATION

To all of my children: Brandon, Josh, Matt & Emily.
Thank you for keeping life interesting and fun.
All I do, I do for you.

ACKNOWLEDGEMENTS

As always to my amazing husband, Brian. You make life a joy. And to the rest of my family: the Harmons, the Russos and the Townsends. And to my critique partner, Barbara Witek, who truly is a goddess! And last but never least, to my agent Christine Witthohn of Book Cents Literary Agency.

Chapter 1

"You're doing it wrong," my mother said, as she looked over my shoulder and inspected my work on a Friday afternoon in October. The leaves had started to turn brilliant shades of orange and red and gold, but the temperatures had risen to unseasonably mild.

It was the day before my best friend Joanne Burnham's wedding. Joanne was marrying our local carpenter, Cole West, on the outskirts of town at Divine Inspiration—a charming inn on Inspiration Lake. I was the maid of honor, but my mother and Jo had bonded since the day she'd met her, so of course Jo had invited her to the wedding.

Vivian Meadows was a highly respected lawyer back in New York City and the queen of high society. She was as chic as she was sharp, but here in the small, quaint, old-fashioned, upstate New York town of Divinity, she was simply a big ole' pain in my behind. Being miles away didn't stop her from interfering. She had pretty much given her input on every possible task that had been assigned to me; and frankly, I'd had enough.

I finished tying a red silk bow to an old-fashioned oil lantern flanking the aisle in the center of the rows of chairs beneath the wedding tent, then stood and faced her. Nothing I did would meet her high expectations about everything in life, so I ignored her comment. "Hello, Mother. Did you have a nice flight?" The city was only around a four hour drive from Divinity, but my parents wouldn't dream of getting behind the wheel. In fact, they didn't even own a car. No need to where they lived.

She waved off my question with her immaculate manicured hand and then patted her chicly styled blond hair. It was a perfect complement to her tailored pale pink suit. "Trust me, darling, there's nothing nice about flying these days. Your father and I should just move here since you insist on staying in this *lovely* little town. Life would be so much easier if we were close by."

My jaw fell open and stomach flipped as acid churned, making me nauseous. If I didn't know better, I would swear my eyes were popping right out of their sockets no matter how hard I tried to hide my anxiety.

"Relax, darling." She arched a golden blond brow, knowing me too well. "I'm kidding." She bent down and retied the bow I had just fixed, even though there wasn't a thing wrong with it.

I blew out the air in my lungs, trying to be discreet, but I was certain my make-up free fair cheeks were blazing red. "Oh, I, well…." I adjusted my burnt orange flowy skirt and cream colored peasant blouse, then curled my bare toes in the ends of my black flats. This was about as dressed up as I got.

"Sylvia speechless. Will wonders never cease?" She stood and faced me once more, smoothing her hands over non-existent wrinkles.

I snapped my mouth closed, stilled my fidgety fingers, and said through a stiff smile, "It's Sunshine now, Mother. Or Sunny if you prefer."

"What I would prefer is that you hadn't changed your name in the first place. You are our only child. Your father and I worked hard to come up with that name. We even waited until you were born to pick something that fit."

Epic fail, I wanted to say. Instead I counted to ten and relaxed my features. "And I appreciate that, but the truth is, that name didn't fit me any more than living in the city did. I wish you could understand that."

She looked down at her hands for a moment. "I'm trying," she finally said in a rare moment of honest vulnerability.

I blinked and then felt an actual genuine smile blossom across my face. "I can see that, Mom. And for the record, I'm trying too."

She sniffed, then straightened quickly, back to her usual self. "Well, dear, I suggest you try harder. These bows are all wrong." She knelt down and redid another perfect red bow on the lantern across the aisle. The rows of white chairs were covered with satin, leading to a gorgeous archway encased in roses. Beyond that was a beautiful white reception tent adorned with twinkling lights with crystal chandeliers hanging from beneath.

And she's back, I thought. "Where's Dad?" I stepped out from under the tent before my mood was ruined completely.

Donald Meadows was a world renowned cardiologist and king of his domain. He had gray-streaked perfectly coiffed brown hair, was highly respected among his peers, and had an impeccable reputation. The only blemish on his bio was having a daughter who made a living as a fortune teller. He didn't believe I was psychic any more than my mother did, but at least he had come around to admitting there were things that had happened even he couldn't explain.

"Oh, he's around here somewhere. Probably talking to Detective Stone, making sure you're not in any more trouble these days."

First our local librarian had been murdered, and I had been accused of the crime. Then the detective's ex-girlfriend had been killed, and he had been accused of murder. And finally the local baker had been murdered while my grandmother and her arch nemesis had been the prime suspects. I couldn't really blame my parents for worrying. I hadn't even lived here a year, yet a crime spree seemed to follow me, making it hard to win this small town over. But everything had died down, and even the mayor was on my side. He was a huge fan of psychics. My business had picked up, and I had a boyfriend. Life was good.

Sort of.

My gaze shot over to the back deck of the Inn, and sure enough my father stood in deep conversation with said boyfriend.

"That can't be good," I muttered.

I took in Mitch's ink black hair, dark brows and eyes, slightly crooked nose, and long jagged scar that ran across his square whiskered jaw. He was so ruggedly big and strong. Not handsome per se, but captivating and mesmerizing. All I had wanted was for Mitch to ask me out on a real date, and instead he'd asked me to marry him.

Mitch was an all or nothing sort of guy. Once he made up his mind about something, he went after it full throttle, consequences be damned. I'd convinced him to give living together a try first, but with Granny Gert and my cat Morty underfoot, I was afraid the honeymoon phase of our brand new relationship would be over before it had even gotten started.

"Trouble in paradise already?" My mother's questioning tone broke through my thoughts. She sounded concerned. My parents were fond of Mitch and worried I wouldn't find anyone else who would accept my "uniqueness." He wasn't exactly a true believer, but I knew he cared about me a lot. After almost losing him, I'd come to realize his belief in my abilities wasn't as important to me as I had once thought.

"Not trouble exactly, just not what I was hoping for when I asked him to move in with me," I admitted.

"Not everything in life is sunshine and flowers, dear. Your father and I are no exception." My parents might drive me nuts, but I knew they loved me, and they truly adored each other. I envied what they had and couldn't help wanting that for myself.

"I'm not expecting sunshine and flowers, but I certainly didn't expect storms and thorns, either. After the mischief Morty and Mitch caused with losing Cole's heirloom wedding rings a while back, they have called a truce of sorts, but it hasn't been easy. And Granny Gert is always underfoot, trying to take care of everyone. Mitch and I don't have *any* time alone." I blew out a breath. "Maybe moving in together wasn't such a good idea."

"Don't even get me started on that demon cat of yours." My mother shuddered.

"Mom, please don't start." I rubbed my temples, easing the headache that nagged me whenever my parents were in town.

"I'm just saying if you're ever going to get married and give me grandbabies, you might have to make some compromises."

"I don't know if marriage is in our future, but compromising shouldn't have to mean choosing between them." I huffed out a frustrated breath.

Morty was a big beautiful mysterious white cat with jet black eyes and my kindred spirit. He knew what it was like to be different and alone. He had come with the ancient Victorian house I'd bought and nicknamed Vicky. Everyone in town thought the old place was haunted, but I'd quickly surmised the cat was the guilty culprit of scaring people away. He moved lightning fast and seemed to appear out of nowhere. I never saw him eat or sleep either, making me wonder if he was immortal, hence the name Morty. He didn't like most people, but for some reason, he'd let me stay. I was more *his* than he was mine, and we both knew it.

That didn't mean he had the right to misbehave and put a claw in my love life.

"As far as your grandmother goes, she can always come back to the city with your father and me. You and Detective Stone need your space."

"I couldn't do that to her. She loves it here, and flirting with Captain Walker keeps her young."

"Young and scandalous." My mother sniffed, making her pinched nose look even more narrow. "Why, the man is young enough to be her son."

"He's in his sixties and she's in her seventies. That isn't that much of a difference. Besides, it's harmless and it makes her happy. I haven't seen her this happy since Grandpa Frank died."

"It's a sin, I tell you," my mother hissed. "Speak of the devil." She shook her head and tsked as she watched Granny Gert flounce over to the captain, who had joined Mitch and my father, and offer them all a cookie.

The rehearsal was only for the wedding party and people who were helping out. Granny had invited Captain Walker as her date. She was an attractive woman with snow white hair and snappy brown eyes. She was dressed in a classy, pretty, floral dress, but that didn't stop her from wearing her usual ruffled apron made from old flour sacks with her ever ready wooden spoon sticking out of the pocket. Granny held onto and reused everything, firmly believing in *waste not want not*. No doubt she'd taken over the inn's kitchen, insisting on baking cookies for the rehearsal dinner party.

According to Granny, there was a cookie for everything.

Peirce Theodore, the tall thin innkeeper with a spotless white suit and slicked-back sandy blond hair, came out onto the back deck, looking like something right out of The Great Gatsby. He frowned at Granny serving cookies before dinner from her orange pumpkin cookie jar—she swore that jar was the secret—and then he motioned everyone inside.

His gaze swept the grounds for any stragglers, stopping when it fell on us. He nodded at me then stuck his nose in the air and ignored my mother. The entire town knew they didn't get along. While she adored his inn, she despised him and constantly criticized him publicly over the way he ran it.

Four and a half stars out of five wasn't good enough for her.

My mother harrumphed. "Did you see that?"

"Mother, be nice for Cole and Jo's sake."

"Oh, don't you worry, I'll be nice. But mark my words, I'll have the last laugh. See if I don't. One way or another, I'll take that man down a peg or two and teach him a lesson he won't soon forget."

***

"You have to do something now!" Jo stood beside me at the dining room table inside the inn. She was a tall, buxom, burgundy haired woman in a forest green dress. Her hair was swept up into a fancy do, but her ladylike appearance wasn't fooling anyone. A warrior lurked beneath and was ready to pounce on anyone who ruined her day. "They've argued over every course so far," she continued. "I can't take it anymore. And the chef, Pierre Desjardins, is ready to quit. What am I supposed to do if he quits? Who will cook the wedding meal tomorrow?"

"You're the one who invited her," I pointed out, tossing my hands up.

"*You're* her daughter," she snapped back, poking me in the shoulder. "And my maid of honor, might *I* point out."

A crash came from the kitchen, followed by a string of angry French. Sally Clark the crisply starched elderly maid went flying by, her gray dress fluttering behind her and her feather duster dropping tiny bits of feathers with every rapid step.

I sighed. "Well, I'm stuffed." I stood and looked at the wedding party, Jo's family, Cole's family, my family, Father Moody and Captain Walker. Pretty much everyone except for Peirce Theodore and my mother, of course, because they were too busy causing all this chaos. "Why don't we retreat to the living room for the evening's entertainment?" I gestured toward the other room, coming up with an idea.

Everyone stood and gladly made their way to the living room, the relief in the air evident.

Jo grabbed my arm, looking panicked. "Entertainment? But we didn't book any entertainment for tonight."

"Lucky for you I know a fortune teller, and I hear she's pretty good." I winked.

She wilted, looking ready to cry. "Thank you."

"You're welcome. I've got the guests. You handle the kitchen."

"Oh, I'll handle it all right." She whirled around and marched away, looking like a fiery redheaded Amazon Warrior Queen. My mother wasn't intimidated by many people, but she hadn't seen Joanne Burnham truly angry.

Now, *that* would be entertaining.

I walked into the contemporary living room with its elegant furniture and classy accessories to a crowd of curious people. Stage fright didn't usually hit me, but then again the people who came to see me were believers and the sessions were private. This group looked more than skeptical.

What was I thinking? I didn't have any supplies with me. I was psychic, but I used fortune-telling tools to help me see the past as well as the future. My visions always came true, though sometimes there were a few bumps along the way to the truth. Usually I let the person's aura dictate which tool would be best for reading them. I always got a gut feeling when I held their hands.

Thinking of hands gave me an idea, and suddenly I knew exactly what I was going to do, no supplies necessary. I smiled and rubbed my palms together, ready to get this show on the road. "Okay, folks. Who's ready for a little palm reading?"

No one spoke.

Many looked excited yet hesitant, and still no one spoke. I didn't dare look at Mitch—not up to him publicly acknowledging he was a non-believer—and I knew Cole was too stressed-out. I met Captain Walker's eyes, but he turned his gaze to the floor. I knew he was a believer, but I also knew he wasn't comfortable with being in the spotlight. Granny Gert was flapping her arms excitedly like the resident swans in our pond, but everyone would think the reading was fixed if I chose her. For that same reason, I couldn't read Sean or Zoe either. I really needed a guest I wasn't that close to.

Just then, Jo walked into the room with a no-nonsense, mess-with-me-and-you're-dead expression on her face, followed by a red-faced Vivian Meadows and a clearly flustered Peirce Theodore.

"Mr. Theodore, you're just the person I was looking for." I beamed, relief surging through all the lines in my entire being. I was banking on there being no way he could say no. Even I was afraid of Jo. "Since you're the head of this fine establishment and you always set a good example, I thought it only fitting you be the first volunteer. What do you say we show these folks how it's done?"

He narrowed his eyes a fraction. "How what's done?"

"Why, palm reading, of course."

He stood a little straighter. "I don't really think that's a good idea…." His voice trailed off as Jo sent him an impressive evil eye. He cleared his throat. "I think it's a *great* idea, since it's the evening's entertainment, and all."

"Fabulous!" I clapped my hands. "And hey, you never know. You just might learn something new and exciting by the time we're through."

"One can only hope I get something out of this charade," he muttered beneath his breath, but I heard him.

Great. Another non-believer. Just what I needed

Chapter 2

Being Jo's maid of honor was quickly losing its appeal, and I was almost ready to give in and let my mother take over. Now there was a thought I'd never imagined having. I stifled a sigh, knowing I would never do that to my best friend, though I had to admit there was something about this wedding that was giving me a bad feeling. Crazy thoughts for sure because Jo and Cole were so happy together. My spine tingled with alarm and I frowned, glancing at Jo. She puckered her forehead, looking worried. So I did what any good maid of honor would do.

I smiled wide and said automatically, "Well, alrighty then. Let's get this show on the road."

Ignoring Peirce's non-believing tone, I instructed him to sit on the couch beside me in front of the window with the last of the day's light setting behind us. Scooting to the edge, we faced each other sideways so everyone in the room could see us. I held out my hands in front of me, and the room grew quiet as a morgue.

"Place your hands in mine, palms up, please."

He moaned, looking bored, but did as I asked. I took his hands in mine and closed my eyes. Breathing deeply, I cleared my mind and focused on his energy. When I felt centered and focused, I opened my eyes and looked down at his palms. I chose his dominant hand because it would reflect the outward expression of his personality while his passive hand was a reflection of his inherited traits. Holding his right hand in mine, I traced the horizontal line from his pinkie to his index finger.

"This is your Heart Line. It's one of the four major lines and indicates emotional stability, romantic perspectives, depression, and cardiac health."

Peirce's Heart Line began below the middle finger, indicating he was selfish when it came to love. It wasn't that he was unhappy with his marriage or didn't love his wife. It was more that he worried about his wants and needs and never put hers first. And there was a distinct circle on the line, indicating depression. Great. By trying to put him in his place, I'd put myself in quite the predicament.

"Why are you frowning?" he asked, and I peeked up at him, noticing his suddenly wary expression.

I glanced out at the crowd, and of course all eyes were glued to us. Relaxing my features and pasting on a smile, I replied, "No worries, Mr. Theodore. I was just concentrating. I see you're in a relationship."

His expression turned from concern to indignation, as if to say, *Duh*. "Everyone knows that, Miss Meadows. I've been married for years. That's hardly new." The unspoken words, *or exciting*, hung heavy in the air.

I ground my teeth to keep from blurting out the truth that he was a selfish jerk, but I couldn't resist adding, "No, that's not new or exciting, but this circle here indicates depression from a number of worries you've had as of late. Is that new, or does everyone know that as well?"

He blinked, and his shoulders wilted a little, taking a bit of the uppity starch out of him. He stared down at his lap. "No I don't suppose they do."

Relenting, I squeezed his hand and sent him a reassuring smile when he glanced up at me. "Let's move on to the next major line, shall we?"

"Please do." The relief on his face was palpable.

I traced the horizontal line below the Heart Line. "This here is the Head Line. This represents a person's learning style, communication style, intellectualism, and thirst for knowledge. Yours is straight, meaning you tend to take a practical and structured approach to most things in life."

He looked pleased.

"The straight line means you think realistically, but there are multiple crosses through the Head Line, indicating a number of momentous decisions you've had to make."

He was nodding, looking lost in thought and weary.

"The next major line is the Life Line," I said. "It's this vertical line near your thumb, and it travels down in an arc toward your wrist."

His face sobered. "Is mine short? Or do I have a long life ahead of me." He asked this casually, but I could sense a level of sincere worry beneath his words.

The crowd fell to a hush.

"The length of a person's Life Line is not associated with the length of their life. The line itself is simply an indication of a person's physical health, general well-being, and major life changes."

He blew out a breath. "Oh, okay. Well, that's good. Not that I was worried, or anything," he quickly added.

"Of course not." I laughed to lighten the mood but couldn't help being curious. The line was short and shallow, meaning he was easily manipulated by others, but I didn't want to say that in front of everyone. "I see a circle in the line, indicating you've been hospitalized or injured recently. I didn't know that." I looked up at him, searching for signs, but he seemed well and fit to me. I glanced at his wife, Linda, but she stared down at the floor, wringing her hands. I'd been around Detective Stone long enough to know that meant she was worried.

"It was nothing," he said a bit too quickly again, bringing my gaze back to him and making me curious as to what he'd been through lately. "What else do you see?" he asked, clearly ready to move away from talks of injury.

I looked back down at the line. "Well, there's a break right here which means a sudden change in lifestyle. If you haven't had one yet, you will." I studied him.

He paled, and I heard rumblings of speculation hum through the crowd.

Returning to the line, I went on. "What's more is I see the Fate Line, or Line of Destiny as some people like to call it. Not everyone has this, but you do. It runs vertical in the center of your palm downward."

"What does that mean?"

"Well, it indicates the degree to which a person's life is affected by external circumstances beyond their control. Yours is deep which means it's strongly controlled by fate. And there are many breaks and changes of direction, indicating you are prone to many changes in life from external forces. And look here." I pointed to where the line began, forgetting myself and my surroundings as I became fascinated with the reading at hand. "The line joins with the life line in the middle, signifying the point at which your interests must be surrendered to those of others."

"Can we get on with the rest of the reading please?" Peirce's tone had me looking up at him a bit startled, realizing I'd revealed too much to the room at large. Who were the others he would have to surrender to and what did they want?

"Of course." I quickly moved on to the other lines worth reading, reminding myself his personal life wasn't my business. I traced the line below his little finger across his palm and down to the base of his thumb. "This is your Health Line. It deals with your material well-being as much as the physical. It's, oh...." I pressed my lips together.

"What's oh?"

"Nothing really, it's just wavy which means potential health problems as a result of anxiety and nervousness."

"Moving right along," he grumbled.

This reading was not going well so far, which wasn't helping Jo since my mother kept making obvious gloating noises with every gloomy thing I revealed. I could only pray this reading perked up with something positive, or Jo would be breaking up yet another argument before the night was through.

"Right. Well, this next line is called the Fame Line." I ran my finger from the base of his hand up to this ring finger, tracing the line that was parallel to the Fate Line. "This line reinforces the Fate Line and influences the social rewards of success. While yours is broken repeatedly, indicating the ups and downs of your success, it is definitely strong and clear, indicating you *will* be successful in the end. Let's just say your inn will be put on the map, so to speak."

He beamed while my mother harrumphed and Jo growled a strong and clear warning, taking *her* down a peg. I sent my mother a look that said, *seriously?* Vivian inspected her fingernails, acting like she'd done nothing wrong as usual, and I went back to my reading, trying hard not to shake my head.

"Next up is the Marriage Line." I quickly moved on, pointing to the line just below the base of his little finger. "Ah yes, strong and clear lines indicating marriage, which as you say, we all know." I shot him a wink and a smile, trying to perk things up, then glanced at his wife who just rolled her eyes.

She was an attractive woman with a caramel, should-length bob hair style and curves in all the right places, but there was obviously even more trouble in paradise for them than Mitch and me. Speaking of Mitch, I glanced at him, but his face was unreadable, yet I felt as though he could read my mind with the way his eyes bore into mine. He hadn't made so much as a peep. I'd almost forgotten he was there. My smile dimmed, and I focused back on the innkeeper's palm, praying for this night to end quickly.

"And then there's a—" *oh, good lord* "—um…" I swallowed hard, "a…."

"Oh, just say it already," his wife blurted, suddenly paying attention.

"Well, it's just a reading, mind you."

"So you're admitting you're a fraud," she scoffed.

"I'm admitting no such thing." My readings always came true. Sometimes I mixed things up a bit and it took a while to figure it all out, but in the end they were always accurate.

"Whatever it is, I can take it." Peirce nodded once, in a sharp concise way, though his complexion had paled several shades.

"Well, there is a line at the end that cuts this line off abruptly, which usually means an end to a relationship due to divorce or…or death." My throat constricted.

A gasp rang out among the crowd, and Mitch frowned.

"Well that's just silly." His wife broke the uncomfortable silence. "Every marriage ends in divorce or death. You either stay together or you don't, and we will all die at some point or another."

"That's true," I replied, though my gut—which was also always right—said there was more to it than that this time, but I didn't owe anything to anyone. I wasn't helping the police or even getting paid for this reading. I was simply helping out my best friend. With that thought, I moved on to the next line. "Next up we have the Money Line."

"Finally, something useful," I heard his wife say.

I was really beginning to dislike the woman. Ignoring her, I continued. "This line runs from the base of the thumb up to the fingers. It represents the person's skill in acquiring riches and provides indicators on how to achieve this."

Peirce perked up on this one. "Go on," he said eagerly, making me wonder if he was in trouble money or if he was like most people: excited with the prospect of getting rich.

I studied the line and then smiled wide. "This one's a good one. Your line runs to the ring finger and cuts through the Fame Line."

"What does that mean, exactly," Peirce asked.

"That you will obtain that success I was talking about, except it looks as though you will acquire your fortune through luck and surprise."

His wife muttered something I couldn't quite hear, and Peirce looked vastly relieved. There was definitely more going on than met the eye with these two.

"One last line worth reading is the Travel Line. It's on the edge of the palm at the heel, opposite the thumb, and it extends in a horizontal direction. It's a major indication of the trips you've taken through your life that have had or will have a penetrating impact on your life. It also indicates your desire to travel."

A snort rang out, and I suspected it had come from his wife.

I tuned her out and studied his hand, realizing I didn't see any travel lines, which meant he didn't travel and had no desire to travel, and suddenly I understood the snort. Obviously *she* wanted to travel. That would explain the selfish part of his reading. "You know what? Since it's getting late, why don't we move on to the four minor lines?" I smiled over-brightly, hoping to defuse the situation.

"You'll get no objection from me," he grumbled.

"First up we have the Lines of Opposition." I traced the lines outside of his palm between the Heart and Head Lines. "These illustrate opposing forces we all must deal with in life," I squinted at his hand, "and I must say you have plenty."

He coughed. "Next," was all he said.

I kept looking for the Line of Intuition which illustrated strong insight, extreme sensitivity, and ESP. He didn't have any. No surprise there.

"Ah, here's the Line of Escape." I pointed to the line at the bottom of the palm near the base. His crossed the Health line, which indicated he could resort to drugs and drinking, which would make sense given his depression and marriage problems. "Just so you know, help is only a phone call away," I whispered for his ears only.

He flinched as though I'd struck a nerve and seen clear into his soul. "I-I don't know what you're talking about," he sputtered.

Desperate to end on a good note, I searched for the last line. The Lines of Influence. They were at the base of the thumb and radiated out into the palm. They illustrated an important event.

I smiled at whatever higher power had helped me out. "The Lines of Influence cross the Money Line."

His brow arched high. "What does that mean?"

"It should show how and where you will come into money."

"Well, get on with it, then. Tell me everything. Am I going to win the lottery? Cash in on the stock market? What?"

I held on tight to his hands and closed my eyes. The world around me faded away as my internal vision tunneled into a scene from long ago. Not the present or the future, but clearly the past, which surprised me. If he was going to come into success, I had assumed it would happen in the future. How on earth was it based in the past?

"I see water," I said. "An ocean...no wait, a river. It travels through the woods and is rough in spots." I felt the wooden planks of a boat beneath my feet. My joints felt stiff and achy as though I had weathered many storms, and it was hard to breathe as if I suffered from asthma or was a smoker. My body filled with anxiety and anger. "Someone is after me. I must escape, must hide, before it's too late."

My body jolted forward to a jarring stop, and I felt the impact with every ounce of my being. When I composed myself, I looked up and gasped. "The inn. I see Divine Inspiration." Suddenly I was somewhere else. "Wait, where am I? It's cold and dark and musty. There's dirt beneath my feet and ropes or webs or vines above my head. I hear a thumping or fluttering. What is that? I think it's—"

A crash jarred me from my trance, and I looked at my captive audience, clearly back in the present. The maid was cleaning up the mess from a serving tray someone had knocked over.

"Sorry," she muttered, looking red faced.

"What did you see?" Peirce grabbed my arms in a death grip, shaking me until my teeth rattled.

"Hey!" Mitch barked and stood by my side in a flash, grabbing Peirce's arm with one hand and balling his fist with another.

A sense of peace and security washed over me, knowing Mitch would never let anything bad happen to me. No matter what our problems might be, I knew he was there for me, always. It was the most comforting feeling I'd ever had.

Peirce let go. "Sorry. I'm just a little excited I guess."

Mitch's look said, *you're a little something, all right.* But he didn't say a word, though a muscle in his jaw bulged. After a tense moment, he let go of Peirce's arm.

"It's okay," I said, feeling calm and back in balance and in control. "Readings have a way of doing that to a person. I don't know for sure exactly what I saw."

"You must know something. How and where am I going to come into money? I need to know now." He looked panicked and desperate, not at all like the composed distinguished innkeeper I'd come to know.

"Calm down, Mr. Theodore, before you give yourself a heart attack." I squeezed his hand for a moment. "We'll find your answers, I'm sure of it."

He responded to my touch and reassurance by taking a big breath and striving for control. "How do you know?" He searched my eyes for an ounce of hope.

Focusing, I did my best to reassure him and do my job. "I might not know what the secret to your success is, but rest assured that I *do* know the secret lies within these very walls here at Divine Inspiration."

Chapter 3

The next morning, I couldn't stop thinking about my reading for Peirce. The secret lay within the walls of Divine Inspiration. What secret? The saying went, *If only the walls could talk*. I was sure that was true with many establishments, but I would bet with a place this old, there were hidden secrets waiting to be discovered. I never could resist a good mystery.

But today wasn't about my readings or secrets. It was about Jo and Cole's wedding. They were so deserving, and I was ridiculously happy for them. If only the sun would shine. I glanced at the overcast sky. The weather hadn't called for rain, but the sky was turning darker by the minute, and the very air had a chill in it.

My gut was telling me it was a sign of doom.

But that couldn't be. I knew without a shadow of doubt that Jo and Cole were meant for each other. For once, I ignored my gut and refused to believe anything could put a damper on this day. Anything other than my mother and Peirce getting into another scuffle, that is. I pushed that anxious thought from my mind and focused on being a good maid-of-honor.

"Are the grounds set?" I stood before Jack Shepard the groundskeeper. He was a decent-looking, tall man with a ponytail, full beard, and even fuller muscles, who had worked for Peirce for over a decade. A tried and true salt-of-the-earth, likable kind of guy.

"Yes, ma'am." He gave me a sharp nod, and a certain amount of pride reflected on his face. It was obvious he cared about this place and the work that he did.

I scanned the landscape. Everything had been groomed to perfection and the tent people appeared to have secured the reception covering to perfection, all under his watch. "Well done, Mr. Shepard. And thank you."

"You're very welcome, Miss Meadows. I'll be around if you need anything." He saluted and walked off as if there was always a purpose in his every stride.

I stopped the next man passing by. Frank Lalone, the maintenance man. "Miss Meadows, isn't it?" he asked.

"Yes." I smiled.

"What can I help you with?" He returned my smile with a pleasant one of his own. I couldn't help liking him as well. It appeared as though Mr. Theodore had surrounded himself with a reliable, competent staff, which made me feel better since that feeling of doom deep in my gut still lingered.

"I'm just checking to make sure everything is okay."

"All systems are a go at full capacity, and the backup generator is working if anything breaks." He stood a bit straighter. "No worries, Miss Meadows. I've got your back. Now if you'll excuse me, I need to speak to Mr. Theodore."

"Of course." I tipped my head and watched him walk away, or more like waddle.

Frank was a short, stocky man with a pot belly, but his apple cheeks and rosy disposition made him somehow adorable. Like a cuddly teddy bear you wanted to curl up with every night. And it didn't hurt that he was a genius when it came to fixing things, an admirable trait to say the least. Word around town was that the inn couldn't run without him.

"We're all set," Zoe came up to me and said with pride and satisfaction. She was Jo's cousin—a shorter, softer replica of her—and the only woman who had ever made Sean O'Malley tongue tied.

Sean was one of my best friends and Cole's best man. He was the one used to flustering women with his blond movie star good looks and killer dimples, not the other way around. He'd gotten Zoe to agree to be his date to the wedding, but she still didn't buy everything he was selling, which made me like her even more. I adored Sean, but Zoe was good for him, whether he realized it or not. He would soon, though. It was only a matter of time.

I took my place in line, right before Jo, and stared out at the audience. They stood and faced us as the music began to play. Between Jo's guest list and Cole's, pretty much everyone in town was there. The groom and his men were beneath the tent at the makeshift altar, waiting for the bride and her maids. We walked down the aisle one by one, smiling and nodding to our friends and loved ones. When it was my turn, my parents beamed. My father looked proud, my mother had hope in her eyes, and Granny Gert was a blubbering mess. But I only had eyes for one person.

Detective Mitch Stone.

The men all wore gray tuxedoes, the women wore burgundy dresses, and the bride and groom were adorned in white. Mitch had such a fierce, possessive look on his face. When his gaze settled on my eyes, a secret thrill shot through me. I smiled tenderly at him, and everything about him softened, giving me hope that this too could one day be mine.

Father Moody performed the ceremony, with several readings by friends and family, and when the bride and groom read their vows, not a dry eye was left beneath the tent. Finally Cole and Jo were pronounced man and wife. He didn't have to be asked to kiss his bride as he bent her over backward and planted a big one on her. I swiped a tear away, so happy for them. Cheers broke out, and the reception was underway.

"Hey," Mitch said, as he came to a stop beside me, standing tall and strong and oh-so-handsome.

"Hey there, yourself." I smiled up at him, my heart skipping a beat. "You clean up nice." His thick black wavy hair had been tamed, his face clean-shaven but shadowed already from his heavy beard, his tux precisely cut, he smelled amazing, and…

He was all mine.

"You look beautiful." He stared down at me with equally dark eyes, and a muscle in his square jaw bulged, pulsing the jagged scar that ran across it.

"Rough, rugged, and oh so right," I mumbled more to myself, but he heard judging from the twitch of his lips.

The DJ began to play, and Jo and Cole danced their first dance as husband and wife. My mother had suggested a string quartet from the city that was all the rage, but I knew Jo. I'd overruled my mother on that one and gave Jo the name of a fantastic DJ I had heard of when I still lived in the Big Apple. Luckily he had been available, and Jo had sided with me on this one, much to my mother's displeasure and my glee.

"So, um, do you want to dance? You don't have to or anything, it's just, you know, I mean, we're here," Mitch said, and I found my lips twitching at him this time. Mr. Tall, Dark, and Dangerous so wasn't good at the whole courting/romance thing, but I had to give him credit. At least he was trying, and it was adorable.

"Sure." I took his hand, letting him lead me onto the dance floor. I slipped into his waiting arms, and it was like coming home. We fit together so perfectly, it brought out my longing for something more.

"I'm proud of you." His soft tone broke into my thoughts.

I couldn't stop the warmth from spreading through me over his words of praise, especially having grown up without much of it in my life. My gaze met his as I breathlessly asked, "For what?"

"You did it." Pride and something more filled the deep timber of his voice. "You pulled off Jo's wedding in record time."

"Well, Zoe planned it, and my mother butted her nose in every step of the way, so I can't really take much credit."

He stilled me with his intense gaze and his big hand tipping up my jaw until I looked at him. "Don't sell yourself short, Tink." I loved when he referred to me by the nickname he'd chosen after we'd first met. Tink for Tinkerbell since he said I was a petite little pixie with way too much attitude and gumption for my own good.

"What you did was much more important," he went on. "You helped Jo keep it together, and as one of her best friends, I know for a fact that's not easy. Not to mention you entertained everyone at the rehearsal dinner. And you kept your mother and Theodore from killing each other, which was no easy feat. All in all, I'd say you're the real hero of the day."

I felt my smile before I even realized I was doing it. "Thank you." I filled those two words with all the tenderness I felt. "That means more than you know."

"So do you." His voice came across soft and husky.

My heart skipped a beat. "So do I what?" I knew what he meant, but I needed to hear the words.

He stared at me for an intense beat. "Mean more than you know."

My lips parted in pleasure. He'd only said he loved me once when he'd asked me to marry him, and of course I'd freaked out. After getting him to compromise on taking a step back, slowing things down, and trying living together first, he hadn't said the words since. I hadn't realized how much I wanted to hear those words again until this very moment.

He stared at my mouth, groaned, and then tore his gaze back up to mine as if what he had to say was more important than any desire to kiss me that he might be feeling. I tamped down my disappointment and smiled at him in an encouraging way.

"Sunny, I'm sorry for the way I've been behaving lately. I love living with you, but it's not easy. I mean, living with *you* is easy, but living with you in that house is damned hard. I'm trying, but the other 'man' in your life isn't making things easy on me."

"I know, and I appreciate that, but you are both so important to me. I can't imagine my life without either of you in it." I stroked his cheeks with my fingertips, studying every inch of his face, realizing just how much I absolutely loved this man. "Please don't make me choose," I whispered.

"Baby, I would never make you choose." He cupped my face in his palms and stared deep into my eyes, the gray surrounding his pupils swirling into thunderous storm clouds that matched the ever darkening sky. "Whatever it takes. I will do whatever it takes to make this work."

"Why?" I sucked in a breath, realizing I'd spoken out loud and now terrified of what his response might be.

"Because you're that important to me," he said. It wasn't, *I love you*, but it was a definite step in the right direction.

I exhaled a huge sigh of relief. "You're important to me too, Mitch. More than you know."

Finally, blessedly, his head lowered until his lips claimed mine.

I was in heaven, feeling him, tasting him, reveling in just *being* with him…until voices raised and shouts rang out over by the buffet line. With reluctance, Mitch and I broke apart, and I groaned. Back to reality.

"Duty calls," I said.

"You get her, I'll get him," Mitch responded.

"Deal." I led the way over to the food table where my mother was wielding a kitchen knife over the fruit tray.

Peirce held the plastic serving spoon as if it were a sword and he were about to shout, *En garde*! "Back off, Mrs. Meadows. The fruit is perfectly fine," he growled.

"Perfectly fine isn't good enough," she snapped back. "Kind of like your inn. It has the potential to be spectacular, but you won't allow it to be. You settle, and today settling isn't good enough. Jo and Cole deserve spectacular, and spectacular is what they are going to get so long as I live and breathe."

"Over my dead body!" he shouted.

"Don't tempt me," she ground out.

"Mother!" I stepped forward and placed myself between them. "I do believe Jo needs you. She's about to cut the cake."

My mother brightened just like I knew she would. "Oh, well then, I mustn't keep her waiting. That cake isn't just any cake, you know. It's from Cake Masters in the city, upon my recommendation, of course. One of their best bakers even personally volunteered to deliver it all the way here. Now that's class. A certain someone could take lessons. Did you try the punch? It's downright awful." With one final glare at Peirce, she set the knife on the table and scurried away.

I let out a sigh of relief as Mitch started talking to Peirce about the fish in the river that fed the lake behind the inn. The fruit looked fine to me. I tried the punch and puckered my face. She was right about the punch, though. Setting down my glass, I hurried after her before she stirred up any more trouble. I wound up watching as she stole the show with Jo once more, pulling off the perfect assistant in cutting the cake, which was pretty spectacular, I had to admit. It was a replica of Smokey Jo's with Cole on his Harley right out front, their Great Dane puppy Biff standing by his side, and Jo welcoming them both to cross the threshold through her open door.

Sam, our local baker, wasn't too pleased Jo hadn't gone with him, but even he grudgingly admitted he couldn't create a theme cake the likes of that one. I did my part by telling each table they could help themselves.

"Nicely done, Cat Woman." Mitch came to a stop beside me a while later.

I grinned up at him. "Ditto, Batman."

"Not sure how much longer we can keep the peace in Tent City."

"I'd settle for just keeping dry." I stared out at the now black clouds as a streak of lightning lit up the evening sky, and the first fat raindrops began to fall.

"Good thing this tent comes with sides. You go left, I'll go right."

"My thoughts exactly."

He winked. "See, I knew we would make a pretty good team."

"There was never any doubt." I winked back.

Ten minutes later, we'd lowered the sides and the entire wedding reception and staff were enclosed inside the confines of the tent. The wind howled and pushed against the canvas, causing the ropes to strain. Seconds later, the loudest crack of thunder I'd ever heard boomed overhead, shaking the ground beneath our feet. Tables toppled, dishes crashed, and guests screamed and suddenly the tent tumbled to the ground.

Tent City was dark, and all chaos broke out.

After much scuffling and panicked conversations and what felt like forever, the yard flooded with spotlights powered from a generator operated by the maintenance man while the groundskeeper and staff pitched in to help raise the tent once more. Tables were righted as people scurried about to pick up broken dishes and make sure everyone was okay.

"What's going on?" someone asked.

"Yeah, what happened?" someone else chimed in.

"Sounded like lightning hit," a third person responded.

"Knocked the power right out," a fourth person added. "Funny thing is, the forecast didn't call for rain."

"This can't be happening." Jo looked like an Amazon queen who'd just lost the most important battle of her life.

"I was afraid that something would go wrong." Cole stood proud and tall with his tattoos covered by an immaculate tux—except for the chain link fence around his neck peeking above his collar defiantly—but his buzz cut and five-o'clock shadow remained firmly in place.

"It's okay, man." Sean clapped Cole on the back. "Every wedding experiences a few glitches. Most people just don't get to see them, laddy. That's all."

"That's not all," Cole said. "Every time I'm finally happy, something goes wrong." The look on his face said everything.

The feeling of doom I'd had the entire day intensified, but I pasted on my best maid-of-honor smile at Jo and tried to reassure Cole. "It's okay. No harm no foul. The party has just begun."

An ear piercing scream came from the other end of the tent, and we all broke into a run in that direction.

Mitch held up his hands as he whirled around to face us. "Don't move," he said, his voice serious and full of authority.

"Why?" I asked, pretty sure I wasn't going to like the answer.

"Because everything's *not* okay. There's definitely harm and plenty of foul...play, that is."

"What does that even mean?" Jo wrung her hands.

"That this is no longer a wedding reception."

"Then what the hell is it?" Sean held his hands up in the air.

Mitch's face turned to granite. "A crime scene."

"I knew it." Cole hung his head. "I'm cursed."

"And Peirce Theodore is dead."

Gasps rang out among the guests as Detective Mitch Stone stepped aside. The innkeeper lay sprawled on his back beneath the buffet table with the kitchen knife buried deep into his chest and my mother standing over his dead body, looking more than *tempted*. She looked downright guilty as sin.

Party officially over.

Chapter 4

Hours later, what had started out as the best day of Jo and Cole's lives was quickly turning into the worst. The beautiful wedding reception was now covered in crime scene tape, and law enforcement individuals scoured the grounds. No one was allowed to leave until everyone was accounted for. Mayor Cromwell had his troll like, flaming red head bent in an intense conversation with Chief Spencer who was a slicked back older version of Mitch. Meanwhile a distinguished, bald, goatee sporting Captain Grady Walker was doing his best to keep the peace.

"Please, everyone." Captain Walker held his hands up high. "Calm down. I promise we won't keep you here all night. We just have to make sure that everyone who was here tonight has been accounted for. It's for your own good. The last thing we want is for a murderer to run around on the loose in Divinity."

People grumbled amongst themselves, but the noise level had lessoned considerably from one of hostility to one of fear. With the storm still raging outside, the tension in the air beneath the tent was tangible. It was clear Peirce Theodore didn't die by accident. There was a killer among them.

"What a nightmare." Jo dabbed the tears from her eyes. "I thought *cold feet* were supposed to strike before a person said *I do*. Cole had no problem marrying me, but now that he *is* married, he's freaking out. Just because his wife died on the back of his bike and now this happens after marrying me, he believes he's cursed. He doesn't want to consummate the wedding, and he offered me an annulment as a way out. Can you believe it? Um, hello, we've already consummated our union and then some! After all he went through to get me to say yes, he's going to wimp out now? I can't take it, Sunny, I just can't."

I grabbed her hands and squeezed them tight with my own. "You won't have to. We'll catch whoever is responsible. I can promise you that."

"I sure hope so." She sniffled. "Because this is *not* the way I intended to spend my honeymoon."

"Land sakes, child. You poor, poor dear. And on your wedding day, no less. Here honey." Granny Gert came to a stop beside Jo, sporting her standard apron over her formal wedding attire. "Have a cookie. It'll fix you right up." She held out a tray of an assortment of her famous cookies. "There really is a cookie for everything, and don't you worry. These things always have a way of working themselves out."

Sean came to a stop beside Jo, with a flustered Zoe. "What the hell just happened?" he asked, loosening his tie and unbuttoning the top button of his shirt.

"My life is ruined," Jo wailed around a bit of Granny's double-chocolate cookie, but even that didn't help.

"Your life isn't ruined, it's just delayed." Zoe tried to keep the calm, but I caught the worried look she shot Sean.

"Tell that to the groom." Jo stabbed a finger in Cole's direction, but he stubbornly refused to look at her *for her own good.*

I grabbed Mitch's arm and pulled him aside. "We have to do something."

"What exactly do you want me to do, Tink? Wave a magic wand?" He crossed his arms over his chest.

"Oh, gee, I don't know…your job, maybe?" I poked him, not liking that Grumpy Pants had inhabited his body once more.

He rubbed his chest and frowned at me. "You're not gonna like what that entails."

"Why?" I had a feeling I knew what he was going to say, but I couldn't quite bring myself to actually believe he would do that.

"Because it involves questioning your mother."

My stomach dropped, and a feeling of dread washed over me. I pushed back the acid in my throat and forced the words out. "Why would you do that?"

"Just doing my job like you asked. I have no choice, Sunny. She has motive and incriminating evidence against her. You know as well as I do that she was the last person seen holding the knife now buried in Peirce Theodore's chest. Not to mention she's made it clear she can't stand him and would love to take over his inn if only to show him how to run it the *right* way." The detective grabbed my shoulders and stilled me so I would look at him. "Do I think your mother is the killer? Hell, no. But if you want me to find the *real* killer, then I have to treat this as a real case. Do you understand what that means?"

I sighed. "That my mother is the prime suspect, so my parents won't be leaving town any time soon."

"Good girl. And do you know what else it means?"

"That you don't want me anywhere near the case."

"Will wonders never cease," he said with a slight grin, trying to ease the tension and lighten the mood. "I guess what they say is true."

"What's that?"

"The more time you spend together, the more you start sounding like each other." He tweaked my nose.

"Sounding yes. Thinking no. And do you know what *that* means?" I raised a brow, my smile more of a smirk.

"That you don't plan on staying away from this case for a single second," he said wearily, looking at me as if he prayed he was wrong.

"Good boy." I patted his shoulders. "You're learning."

He sighed in resignation. "And you're playing with fire."

"It wouldn't be the first time."

***

"Well, this certainly isn't Divine Inspiration." My mother ran her white gloved fingertip along the top of the check-in counter at The Divinity Hotel.

Divinity was an old-fashioned town with big Victorian homes and various businesses that showcased different eras throughout history. Some newer businesses opted for a more modern décor, but many of the older ones stuck to tradition. The Divinity Hotel was a large brick building with a 1930's Art Deco theme inspired by the artists of Paris.

Lacquered wood furniture trimmed with brushed steel and lined with exotic Zebra skin upholstered fabric was placed strategically throughout the lobby. And the colorful starburst motifs in various shades of greens and oranges with small bits of black and gold arranged in geometric shapes that covered the floors and walls was eye catching.

I thought it was charming, but my mother thought the place was over-the-top and tacky. With the inn shut down as a crime scene and no other hotel in town, she didn't have a choice unless she wanted to stay with me. Under strict orders from the captain not to leave town, she'd made it more than clear that jail would be preferable before she would go anywhere near my demon cat.

Chuck Webb's hard eyes narrowed. "I don't know why I'm letting you stay here. You being a criminal, and all. You're lucky Abigail and I have a baby on the way."

He was a muscular man in his fifties, with a brown military haircut, and he looked scary intimidating. I avoided him whenever possible after our rocky past encounters, though his recent marriage to Abigail Brook had softened his edges a bit. Except my mother had a way of scraping her perfectly manicured nails over anyone's patience.

"Last I checked it was innocent until proven guilty, darling. Don't you know anything?" my mother fairly purred, but her eyes gave her away. She might act all calm and cool, but she was worried. I could tell. People might be more sympathetic to her plight if she would allow them to see that vulnerability, but showing weakness wasn't in her nature. "No, you're the lucky one, Mr. Webb. It's a wonder your wife lets *you* stay here."

He curled his hands into fists, but my father stepped between them, looking as dashing and important as ever. "Mr. Webb—Chuck—Donald Meadows here." He held out his hand, and Chuck warily grasped his palm and shook after a long hesitation. "I really appreciate you letting us stay in your fine establishment. My wife has had a rough day and isn't quite herself. You know how it is with women."

My mother was about to say something, but my father shot her a warning look, and she backed down. He was the only human being on this planet who had that effect on her. It was one of the things I admired most about him. He truly loved her, and she knew it, but more importantly respected it. They respected each other. She knew he *always* had her best interest at heart, therefore she trusted and listened to whatever he said. I felt I had that with Mitch, it was just terrifying to give in to.

"Women." Webb chuckled. "They truly are from another planet."

"Exactly." Dad clapped him on the shoulder as if he felt his pain. "Now if we could have your finest room, I will make it more than worth your while."

"I'll see what I can do," Chuck said.

"So, how far along is the Misses?" my father asked as if he genuinely cared. His admirable bed side manner was one of the things that made him such a great doctor. His patients adored him.

I pulled my mother away while my father worked his magic to smooth things over. We sat in a couple of chairs by a cozy fireplace. It wasn't just a fireplace, it was the focal point of the lobby. A combination of mahogany, walnut, and oak wood had been used to create the mantel. Those woods were easy to carve and featured contrasting grains as part of the design. Carved flowers, leaves, and beading lined the frieze, and a beveled mirror had been built right into the center, surrounded by hand painted tiles.

My mother's shoulders slumped just a hair, and only for a moment, but I saw. "Mother, what were you thinking?" I couldn't help but ask.

She waved her hand at me. "He's harmless."

"I'm not talking about him, Mom," I sputtered. "People heard you say on several occasions that you should buy the inn because you could surely run it better than that imbecile, and then you threatened to kill him."

"I'm not worried because I'm innocent, darling. I wouldn't be in this God forsaken business if I didn't believe in it. Detective Stone will catch the real killer soon, I'm sure of it. This is simply an inconvenience."

"It's more than an inconvenience, and you should damn well be worried." As my voice raised, I could feel my blood pressure rise as well. I couldn't help it. I was worried sick. She was my mother and no matter how much she drove me crazy, I was terrified. She might act all tough, but there was no way she could handle jail. If anything bad ever happened to her, my father would never survive and I would never forgive myself.

She blinked up at me startled.

I took a deep breath and continued in a lower voice. "You kept pushing Mr. Theodore and arguing with him relentlessly in front of all the guests. Half the town was at that wedding. Everyone saw you two argue over the fruit bowl, and how on earth did the kitchen knife you were using end up buried in his chest? Answer me that." My voice squeaked despite my efforts, so I looked away and practiced my yoga breathing. Wally's World gym had to start paying off somehow.

When she remained silent, I glanced back at her. She would draw her sleek eyebrows together if she could, but the Botox prevented it, I was sure. "You don't honestly think I killed him, do you?" she finally asked, as if my belief in her mattered that much. Sitting on the edge of her seat, she stared at me.

I blew out a breath and fell back against the cushions in my chair, because I knew it did. I knew she loved me as much as I did her. "Of course not," I finally said, "but why were you standing over him when the tent was raised?"

"Like I told Detective Stone," she replied, more composed now. "I helped Jo cut the cake and then just before the tent collapsed, someone shoved me hard in the direction of the fruit table. I had just regained my balance when I found myself face-to-face with the innkeeper. I admit we were about to pick up where we'd left off earlier in our argument but the tent suddenly fell."

"What happened after that?"

"Quite honestly, I'm not really sure. There were all kinds of skirmishes taking place beneath that tent before it was lifted. Once it was, I was as shocked as everyone to see Mr. Theodore dead at my feet and the knife in his chest. I don't recall how it got there. To think the real killer must have been right beside me when he or she committed the heinous act. I don't know who it was, but one thing is clear. Someone is trying to set me up."

"They're not *trying*, Mom, they've succeeded. Can you think of anyone who would want to set you up?"

"No one knows me which makes me an easy target. It was pretty clear Mr. Theodore and I disliked each other, and I'm an outsider. The real question you should be asking is who might want Peirce dead or even who might want to ruin Jo and Cole's wedding. Speaking of them, where are they now? On their honeymoon?"

"No, unfortunately. The honeymoon is on hold. They aren't allowed to leave yet, either. No one who attended the reception can leave for the time being. It wouldn't have been much of a honeymoon right now anyway. Not with the memory of a man getting murdered on their special day. And Cole is having a hard time not blaming himself."

"What on earth for?"

"He thinks he is cursed, so now he's trying to get Jo to leave him." I shook my head and sat back to rub my throbbing temples.

"Oh, that's just ridiculous." My mother threw her hands up.

"Mitch and Sean are on their way to find him and try to talk some sense into him."

"Poor Joanne. She shouldn't be alone at a time like this." My mother's face suddenly looked every inch her age. She really cared about Jo, and I couldn't help but feel a smidge of jealousy. I wasn't sure she had ever expressed that kind of genuine concern for me. At least she never showed it.

"She's not." I pushed my jealousy aside because Jo was pretty awesome and deserved everyone's affection. "Her cousin Zoe is with her. She'll be okay. They went back to her new house to check on her dog Biff."

"Now there's a pet worth having." My mother smiled in fondness, then her lips tipped down and her face looked pinched as she studied me in a most disapproving way. "And why aren't you with them? You're not being a very good maid-of-honor and best friend now, I'd say."

And there was the mother I'd known my whole life. No "thank you" for staying with her because, heaven forbid, she admit she might actually need me for a change. Or the world might come to an end if she admitted she was the one in trouble this time. After all these years of knowing how she was, you wouldn't think I would continue to let her get to me, but I did.

I just sat there too numb for words.

As if reading my thoughts, she responded. "Don't worry about me, darling. I have your father." *And that's all I need* was left unsaid, but we both knew it had been implied. She didn't need me, didn't appreciate me, and probably never would.

I snapped my jaw closed and stood. "You know what? You're right. I think I'll go where I can actually do some good. Good luck, Mother. I hope you like orange. I hear it's the new black and all the rage behind bars." Waving my fingers at her eye-roll and head-shake, I turned my back and walked out the door, but I wasn't going to Jo. And I wasn't going home. I was on a mission.

Mother wasn't the only one who could stir things up.

Chapter 5

It was Saturday evening, but not too late. I was hoping Mitch thought I was still settling my parents in at the Divinity Hotel. He had been busy securing the crime scene and questioning the guests at Jo and Cole's wedding reception, but everyone had dispersed, and he was probably home by now. Leaving him alone with Morty was risky, but I needed answers. This was my mother we were talking about. As much as she drove me nuts, I still loved her and didn't want to see her go to jail for something she didn't do.

There had been something in the reading I had given to Peirce that made me want to question Linda Theodore more. She had definitely seemed like a wife who wasn't happy. She had rolled her eyes at Peirce not wanting to travel and didn't seem entirely content in their marriage. It was late when I arrived back at Divine Inspiration. The wedding and reception had long since been over, the crime scene was secured, the detectives were gone, and my parents were settled. I only had minutes to play with.

I rang the doorbell without hesitation. The door swung open and Linda Theodore stood there, her eyes wary and calculating but not red-rimmed like you would expect from someone who had just become a widow.

"I'm Sunny Meadows, consultant for the Divinity Police Department." I stuck out my hand.

"I know who you are." She didn't shake my hand. Instead, she tightened her long, satin robe around her.

"I see." I dropped my empty palm to my side.

"What are you doing here so late, Miss Meadows? The police have already questioned me thoroughly and shut down my place of operation, I might add. Do you have any idea the amount of money I will lose by closing my doors until this investigation is solved? I can't afford that. We were fully booked for the fall leaf peeping season. This will ruin us."

"I do understand, and I'm so sorry. I get it, believe me. It wasn't long ago that I had to close my doors until a murder investigation I was involved with was solved." I tried to play on her sympathies. "I understand first-hand what you're going through. I'm just here to try to help you if you'll let me."

"I'm not a fool, Miss Meadows. You're here because you want to save your mother." I could tell she didn't trust me. She tucked her brown bob behind her ears.

"True, I do," I chose my words carefully, "but not at your expense. I can promise you that. I really do want to get to the bottom of whomever the real killer is."

She stared at me for a long minute, and then finally stood back and pushed the door open wider. No words were necessary to know that she believed me or was at least curious enough to hear me out.

I stepped through the threshold and followed her into the living room. The same living room where I had given Peirce his reading.

"Normally this room would be filled with guests right now." A note of wistful longing filled her voice as she sat on the very same couch.

I sat down on a chair adjacent to her.

"I'd offer you refreshments, but since I'm not allowed to entertain any guests, I can't exactly afford any staff at the moment."

"But I thought I saw a few of your regulars just minutes ago."

"I have a few diehards who refuse to leave whether I can pay them or not."

"That's sweet. You hold onto that. And don't worry about me, I don't need any refreshments."

"I plan to hold onto that." She appeared stronger than I had originally thought. "Now, what can I do for you, Miss Meadows?"

"Listen, I just want to help you. Sincerely, I do." I studied her, taking in her appearance. She was a petite brunette with a cute, sassy, wavy brown bob and pretty amber eyes. She could have any man, but she'd remained true to her husband, who obviously hadn't treated her as nicely as he should have, according to the vibe I'd received from his reading.

"And how can you do that?" she asked with a surprisingly calculating gleam in her eyes. "You're reading was a joke. Where's all the money Peirce was supposed to come into? I certainly haven't seen any of it."

"These things take time before they reveal themselves fully."

"Well time is something I don't have. Let's just say my husband had more enemies than friends, I'm discovering. And more debt than I was aware of."

"What kind of enemies? Are you in danger?" I pulled out a notepad and pen. For the first time, I realized there might be more danger involved than I had first thought and more people might be in jeopardy of losing their lives.

She shrugged. "I was never afraid for myself, but he seemed terrified. Whenever I asked him about it, he told me I was imagining things, but I wasn't. I was married to him for long enough to know when he was stressed out."

"I'm listening."

"At first I thought he was seeing another woman with all his late night hushed phone calls and secret meetings, so I followed him. Turns out he had been meeting with his accountant. Then when we kept getting prank phone calls, I knew his problems were much bigger than a simple affair." She finally sniffed, pulling out a hankie and dabbing at the corners of her eyes. "I just don't know how I'm going to get through all of this. I sometimes worry that his thugs are now after me."

"I'm sure you'll find a way," I said because I didn't know what else to say.

Her calculating gaze cut to my eyes. "I don't know what you mean."

"I think you do." I narrowed my own gaze. "I do my homework, Mrs. Theodore," I added, deciding to cut to the chase.

She arched a brow. "And what exactly does *that* mean?"

"That I know you took out a big life insurance policy on your husband recently." Okay, so I didn't do my homework, but

I'd overheard Mitch and Captain Walker talking earlier, but she didn't have to know that.

She stiffened and a flash of concern crossed her features, then she sat up straighter, donning an unreadable expression. "So what? That doesn't prove anything."

"I'm not trying to prove anything, Mrs. Theodore. I'm trying to point out what any prosecuting attorney is going to jump on in a court of law. Do I think you're guilty?" I studied her carefully and answered as honestly as I could. "No, I don't. However, that doesn't mean I don't think you're hiding something."

Her eyes shot to the floor, her body language saying it all even if she hadn't uttered a word of guilt. "There's nothing wrong with planning ahead."

"No, especially not if you think your husband's life is in danger. Is that what happened?" I watched her eyes closely to gauge her reaction.

She sighed and the first unguarded, honest expression of worry crossed her features. Her shoulders slumped as though she had the world resting upon them. "Look, Miss Meadows, I actually loved my husband. Did I make mistakes in our marriage? Of course. I'm only human. But I didn't kill him or have him killed, if that's what you're wondering."

"Then why the policy?" I asked in a quiet voice.

"Because he wasn't himself at the end. He wouldn't talk to me, but I could tell something was bothering him. He was never big on travel, but at the end, he was adamant we not go anywhere. And he was constantly on his phone, whispering in a heated voice and looking more stressed than I'd ever seen him. It was after I received those few threatening phone calls in his absence that I finally took out the life insurance policy. I knew we had a lot of debt, and the last thing I wanted was to go bankrupt for whatever he was involved in. That doesn't make me a murderer, Miss Meadows."

"I never said that it did, Mrs. Theodore. I am truly sorry for your loss. Here is my card if you can think of anything else. I really do just want to help you. I owe that to your husband. Thank you so much for your time." I stood and let myself out. Peirce was obviously involved in something much bigger than anything to do with Joanne's wedding. The question of how much his wife knew about it remained. Maybe it was time I paid his accountant a visit.

I stepped outside and shivered as I walked to my car. The temperature had dropped considerably, as was the case in upstate NY in the fall. Fishing out my keys, I unlocked my bug and reached for the door handle. A body pushed me up against the door, my cheek pressed to the roof, my arms trapped at my sides. The hard confines of the much bigger form pressed snugly against my backside. My heart began to race and my stomach jumped into my throat. Had someone been watching and waiting to attack Linda, only to wind up attacking me instead? Why hadn't I paid more attention in self-defense class?

I could hear my pulse beat in my ears and squeezed my eyes shut. "Wh-what do you want," I asked. I tried to think about what to do, but my mind went blank.

The form didn't say anything, it just pushed into me harder, letting me know I was vulnerable and he was in control. Finally, he spoke. "Have you had enough? Are you ready to listen to me now?"

I gasped. "Mitch?" I squeaked out, nearly wilting in relief.

"Dammit, Tink, this could have been anyone!" Anger vibrated through his pores. "Now do you see why I'm so worried?"

The tension eased out of my every cell immediately, my pulse returning to normal and my breathing finally regulating. No matter how angry he got, he would never hurt me. "Mitch, oh my God, you scared the heck out of me."

He turned me around to face him and nailed me with an icy gray glare. "My point exactly. When are you going to learn to use common sense and leave the police work to me? Jesus Tink, you are going to be the death of me yet."

I sucked in a breath as he leaned into me, trapping me against the car. "Wh-what are you doing?"

"Making a point."

"Oh, I got the point. Felt it with every ounce of my being." My grin came slow and sweet.

"This isn't funny, Sunny," he said in a soft but deadly tone. I could feel all of his hard body pressed intimately against mine. As much as I wanted him, I knew he was serious. "Someone could have done a whole lot more to you than kill you. In the end, death might have been preferred."

My smile faded. "I'm not laughing, Mitch. You caught me off guard, but it won't happen again. I know what I'm doing."

"Do you?" he ground out. "I could have been someone else. You aren't supposed to be anywhere near this case. Not to mention, we made a commitment to each other."

"Did we?" I asked, dying to know why he hadn't said he loved me since that fateful day so long ago. The day I'd asked him to take it slow. The day I'd said no to marrying him. The day I'd regretted ever since.

"Yes, Miss Meadows, we did. When I moved in, I assumed that meant you would do me the common courtesy of letting me now when you wouldn't be coming home. Do you know how worried I've been? I called the hotel an hour ago, and your mother said you'd already left. Yet you didn't bother to call me and tell me where you were going. Why is that? I don't ask for much, Sunny."

"I know, and I didn't call you because I knew you would stop me," I said honestly. I blew out a breath. "I knew you would be worried and you would come after me and you would make me go home. It's my mother, Mitch. I can't help but want to be involved in this case. I need to know she's going to be okay. I need to know I'm doing all that I can. I need to clear her name before it's too late."

"And I need you to trust me to do my job."

I reached up and cupped his face with my hands. "I do trust you." I pressed my lips softly against his. "I just need you to trust me, too. I can be a help to you. Please let me."

He dropped his forehead to mine and tried to control his breathing. "Goddamn this is hard."

I bit my lip, afraid to ask, then finally said, "What? Working with me or living with me or just being with me?"

He raised his head and answered point blank. "All of the above."

"Oh, I see," I said in a quiet voice and dropped my hands.

"You don't see anything," he ground out, stepping back from me and pacing the driveway.

"Then tell me. I might be psychic but I can't read your mind, Mitch, or haven't you figured that out yet. You're grumpier than ever these days."

He stopped pacing and nailed me to my car with just a look from his stormy gray eyes. "You want to know why I'm so grumpy?"

"Y-Yes?" I asked, suddenly second guessing if I really did or not. He looked like he was on the warpath and I was his target.

"I—I—oh, hell," he said, then picked me up to straddle his pent-up frustration as he pushed me back against my car and his lips slammed down on to mine and his body pressed tightly against me.

He kissed me with all his emotions flying raw and at the surface. I tasted Morty driving him crazy, Granny Gert underfoot, my obsession with Jo and Cole's wedding, my insistence on clearing my mother's name, and just exactly how much he had missed me. By the time he tore his lips from mine, I felt ravaged and raw and oh-so-wanted.

"Awww, honey, why didn't you say so," I said, stroking his cheeks and pressing tender kisses all over his face.

He closed his eyes and his lips tipped up a hair. He turned his face into my palm and kissed it softly. "You're going to be the death of me yet, Tink."

"Nonsense," I said in a breathy voice. "I'm going to be the thing that makes you finally start living. Now take me to the nearest hotel room and love me forever, baby."

He blinked. "Seriously?"

"Yes, detective. I *seriously* need some alone time with my boyfriend, and something tells me you need alone time with me as well. I say it's time we put each other before everything else for a change."

"You're boyfriend, huh?"

"Um, hello, we *are* living together."

"And taking it slow." He eyed me carefully.

"Slow, yes. A step backward, no. I miss you, Detective Grumpy Pants."

"I miss you, too, Tink. And I say making love to my *girlfriend* has never sounded better."

Chapter 6

"Isn't this just the bees' knees?" Granny Gert hummed, as she lit the small fireplace in the corner of the kitchen in my ancient Victorian house.

She set the tea kettle atop the gas stove that had replaced the old coal burning stove that used to sit there years ago. Next she set dessert—a big plate of cookies, of course—in the center of the long wooden harvest table. Out in the formal dining room there was a fancy large, round dark wood table with pedestals, but I preferred the coziness of the kitchen with its old-fashioned root cellar and scullery where the servants ate once upon a time.

The charming house had come fully furnished with overstuffed chairs, oriental rugs, draperies in heavy fabrics, and all sorts of knickknacks. As much as I wanted privacy with Mitch, I honestly didn't know how I would keep up with taking care of Vicky by myself. On Mondays Granny cleaned, on Tuesdays she tackled the laundry, on Wednesdays the ironing, and Thursdays she baked for the weekend's entertainment, leaving Fridays for herself and all the fads waiting to be discovered in the magazines at the hair salon. Everyone at Pump Up the Volume Salon and Spa loved her. Granny Gert loved being needed, and I wasn't too proud to admit I needed her in a big way.

Mitch and I had invited Sean and Zoe as well as Cole and Joanne over for dinner. My parents had refused to step foot in the house with Morty under the roof. Besides, my mother was busy calling in every favor owed her from various lawyers and judges back in the city, while my father was reaching out to a few contacts of his own. Meanwhile, none of us had said much throughout dinner, and I'd barely even tasted the delicious smelling pot roast, and that was a downright shame.

"It's wonderful, Granny." Jo's tone was thankful and appreciative, but her smile didn't quite reach her red-rimmed, puffy eyes.

Sean and Mitch had talked Cole into coming to his senses and going home with Jo on their wedding night. But it was clear that Cole still harbored many doubts. He was here, but not present. Married, but holding back. Physically sitting right beside Jo, yet mentally and spiritually so far away. It was hurting her. The dark circles under her eyes bespoke of sleepless nights, and she looked exhausted. I knew hurting her was the last thing Cole would ever intend to do, but in trying to save her from harm, he was harming her more than anything else ever could.

"Oh, you're welcome, sweetie. But land sakes, you hardly ate a bite." Granny tsked. "A newlywed needs to keep up her strength." Granny snickered.

Jo humored her by smiling, but her eyes still looked so sad and hopeless. "I'm sorry. It really is delicious, I just don't have much of an appetite today."

Cole's worried gaze shot to her. "You okay?"

"As good as can be expected, given that somebody was murdered at our wedding and then my husband spent our wedding night on the couch." She glared at him, revealing a shadow of the Amazon we all knew and loved. "Why bother caring now?"

"You know I care, Jo," he said softly. "You also know why I spent the night on the couch. If we don't consummate our marriage, it will be easier to annul. Trust me, you'll want to once you've had a chance to think about it. I'm cursed. The last thing I want to do is saddle you with that and make you be a part of my life forever."

"Too late, you numbskull." She threw down her napkin.

"What are you saying?" he paled. "That you're cursed now too? The last thing I ever wanted to do was ruin your life."

"Consummation or not, it doesn't matter. You'll always be a part of my life, but you're right. You did ruin everything when you walked away from me, from your vows, from what we had. I was going to wait to tell you until after the honeymoon, but since that isn't likely to happen, I might as well tell you now. I'm not cursed, Cole, I'm pregnant. But don't do me any favors. You're free to leave because guess what…I'm the one who doesn't want *you* anymore. Not now, not ever."

All sorts of commotion happened next. Granny dropped a tray of cookies, Mitch jumped up to help Granny, and Morty hissed at him. Jo burst into tears and stormed out, leaving Cole speechless and frozen to his chair with his jaw hanging wide open. Sean stood but Zoe stopped him, telling him if he was friends with Cole, then he was no friend of hers, and then she stormed out after Jo. Cole whispered, "What have I done?" And a pounding headache hit me hard right behind the eyes.

***

I couldn't believe Jo was pregnant. Married, pregnant, yet so alone. I sat in Smokey Jo's Tavern, having guessed that would be where I would find her. Sunday nights weren't busy to begin with, and she was supposed to be gone on her honeymoon, but this was as much a home to her as her new house. This was her first born.

"Seriously, are you okay?" I asked, then reached out and grabbed her hand to stop her from rubbing the varnish right off her rich mahogany bar. Soft seventies folk music filtered out of the speakers in soothing tones, and warm amber lighting cast a pleasant glow of ambiance, making Smokey Jo's a hit with most people in town.

She sniffed and blinked, but she refused to cry any more. "No, I'm not alright. Do you know how long I waited for this? I've dreamt of my wedding day and reception and honeymoon for half my life, but I never really thought it would happen. When Cole asked me to marry him, it was like a dream come true. I should have known it was too good to be true. I pushed him too hard to get over his first wife and move in with me and play house with Biff. If he wasn't ready for any of that, then he certainly won't be ready for a baby. What have I done?" Her voice hitched despite her best efforts.

"You didn't do anything wrong, Jo." I squeezed her hand before letting it go. "And I don't believe for a second that Cole didn't want this or isn't ready for it. I think he's running scared because he loves you so much. He doesn't care about his own well-being. He is petrified of making another mistake and putting your life at risk. All because of some silly superstition that his life is cursed."

"Well, he can't afford to be silly." She thrust her chin in the air. "He's going to be a father, whether he likes it or not."

"Did you mean it when you said you didn't want him anymore?" I asked gently.

She burst into tears. "No!" she wailed. "I love him more than I've ever loved anyone. I don't want to live a single day without him. I just can't seem to stop crying."

"It's the hormones," I said and couldn't keep my lips from tipping up at the corners ever so slightly. "You're a hot mess, you know that?"

She laughed despite herself and eyed me as if she knew something I didn't. "You just wait until you're in this condition."

I sobered at that thought and crossed my arms over my front as if that would somehow protect me. "Um, yeah, that's not likely to happen anytime soon."

"Oh, please. Mitch has already proposed once, and he's living with you, for Pete's sake. All I can say is be ready for a little payback from me when you become a blubbering fool. Like it or not, it's going to happen, and soon if I'm not mistaken." She started restocking the glasses behind the bar.

"Whatever you say," I responded almost numbly. The thought of having a baby had never crossed my mind, yet marrying Mitch had. What if he wanted children? I had never thought to ask. Probably because I didn't even know if I did yet. My parents certainly weren't the best role models. Who's to say I would be any good at it? All I knew for certain was that I couldn't imagine my life without him.

"Earth to Sunny." Jo waved her hand before my face.

"Huh, what? Sorry," I muttered with a sheepish expression on my face. I was the one who was supposed to be giving her advice, yet Jo was always in counseling mode when behind the bar. It was one of the things she did best.

"I said, how are things going with you and my favorite detective?" She looked at me as if she could see straight into my soul.

"Everything's fine," I answered automatically. "The last thing you need to worry about is me."

"Trust me, I need to focus on someone's relationship other than my own at the moment. So fess up, okay? Don't make me think I'm alone in this insane thing called life." She rubbed her aching back and leaned on the bar for a moment.

"Okay, okay." I sighed. "Honestly, I'm not sure how things are going between Mitch and me."

"Why?"

"Well, for one, he hasn't said he loves me since he proposed and I told him to take it slow."

"Um, can you blame him?" she said gently.

"No. And I regret not saying yes right away. I wanted to. I guess I just wanted him to be sure. Mitch is an all or nothing, black or white kind of guy. My life is far from black and white. I wanted to make sure he could handle the gray area in between."

"Gray area meaning Morty and Granny?" Jo popped the top on a beer for me and a root beer for her, coming around the bar and sitting on a stool beside me.

"Precisely." I took a grateful sip before continuing. "They're not exactly easy to live with, but they are a part of me.

I know he wants me. He proved that the other night, several times." I blushed. "But can he live with *all* of me?"

"That is the question, isn't it? Same question Cole has to decide. I know he thinks he's saving me from himself, but it's not just me he has to worry about anymore. Our baby deserves a father, but if he doesn't get his act together soon, I won't have him. I'm a strong woman. I don't need a man to complete me."

That gave me pause, and suddenly, I realized I didn't need a man to complete myself either. "You know what, you're right. I don't need Mitch to complete me, either. If he doesn't get *his* act together soon and realize Morty, Granny, and I are a package deal, then it's his loss." Now that I had said the words that had been buzzing about in my mind for weeks, I suddenly felt free.

"I hear that." Zoe came to a stop beside us, and Jo and I both jumped. Neither one of us had heard her come in.

"Men! They're all more work than they're worth." She plopped down on a stool with a glass of wine already in hand. "Your bar-back has officially driven me to drink, and I don't even really like alcohol." She took a dainty sip. It was clear she was starting to get tipsy, yet she still looked as stylish as ever in her Sunday best. She finished with, "But it's growing on me I must say."

"What's Sean done now?" Jo asked.

"What *hasn't* he done?" I laughed.

"Taken me out on a proper date, for one." Zoe shook her head in disgust. "And then he has the nerve to freak out over the word baby and sputter, '*You're* not pregnant, are you?' I mean, seriously?"

"He did not," I said, my jaw falling open.

"Oh, yes he did." Zoe scoffed.

"How did you respond?" Jo asked, a spark of curiosity and something more than depression entered her eyes.

"I told him considering I've never been with *any* man, my baby would be truly blessed. Can you say Immaculate Conception? To which he freaked out even more. I guess me being pregnant would be less scary than me being a virgin. Ugh. I repeat, Men! Way more trouble than they're worth." Zoe took a hearty sip this time.

I couldn't help but giggle. "I'm sorry. I'm not laughing at you, I promise. I'm laughing at Ladies' Man Sean falling in love with a virgin. He's gonna need Doc Wilcox, stat!"

Zoe blinked. "Love?" Then she shook her head, wobbling a bit. "Oh, I don't think he's in love with me. He hasn't even kissed me."

"That's what makes it all the sweeter." I grinned.

"Honey, we know that boy better than anyone. He's got it bad, and you are oh-so-good for him, my darling. Now take my root beer and give me that wine before you fall on your butt. My goodness, but we are all a mess."

"You don't need wine, you're pregnant." Zoe blinked up at Jo, confused.

"Oh, I *need* it all right, but I'm not going to drink it, and neither are you. The last thing I need is another light weight falling off my barstool." She gave me a pointed look as she slid the drink away from Zoe. Zoe shrugged then took a sip of the root beer as Jo continued to talk. "Speaking of needing something, I know someone who needs you more than ever." Jo gave me another meaningful look.

I groaned, knowing exactly who she meant. "My mother, right?"

"You're luckier than you know. She really is a great woman. And right now, she must be freaking out. As much as I wanted to smack her for starting crap with Mr. Theodore, I know in my gut she isn't capable of murder. And being a top notch lawyer, it must kill her being the one accused."

I sighed long and deep. "I know, you're right, and it does. Of course she refuses to admit she's worried, and she would never dream of asking for my help, so the burden is once again left up to me."

"Families aren't easy, Sunny. I get that. Trust me, mine is huge and a big pain in the butt half the time, but…family is family, for better or worse."

"I know, and I'm on it. She might not appreciate it, but I will do my best to clear her name. At the very least it will free her to leave town, which is never a bad thing. I love my parents, but we get along much better long distance."

"Amen to that, sister." Jo raised a glass of water.

Zoe raised her soda. "Amen to the sisterhood."

And I raised my beer. "Amen to the future…whatever it may bring."

Chapter 7

On Monday morning I pulled into the parking lot of Benedict and Rossetti, the accounting firm that handled Peirce Theodore's inn, Divine Inspiration. My slightly rusted but well-loved VW bug with the orange, yellow, and pink flowers on the sides sputtered and then died as I cut the engine. She'd seen me through some pretty rough times. Thanks to Big Don of Don's Auto body, she still had some life left in her.

Unlike Peirce Theodore.

I still couldn't believe he was dead. I had just done a reading for him a couple of days ago and had given him so much hope. How was he supposed to come into money if he was dead? But then I remembered the reading had shown that his inn would finally be put on the map from something in the past. I had assumed that something had to do with Peirce, but apparently not. I felt more obligated than ever to find out what it *did* have to do with.

I still wondered if his widow Linda had arranged to have him killed somehow. She had conveniently taken out a large life insurance policy right before he died. She claimed it was because she was worried. That she had received threatening phone calls, and he had been arguing with his accountant, Brice

Benedict, a lot as of late. So here I sat, ready to talk to Brice, even though I knew Mitch wouldn't be happy about it.

I got out of my car and made my way to the front door of the quaint brick building. The air was crisp, and the sun shining bright and clear, as though nothing were wrong whatsoever. A beautiful, picture perfect, fall day. But pictures could be deceiving. I'd learned that the hard way throughout my life and especially since I'd moved to Divinity just nine short months ago. Nothing about this town was picture perfect.

I reached for the doorknob, and it swung open of its own accord. A man I had never seen barged outside with an angry look on his face. I nearly bumped into him, and his face registered surprise and then quickly masked any expression at all. He was tall and distinguished with a full white head of hair and a tailored suit. He looked like the perfect businessman, but it was the piercing in his left ear that made him seem out of place.

He grabbed my arm with a firm grip to steady me and donned a look of concern as he asked, "Are you okay, ma'am?" A whiff of expensive smelling cologne wafted past my nose. He looked like someone who would fit into my parents' world more so than our charming small town.

I smiled despite my uneasy feeling. He looked completely respectable, but he didn't seem genuine somehow. "I'm fine." I gently pulled my arm from his rather large hand. "Thank you for asking."

"You're welcome. And what did you say your name was?" The question itself wasn't really all that odd, given we had just run into each other. Introductions were usually a part of first meeting someone, but it somehow felt out of place.

"I didn't." I frowned in response, my uneasiness increasing. Alarm bells were telling me not to tell him my name, though it wouldn't be that difficult for him to find out in such a small town. Hopefully he was passing through and wouldn't stick around for long. Maybe he was a client from out of town. "Well, I've gotta run."

He narrowed his eyes for a second, and I could have sworn a flash of that scary look crossed his face again, but then he pasted on a bright smile, making me wonder if I had imagined it. "I'd better not keep you, then." He tipped his head and went about his business, heading down the street.

Hurrying into the office, I climbed the stairs until I reached the second floor suite. "Mr. Benedict, I presume." I held out my hand to the frazzled looking man pacing the room. "You're the exact person I've been looking for."

He blinked, looking startled, his thinning red combed-over hair was slightly askew and his spectacles were perched on the end of his beak-like nose. He checked his watch. "Do we have an appointment?" He stared at me like he was scared to death.

"Well, no, not exactly." I looked around the nicely furnished suite, thinking his business must be booming.

His forehead puckered. "I'm sorry. Who are you?" His terrified look remained, and beads of perspiration had started to form on his upper lip.

"My name is Sunny Meadows, and I'm a consultant for the Divinity Police Department." I held out my hand, but he stood there, growing paler by the second. I lowered my hand, and that seemed to jar him out of his stupor.

He cleared his throat and stood a little straighter. "What on earth could the police possibly want with me?"

"Oh, I'm sorry. I didn't mean to give off the impression that you're a wanted man." I chose my words with a definite strategy in mind.

"Wanted man? But you can't prove anything. I mean, I didn't do anything," he sputtered, looking on the verge of hyperventilating.

Interesting. "I didn't say you did anything, Mr. Benedict, and neither did the police." I had to make sure I chose my words carefully or risk the wrath of Detective Grumpy Pants. He wouldn't be happy with me if I screwed up his case.

"That's right, you're not the police. And since you're not the police, then what do *you* want with me?" he rephrased his question, looking less alarmed and more annoyed now. I needed to put him at ease and gain his trust. The last thing I needed was to frustrate him and have him throw me out, which technically he had every right to do, since I really didn't have any business being there.

"Well, I was talking to Mrs. Theodore, and she happened to mention that you were the accountant in charge of their inn. I know Mr. Theodore would settle for nothing but the best, God rest his soul."

"I read about what happened in the paper. What a shame. I liked Peirce." Brice stared off into the distance and sounded surprisingly genuine.

"I'm not sure if you know this, but I happen to own my own business as well." I interrupted his thoughts.

"Sunny's Sanctuary, right?" His eyes widened warily and they focused on me as recognition dawned. "You're the fortune-teller lady. There aren't many people in Divinity who haven't heard of you," he said, but his face read, *And all the trouble that follows you.* "I'm not taking on any new clients, if that's what you're wondering," he quickly added.

"Is that why the man I ran into outside was angry?" I asked, point blank, knowing I was running out of time and not really sure how to get to the bottom of why he and Peirce had been arguing right before he died. I wasn't officially working with the police on this case, so Brice wasn't obligated to tell me anything. I was banking on him not knowing that.

"I don't know what you're talking about," he answered a little too quickly. "The man was probably Rossetti's client, not mine. Now if you'll excuse me, Miss Meadows, I have to get ready for a meeting."

I handed him my card. "If you change your mind, I would love to talk to you more. Financial decisions are so important. I would hate to make a bad investment. Things like that can affect a person's future in a big way, don't you agree?"

"Yes, yes, of course. I will give your name to Rossetti and have him call you." Brice ushered me toward the door.

"That would be wonderful. Thank you so much. I'm sure he'll be a big help, like he was for that man I saw outside." I paused and scratched my head. "Then again, maybe not. The guy did seem rather angry."

Brice paused at that, as if weighing something of grave importance. "You know, we don't need to bother Rossetti," Brice said. "He's been under a lot of pressure lately. Health issues. Maybe I can squeeze you in after all. I'll have my secretary call you to set up a time to talk. But I really must get back to work now."

I blinked, trying to appear innocent, and then donned a pleased expression. "Today must be my lucky day. I'm so glad you changed your mind, Mr. Benedict, and I can't wait to hear what you have to say. Something tells me you're the key to solving my problem."

"One can hope," he grumbled and waved me off as the shut the door behind me with a resounding thump.

But I didn't have to hope. I knew. He was definitely hiding something, and my gut told me that something had to do with Scary Guy. Now if only I could figure out what and how it was connected to Peirce, it just might be the key to setting my mother free.

***

I pulled into my driveway with a sigh of relief. Detective Stone was at the office. I felt pretty good about Mitch not discovering I had been at Benedict and Rossetti's this morning. It was nice to know I could dodge at least one bullet. I loved Mitch, but my safety was one subject we would never agree on. He still wasn't a true believer and he wasn't crazy about me working with the police, no matter how many times I had proven myself to be an asset. But mostly he drove me crazy trying to protect me, especially when I was too close to a case. This time was no exception.

I wasn't stupid. Yes, I took chances and often found myself in the most bizarre predicaments, but I knew enough not to willingly put myself in danger. At least I now had a lead, which was probably more than he had. Although I couldn't know for sure because as usual he refused to share any details with me. If we were ever going to work, he needed to start treating me as a partner. In work, in life, in general. I headed inside and heard the vacuum cleaner running. Today was Monday. Granny always cleaned on Mondays.

She shut the vacuum off. "Hi, Sunshine. You slipped out mighty early this fine morning. Detective Stone left shortly after you. Busy little bees, you two." She looked at me with sharp, knowing, brown eyes. "Not too busy to make time for each other, I hope."

"We're trying," I replied honestly.

"Well, that's good. Relationships are work, but they are so worth it in the end." She smiled wistfully, remembering Grandpa Frank I was sure. "I'm going to go apple picking after I finish my chores," she finally spoke again. "Do you want to come along and help? It's a beautiful day. I'm thinking homemade apple crisp tonight and a lovely apple pie for this weekend. What do you think about that?"

"You mean you're not making apple cookies?" I stared at her in mock shock, avoiding answering her about going apple picking. I had way too much to do like solving my mother's case. Knowing Granny, she would slip up and tell Detective Stone. Something I so did not need to happen right now.

My granny always wore her recycled apron made out of flour sacks, with her wooden spoon at the ready sticking out of her pocket, and the oven was almost constantly on pre-heat. She truly believed there was a cookie for everything. Ever since Grandpa Frank died, she had stored her money in shoe boxes and freezer bags, hoarding it away for a rainy day and reusing everything she could get her hands on.

Poor Morty had taken Grandpa Frank's place as her companion, being such a good sport about her dressing him up in bowties made out of old draperies. Granny Gert had been lonely before moving in with me. Now she felt needed. She had a purpose. Taking care of Morty and flirting with Captain Walker kept her feeling like a feisty kitten—her words not mine.

"Oh, don't be silly. You know there will be cookies. What's a party without cookies?" She started humming as she dusted the knickknacks, her perfectly styled snow white hair not moving an inch. It had turned snow white after having scarlet fever at sixteen, but she'd never dyed it. A firm believer in everything happening for a reason, she said she didn't want to mess with what the good Lord had given her. A wise choice since it had become the envy of most people she met.

Her words set in, and my grin faded away. "A party? What party?" The words party and Granny Gert did *not* mix.

"Well, seeing as how it's fall harvest and apple season and the leaves are simply lovely, I thought a party was in order. Besides, your mother could use a little pick-me-up."

"B-But she won't go anywhere near Morty," I stuttered, desperate to stop my granny's idea of a fall harvest party.

Every time Granny planned a party a fiasco happened, and I was left cleaning up the mess. I already had a big enough mess to get my mother out of. I certainly didn't need any Granny trouble. Not to mention Jo was still in need of help, and now Zoe was having guy trouble, and my relationship was pretty much at a stale mate. I couldn't imagine what could possibly happen next.

"Oh, don't you worry about a thing, dearie. I'll take care of everything. In fact, I already thought of your mother and Morty not being overly fond of each other. So I organized a committee, and we're throwing the party in Mini-Central Park."

"That's what I was afraid of," I muttered, but she had already turned the vacuum back on, humming and singing as she twittered about.

The doorbell rang, and I headed in that direction, knowing Granny would never hear it. Morty appeared out of nowhere wearing a red, orange, and yellow leaf-patterned bowtie. He hissed, and I couldn't blame him.

"Sorry, buddy. I have about as much control over Granny as you do." I took a step toward the door.

Morty hissed louder.

"Honestly, Morty, what is the matter with you? Mayer Cromwell is here for his reading. Now step aside and be a good boy."

He refused to step aside or be good, so I walked around him.

Shaking my head, I shot him a frown and then took a deep breath and formed my lips into a welcoming smile. I opened the door and started to say hello, but the word died on my tongue. Mayor Cromwell was *not* at the door.

Scary Guy was.

Chapter 8

Later that day I stopped by the Divinity Police Station to bring Mitch his lunch. Granny Gert was right. Relationships couldn't be taken for granted, so if I ever wanted to move beyond our stale mate, I needed to take the initiative. Cutting the engine to my bug, I picked up a basket filled with a steaming bowl of homemade chili, still hot-from-the-oven rolls, and a big slice of apple pie. Granny always says the way to a man's heart is through his stomach, but I am no fool.

I had Granny do the cooking.

I walked down the long hallway, nodding hello to the dispatcher as I passed her, and I made a pit stop by Captain Walker's office to drop off some apple cookies, much to his delight. He mumbled a thank you around a mouthful of sugar, his eyes rolling back in his head. He sure did love Granny's cookies, and if I had to guess, I would wager he enjoyed flirting with her just as much.

Pausing at the door to Mitch's office, I took a moment to study him since he didn't see me right away. He ran a hand through his shaggy black hair and rubbed his temple, his shoulders looking tense and his profile tired. He picked up a picture of me—the only personal touch he'd added to the space since I'd known him—and his brows pinched together, making him look troubled. His desk was cluttered with files and crumpled up pieces of paper as if he'd been working all morning but not having much luck. I was about to change that if he would let me without locking me up and throwing away the key.

I tapped my knuckles twice and he looked up as he set down his picture, his face transforming into a pleased expression. "You are the best thing I've seen all morning, and whatever that is, it smells amazing."

I smiled tenderly as I walked into the room, set the basket down on the desk, slipped my arms around him, and sat on his lap. "You work too hard." I kissed his cheek. He smelled of soap and after shave and Granny Gert's sugar cookies.

He took a moment to wrap his arms around me, bury his face in the crook of my neck and inhale my scent, sending chills up and down my spine. I threaded my fingers through his hair and massaged his scalp. He allowed it for a moment and I could feel him start to relax, but then he pulled back.

"You don't know how much I needed that right now, but if I don't work harder, I'm afraid your mother's case will look even worse than it already does. I need to find another lead and soon."

"Funny you should say that." I stood up from his lap and pulled out the food to distract him. I placed it on the desk in front of him, including real silverware and an embroidered linen napkin at Granny's insistence, and then stood back. Only after he started to dig in, did I add, "I ran into Brice Benedict this morning."

Mitch paused with his spoon full of chili halfway to his mouth. His eyes narrowed. "Ran into? And where exactly did this encounter with the deceased's *accountant* happen to take place? At the grocery store? Oh wait, you don't cook." He set his spoon down and pushed the bowl away, sitting back and crossing his arms. "Let me guess, this is all a bribe so I won't get angry at you for sticking your nose in where it doesn't belong and putting yourself in danger yet again. I'm right, aren't I?" He raised a brow and waited.

I sighed, knowing it was pointless to deny it. "Fine, you win. What you call a bribe, I call an offer of peace. Although, I do think you work too hard, and I knew you wouldn't take time to get lunch yourself. It's my job as your *girlfriend* to care about your Health Line."

I could see his mind and body were at war. His hunger won out, pushing the last remnants of his stubborn streak to take a backseat until lunch was over. He grabbed the bowl and grunted while he finished the food, gesturing for me to start talking.

"Okay, so when I was speaking with Linda Theodore, she mentioned something about Peirce making late night phone calls and whispering and acting sneaky. At first she thought he was having an affair, but then she found out the calls were to his accountant."

"So naturally you just had to go see him yourself instead of telling me." Mitch scowled, his tone screaming pure frustration.

"I'm telling you now. Doesn't that count for something?" I flashed my pearly whites and fluttered my eyelashes at him, attempting to look adorable.

He just rolled his eyes and shook his head.

Giving up on a lost cause, I continued. "Anyway, in my efforts to *help* you, even though you don't appreciate it, I stopped by his office this morning. I have to say Brice acted even more nervous than Peirce."

"People generally act nervous when murder is involved. That's hardly newsworthy, Tink."

"No, but I ran into this big scary guy I've never seen before who showed up at the house later and—"

"Wait, back up. What?" Detective Stone gaped at me in pure cop mode, Boyfriend Mitch all but gone.

"I was fine." I held up my hands. "Granny was there, and Morty."

"Yeah, and we see how well that worked out for you last time when you got kidnapped," he growled in exasperation, worry lines bracketing the corners of his wide firm mouth once more.

"The point is, Scary Guy really wasn't all that scary. I did some digging and word around town is he's actually from the IRS. Apparently Peirce files quarterly, and something in his books didn't add up. This guy is here investigating, but Mr. Benedict isn't exactly cooperating. When the IRS agent saw me talking to Brice, he thought I might know something. I don't, of course, but I thought that you might want to look into this as well. What if Brice was involved in something illegal and Peirce found out about it? Brice might have killed him or hired someone to kill him before anyone else could find out. He probably didn't anticipate the IRS catching up with him first."

"You have one active imagination, Sunny, but I *am* glad you told me. At this point I'm grateful for any lead that points away from your mother."

"Amen to that. You're not mad then?" I smiled at him hopefully.

"I wouldn't go that far," he replied, but the corner of his lip tipped up a hair as he added, "we'll work out your punishment later."

"Is that a threat, Detective?"

"That's a promise," he said with a serious tone, but something in his eyes told me this was a punishment I just might enjoy.

***

The leaves were changing rapidly this season, and many had already fallen in my back yard. I didn't have any appointments this afternoon, and Granny was driving me nuts planning her fall harvest party to cheer up my mother. Something told me Granny's attempt to *help* was only going to make matters worse. She promised it wouldn't get out of control this time, and Mother wouldn't have to deal with Morty if it was at the park, but still....

I chuckled as Morty popped out of a pile of leaves I had just raked, as if he were practicing a magic act. Knowing him, he was planning on terrorizing my parents anyway. It didn't matter if the party was inside or out or on a different planet. Everyone knew Morty went where he wanted and did as he pleased. He had a leaf stuck to his eye, making him look like he had an eye patch on. I peeled it off, and he just stared at me, then started digging in the dirt as if I were insignificant.

"Behave yourself, Mister." I pointed my finger at him, but he just hoisted his chin high in the air and walked away, messy paws and all.

"Need some help?" came a welcome voice from behind me.

I spun around with a genuine smile on my face. Now this was the kind of help I could use right about now. "Why, Sean O'Malley in the flesh, offering to do manual labor for free. Mark the calendar."

"Who says my offer is free? Spending time with all of this," he swept his hands up and down his impressive body, "will cost you, love." He grinned wide, his charming dimples sinking deep. He really was a character.

"Um, you came to me. Not the other way around, Romeo," I pointed out. "Besides, aren't you taken?"

His dimples faded and sparkling blue eyes dimmed. "I wish. The stubborn lass is giving me the cold shoulder. Can you believe it?"

"Well, come on, Sean. You *did* ask her if she was pregnant. I still can't believe you did that." I put my hands on my hips and gave him a look that said it all. "What did you honestly expect?"

"I'll tell you what I *didn't* expect. For her to be a virgin, that's what." He raked a hand through his blond curls and began to pace. "What am I supposed to do with that?"

"You're supposed to cherish that and thank your lucky stars you found such a gem of a woman to put up with you." I swatted him on the arm.

"She really is an angel, isn't she?" He scrubbed a hand over his stubble-covered face, looking more unkempt and flustered than I had ever seen him. "Trouble is I think I've lost her for good, Sunny." He stopped pacing and looked at the ground, his shoulders wilting a little. "She's different than any woman I've ever dated. I didn't know I could feel this way, and it scares the hell out of me."

My heart went out to him. He really was a mess, and that made him all the more endearing. "So why are you telling me?" I poked him in the shoulder. "Zoe is the one you should be telling, you numbskull."

He rubbed his shoulder. "I tried talking to her, but she won't listen to me. I think it's too late."

"Nonsense. It's never too late when you care about someone." I patted his cheek until he looked at me. "It's not what you say, Sean, it's *how* you say it. Quit feeding her lines. They don't work on someone like her. Speak from your heart and just talk to her. She'll listen, I promise. What do you have to lose?"

"I'll rake your entire yard if you do it for me." He gave me such an adorable expression, I almost caved. Not to mention my yard was really big, and his offer was extremely tempting, but I knew Zoe.

I let out a deep sigh and replied, "Sorry, pal, but I'm doing this for your own good. This is one conversation no one can have but you."

He shoved his hands in his pockets and hung his head. "That's what I thought you were going to say."

"You're a big boy. You can do this." I gave him a hug. "Who knows? Maybe you'll be planning a wedding of your own soon."

His face paled. "Baby steps, Sunny. I'd settle for a real date and a first kiss. Good God, I never thought I'd hear myself say that, but damned if I don't mean it. I haven't looked forward to a simple kiss since I had pimples."

"*You* had pimples?" I gaped at him in mock horror.

"Seriously, love? My pimple status is what you got out of all of that?" He scowled without much venom. Sean was a lover. He couldn't be mad if he tried.

"No, I'm just playing." I laughed. "What I got out of your endearing confession is that she's changing you for the better, my friend."

He took a moment to ponder my words. "You think so?"

"I know so."

"Thanks, Sunny." He turned around and started to walk away, looking more like himself with a spark of hope in his step he couldn't quite hide.

"Hey, wait a minute. Where are you going?" I held up my rake after realizing what I'd just done. Why was it every time I tried to help someone, I only ended up hurting myself in one way or another?

"You were right. All this," he turned around and swept his hand down his frame once more, "isn't suited for manual labor." He winked, then spun back around and kept walking now as if he had purpose in his ever stride.

He had purpose, all right. To get far away from a little thing called hard work. "I take it back. You haven't changed at all," I hollered after him. He just laughed and kept walking and even started to whistle and dance an Irish jig.

Mitch passed by Sean, shot him a wave with an odd look, picked up a rake without having to be asked, and joined me.

"Now here's a *real* man," I said and gave him a kiss when he came to a stop by my side, thinking, *My man.*

"Was there ever any doubt?" he replied with his rich deep tone that never failed to give me shivers. "What's Granny Gert doing with all those apple desserts? It's not even her baking day."

The mention of Granny Gert put the kibosh on my shivers in a hurry. "Planning a fall harvest party to cheer Mother up." I groaned.

"Please tell me you're kidding." His face looked pained.

"I wish. She even put a call into her Sewing Sisters as well as Fiona and the Knitting Nanas for help."

"Great. I'll tell Fire Chief Drummond down at the firehouse to stay alert. Remember last time those two worked together?"

"Don't remind me," I responded, thinking of the kitchen fire they'd set in my house and then Fiona getting stuck in a tree while they were under house arrest. "It doesn't matter if they are friends or foes. The Dynamic Duo are more like the Disaster Duo if you ask me, but never mind that." I pushed those scary thoughts away. "You're home early. How come?"

"After you left I paid your IRS guy a visit, and together we made a little stop in to see Brice Benedict. It didn't take much for Benedict to confess. Turns out he invested money from Peirce Theodore without his consent into some bad deals. The deals went south and Brice lost Peirce's money."

"Wow, that's terrible. No wonder Peirce was stressed out and looking for money. He had to be on the verge of losing the inn."

"That's not all. The people Brice was in bed with are shady at best and downright dangerous." Mitch gave me a stern look that said, *Now do you see why I worry?* "I think they're the ones who were roughing Peirce up, trying to squeeze more money out of him. Brice confessed because he's more afraid of them than being behind bars."

"So what happens now?"

"Now you stay away and let me do my job."

"And?" I said noncommittally.

"And Brice will probably go to jail while Linda's life insurance money will go to the IRS, putting her back at square one. She will probably have to sell the inn unless she comes into some magic money somehow."

"Magic money," I mumbled, thinking of a plan. I was trying to be good and stay out of this case, but I had to do something to help or I would go crazy.

"I know that look, Sunny." Mitch tipped up my chin. "Please tell me you aren't thinking of doing something stupid?"

"Me, something stupid? Of course not." I laughed a little too loudly. "Why would you even think such a thing?"

"You seriously have to ask?" he sputtered.

"You do your job, honey." I patted his chest. "And let me do mine."

I left him with the rake as I made my way back to the house with him shouting, "That's what I'm afraid of," from behind me.

I smiled warmly. He knew me so well, because that was exactly what I was going to do. My job. Peirce's reading had said he was going to come into money and the inn was going to be put on the map. I somehow felt guilty for Peirce dying, even though I knew I had nothing to do with it. I might not have been able to save him, but I could certainly help save his business. Besides, ever since giving him that reading, one thought kept rolling through my brain. I knew I wouldn't rest until I found out what it meant.

The secret lies within the walls of the inn.

Chapter 9

"Do you think this is a good idea?" Zoe asked as we stepped out of Jo's suburban.

Jo always drove when we went somewhere together because Jo liked being in control of everything in her life, which was especially important at the moment since it was obvious she felt like her world was spinning out of control. It was Monday night and Sean was manning the bar, trying to make Jo happy. He might be a devil, but no one could deny he was an amazing friend. Meanwhile Cole was home dog-sitting Biff, cleaning the house, and basically doing anything he could to get back in her good graces.

"Good idea or not, we're doing it." Jo zipped up her fleece over her rapidly thickening middle. "I need to get out of the house before I throw up or kill my husband. You're avoiding Sean and having to *talk* to him seriously for once, so don't even try to deny it. And Sunny needs to stay out of trouble and let Mitch do his job. What better way to do that than to see if we can solve a good mystery that has nothing to do with murder. It has to do with the future. Nothing dangerous about that."

"Thank you both for being with me. I feel really bad that Mr. Theodore died and I wasn't able to help him." I shivered over the quickly dropping evening temperature. As I tightened my fringed sweater coat, I wished I had put a pair of socks and boots on instead of sandals. I tended to be impulsive, which did not serve me well when planning a mission—something I vowed to work on and soon. Focusing on the task at hand instead of my freezing toes, I added, "If I can just figure out what his reading meant, then maybe I can help save his inn."

"While you're at it, maybe you can figure out what I'm supposed to do about Sean," Zoe grumbled, not looking cold at all in her sensible yet stylish wool coat. "Actually, never mind. You guys are friends with him, so I highly doubt you could remain impartial."

She started walking toward the Divine Inspiration Inn that looked deceivingly normal now that all traces of the wedding and murder had been removed. The crime scene had already been investigated, and Peirce had been cremated in a private ceremony. Loyal workers still wandered about the grounds. The only thing missing were the guests.

"Yeah we're friends with Sean, but you're family." Jo draped her arm over Zoe's shoulders. "I adore Sean, but I love you. I would never steer you wrong. You have my word on that. Right now men don't rank very high on my list."

"Well, I'm no expert when it comes to love." I snorted. "Just look at Mitch and me. We don't do anything the normal way. I'm not even sure exactly where we stand right now. But I do know that Cole loves you, Jo. He might be afraid, but you know he's crazy about you and he will make an amazing father. Just look at how he is with Biff."

"I know that, but still, I'm not through with making him suffer after what he did to me." Jo raised her chin a notch. "Blame it on the hormones, but I figure I'm entitled to a little revenge. I only plan to get married once and you only get one wedding night and honeymoon. He ruined that. I'll come around eventually, it's how we do things. And then he will spend the rest of our lives making it up to me." She winked.

"You're so bad," I said half laughing. "And, Zoe, you really are lucky. Sean might be a lover of all women, but he's never fallen for a single one until you. I always knew once he met the right woman, he would be a goner. He would hang up his roving ways and be the most loyal, doting man on the planet. He'll treat you like gold if you just give him a chance, I promise." At least Sean couldn't say I didn't try. The rest was up to him.

"Maybe." She looked hopeful yet doubtful at the same time. "But I'm with Jo. I deserve a little payback, and that boy deserves to beg. I don't think any woman has *ever* said no to him regarding anything. I have been saving myself for a special man. If he wants to be that man, he's going to have to earn it." She snapped her spine straight, and the family resemblance between her and Jo was suddenly crystal clear. "Speaking of earning it, don't you think Detective Stone has proven he's worthy to be the man in your life?"

"Absolutely," I answered easily. "The problem is getting him to say he loves me and ask me to marry him again. I never should have said let's take things slow because now I'm afraid he will never propose."

"Who says he has to be the one to propose?" Jo asked.

I blinked, and my heart did a funny little flip. "I don't know," I finally responded. "I wouldn't have a clue where to begin, and I tend to make a disaster of pretty much everything. You really think I should do it?" I chewed my bottom lip as the idea took root and nestled in my belly where it began to grow and blossom and push my doubts aside.

"Why not? You're a modern, free-thinking woman. If anyone can pull it off, you can." Zoe beamed.

A slow grin spread across my face. "You guys are right, darn it." I felt excitement and nervousness battle within me. "I'm going to do it. I am going to propose to Mitch just as soon we clear my mother's name. I want the moment to be perfect with no distractions or worries hanging over our heads."

"Then let's get this show on the road, ladies." Jo knocked on the door to the inn. It had remained locked since Linda had shut her doors.

The door swung open and Sally Clark the crisply starched elderly maid stood ramrod straight and eyed us warily. "May I help you?"

"Is Mrs. Theodore home? We would like to have a word with her." I smiled.

Ms. Clark did *not* smile back.

"You already did just the other day." She started to close the door in my face, but Jo stuck her foot in the way.

"Well, I didn't." Jo stood to her full Amazon height, and the maid's eyes widened a fraction.

"We'll be happy to wait here while you go ask her," Zoe said. "And please let her know I have a business proposition for her."

Ms. Clark nodded once, then closed the door in our faces with success this time, but only because Jo allowed it.

"You have a business proposition?" I asked.

"Well, *we* do, but I thought she might take us more seriously if the idea came from me. No offense, but she doesn't seem to like you or your business." Zoe shrugged.

"None taken," I said easily. I was used to people not taking my profession seriously. "I'm all for anything that will get us inside."

Five minutes later the door opened. "Follow me," Ms. Clark said.

We followed her into the dining room where Pierre Desjardins the chef was trying to get Linda Theodore to eat something. She looked like she'd been crying. He backed away, appearing defeated. When he spotted us, he blinked in surprise and then a little wariness, but other than that his features were a mask of charming civility. He bowed a bit at the waist, looking dashing and debonair with his black slicked back hair, and then he left the room with the tray of food still in his hands. Jo nearly swooned over the delish aromas of beef and burgundy wine and spices wafting by. I had to grab her arm to keep her from running after him.

Frank Lalone the maintenance man stopped by and whispered something in Linda's ear. She frowned and then shook her head no. He nodded, gave her shoulder a quick pat, and left the room.

"Have a seat, ladies." Mrs. Theodore held a full glass of wine in her hand. It didn't look like the first one she'd had. "Ms. Clark mentioned something about a business proposition? I'm open to anything at this point."

"I heard about what happened with Mr. Theodore's accountant. I'm so sorry," I said as we all sat.

"I should have known something like this would happen. Peirce was always way too trusting of Brice. I knew we were having financial problems, but nothing to this extent. I had no idea our money was all gone. I don't even get to keep the life insurance policy. It's not fair. It will take a miracle for me not to lose my home. I hate Peirce. I'm glad he's dead." Her voice hitched.

Jo raised an auburn brow at me.

"I'm sure you don't mean that, Mrs. Theodore," Zoe chimed in.

"Hell yes I do," she said with venom. "I'd gladly sell this place and move on. I never wanted it in the first place, but I need something to live off of. Since the murder, I will be lucky to get enough to break even. How am I supposed to live after that? I don't have any skills, and I'm too young to retire. For now I need to keep this place running."

"That's where we come in," I said.

"Ah, yes, the business proposition." Mrs. Theodore looked at Zoe. "Perhaps you want to book another party?"

"Actually, *we* had something else in mind." I smiled encouragingly.

Mrs. Theodore frowned. "I'm listening."

"Well, the way I see it, we only have one choice. We have to find out what my reading for your husband meant. If we can do that, then I am certain we can find the money he was to come into."

"Are you kidding me?" The widow gaped. "You came all the way here to chase some hocus pocus pipe dream?"

"I understand it's hard to believe in what I do, but if you could just give me a chance, I would—"

"It's a bunch of nonsense, is what it is," she spat. "We'll never find the money, if there's even money to be found. Especially if the key is in the past."

"Listen, toots," Jo snapped back and slapped the table with her palm. "My back hurts, my feet hurt, and that wine smell is making me nauseous. You don't want to mess with a hormonal pregnant woman, trust me. You need us and we need you. End of story. If it will help, let Sunny read you and then you'll see. If you believe after that, then you let us worry about finding the money. What do you say?"

There was a long pause.

"You're on," Mrs. Theodore finally agreed with a smirk.

"Gee, no pressure, Jo." I glared at Jo, and she shrugged while wearing a *whoops* expression.

"Just do your thing, Sunny. You'll be great." Zoe smiled wide, but even she looked nervous.

"Here goes nothin'," I said, and for the first time ever, I doubted my own ability.

***

Ten minutes later we had moved into the living room to the exact spot where I had given Peirce his reading. Only this time his widow Linda sat next to me on the couch. I knew she was a non-believer and the odds were stacked against me from the get-go, but I had to give it a try. I owed Peirce that much. I dimmed the lights, lit some candles, and had the staff put on some soft new-age music in the background in hopes of relaxing Linda as well as myself.

"Are you ready to begin?" I asked.

She shrugged. "Sure, I guess. I mean what else do I have to lose? Besides it's going to be fun proving you're a fraud." She sneered.

Great. I might be psychic, but I wasn't a miracle worker, and if she wasn't open at least a little bit, I feared this reading was going to be a disaster. I was a professional. I could do this. I just had to remind myself I was in control.

"Okay, then." Sucking in a deep breath and exhaling slowly, I took her dominant hand in mine and turned it over so her palm faced up. I studied the lines and located the four major ones. Tracing the horizontal line from her pinkie to her index finger, I said, "Here is the Heart Line." Tracing the horizontal line below the Heart Line, I said, "And here is the Head Line." Moving on to the vertical line near the thumb that traveled in a downward arc toward the wrist, I continued. "Here is the Life Line." I searched the rest of her palm. "Let's see, it looks like you don't have a Fate Line."

She raised a brow and gave me a look that said, *How convenient.*

"Don't worry, not everyone has a Fate Line." I smiled reassuringly, refusing to let her rattle me. "It won't affect anything. I can still do the reading."

"Trust me, I'm not worried, Miss Meadows," she said dryly. "Let's just get this farce over with."

Jo looked like she really wanted to say something, but she knew me well enough to know not to speak during one of my readings. It disrupted the mood and the flow of energy. Zoe followed Jo's lead, but that didn't mean I couldn't feel their anger on my behalf. That alone warmed my heart and gave me strength.

"As you wish." I focused on the task at hand, tuning everything else out and studying her palm closely. "Let's start with the Heart Line which indicates a person's emotional stability. It doesn't take a psychic to see your emotions are in complete turmoil with the death of your husband and the financial crisis of your business."

"Gee, ya think." She snorted.

"It can also indicate depression and the cardiac health of a person as well as a person's romantic perspectives. A certain degree of depression is to be expected, but I don't see anything to indicate an unhealthy heart. I'm feeling a strong pull toward your romantic perspectives, though. Maybe your future will be filled with new hope and a new love." I glanced up at her encouragingly, but her face paled. My brows drew together as I restudied her palm and suddenly my psychic ability kicked in.

Everything around me narrowed to tunnel vision like it always did when I fell into a trancelike state. "I'm outside in the garden," I said out loud and smiled. "He's here. I can feel him behind me. My rock. This is our special place. I knew he would come. He wraps his arms around me and I feel safe, loved, wanted. I can get through anything as long as he's by my side. He kisses my neck and a warm familiarity engulfs me like I've known him for a long time. My eyes flutter closed as he turns me around and kisses me deeply. It's not the first time, and I want him more than ever. When he pulls away, I smile tenderly as I start to open my eyes so I can look into his and see—"

"Enough!" Mrs. Theodore barked.

I blinked, startled, and came out of my trance. Our eyes met. No words were necessary in the silent conversation that passed between us. She knew that I knew that this man wasn't her husband, and she now *believed* no matter what she might say. I could see it in her eyes even though I was pretty sure she would deny it all.

"But don't you want to know who you are going to fall in love with?" Zoe asked. "It's so romantic."

"My husband just died." The widow's face grew flushed. "I'm not going to fall in love with anyone anytime soon."

"But that doesn't mean you didn't already," Jo said. "That's a guilty face if ever I've seen one, and I've seen plenty in my line of work. That reading wasn't from the future, was it, Sunny? That was from the past, and I'm guessing the man of your dreams wasn't your husband."

"This is outrageous. You don't know what you're talking about." Mrs. Theodore surged to her feet, albeit a bit unsteady. "Do whatever you want with Peirce's reading, but leave me out of it."

"Except if we find money, right?" Jo eyed her knowingly. "I'll bet you want to be *in* it then, won't you, Mrs. Theodore?"

Regaining her composure, Linda hardened her jaw and said through her teeth, "Everything on this property belongs to me. Of course I want whatever you find. I hope I make myself clear."

"Oh, I think it's pretty clear," Jo said.

"Does this mean you're a believer?" I asked with a quiet voice, seeing if she would admit it out loud.

"Let's just say I'm no fool. Now if you'll excuse me, it's getting late. You can come back tomorrow. I will inform the staff. Good night, ladies. I trust you can find your own way out." She left the room with a calm outward appearance, but she wasn't fooling anyone. My reading had rattled her big-time, and I couldn't help but wonder what other secrets she was hiding.

"Was she really having an affair while Mr. Theodore was alive?" Innocent Zoe looked shocked.

"She sure was," I said.

"Did you see the man's face?" Jo asked.

"No, and I was so close." I met their curious gazes. "But it definitely wasn't her husband. When I talked to the staff the other day, a few had said there were rumors Mr. Theodore was going to fire someone. Maybe he found out who she was having an affair with, so her lover killed him before he could follow through."

"Maybe. Especially if this person knew she had taken out a life insurance policy. Do you think that was the secret that lies within the walls of the inn?" Zoe asked.

"I don't know," I responded. "Somehow the reading gave me the feeling the secret was something bigger than a mere affair, but at least Mrs. Theodore gave us free reign to dig into that mystery."

"An unsolved mystery and a new murder suspect, if only we could figure out who it is," Jo mused. "Not bad, ladies. Not bad at all. This is the exact kind of distraction I need right now to take my mind off murdering a certain man in my life these days."

"Amen to that. Count me in." Zoe grinned with excitement.

"Whoa, wait just a minute," I said. "Mitch is going to kill me, not to mention Cole and Sean will have my head if anything happens to either of you. I only needed your help in convincing Mrs. Theodore to let me look around. Now that this might have to do with the murder, Morty and I can take it from here."

"Yeah, that's not happening." Jo ignored me and she unlocked her truck.

"But…"

"Don't waste your breath, Sunny." Zoe set her jaw. "You know Jo. Once she's made up her mind about something, that's that. Same for me. Let's just say it runs in the family." She winked, but her jaw was set as she climbed into the truck.

I just stood there, numb. First Granny Gert and her fall harvest party and now the Amazon Twins thinking we're all Morty's Angels or something. I could feel a massive headache settling in already as I thought, *What kind of mess have I gotten us into now?*

Chapter 10

"How are you doing, Mom?" I asked the next morning at Warm Beginnings and Cozy Endings Café.

I sat across from my mother at a small, round, cast iron table, sipping hot cocoa and trying not to let the worry gnawing away at my insides show. The café was pretty empty this morning, but it would fill up soon I was sure. The smell of fresh baked pastries was too hard for most normal people to resist. Then again, my size two mother wasn't normal. She ate like a bird and never let me forget that I didn't.

"As well as can be expected, I suppose." She sniffed yet still looked dainty and picked up her delicate china coffee cup, taking a tiny sip. She took a moment to set her cup down and dab the corners of her mouth. When she met my gaze, her eyes were as sharp and cunning as ever. "No need to worry about me, Sylvia. I'm tougher than I look. It's my secret weapon. You of all people should know that."

What would normally rub me the wrong way actually made me breathe a sigh of relief today. "That's good." I sank my teeth in for a big bite of a chocolate frosted donut and moaned over how good it was.

My mother's perfectly plucked, golden blond eyebrow arched high, but she didn't say a word. Instead she took a small bite of her dry wheat toast followed by a nibble of strawberry and another sip of espresso. "Now, *that's* a cup of coffee." She smiled in appreciation at the café owner Natalie Kirsch's skills.

I gave my mother credit for not outright speaking ill of the dead, but I could tell she wanted to. Natalie waved at us, and I sighed, suspecting my mother would trade me in for either Natalie or Jo if given the chance. I ripped off another big hunk of donut on purpose. A small bit of defiance that made me feel more like a child than vindicated.

My mother's lips parted as if she were about to make a comment, so I blurted with donut still in my mouth, "By the way, where's Dad today?"

"Fiona and Harry are back in town."

"Ahhh," I replied, understanding perfectly.

Fiona Atwater was Granny Gert's arch nemesis and head of the Knitting Nanas who had recently become Granny's best buddy, and Harry Dingleburg was a former judge and Fiona's ex-recently-turned-present husband. My parents were fond of them both as they ran in the same circles back in the Big Apple.

As for Granny, she was more like me and not on my mother's good side either, ever since she'd permanently moved to Divinity to stay with me. My mother truly believed we conspired against her to purposely leave her out. We didn't want to leave her out, we simply got along better. Granny Gert and I were kindred spirits. That was something my mother could never seem to get over.

"Can you believe they came all the way here for your grandmother's silly cheering up party?" My mother went on. "Like I need a party." She scoffed. "I keep telling everyone I'm fine, but they insist on fussing over me anyway. They are here for me yet they won't let me help, even though they clearly need it. The only right thing they did was get my cake lady to agree to bake a theme cake for the party, but they haven't even asked for my input on the theme. And they actually talked your DJ guy into controlling the music. They really don't know me at all." She sighed.

"Well, they *are* both stuck here for the time being, so it makes sense. I mean, who else would they have asked?"

"You mean who else would be willing to come to Divinity during a murder investigation. You're right, of course, but that doesn't mean I have to like it. The men are smart. They headed straight to the lake to fish, leaving me to fend for myself. I called Joanne and Zoe but they weren't answering their phones, which is strange because they always answer my calls." She stared off thoughtfully. "Must be they're both busy as well, though what they're doing this early is beyond me."

They're probably getting ready for our secret mission, I wanted to say, but another thought came to me. "So that's the reason you asked me to meet you for breakfast. I was the only one left who wasn't busy."

"Nonsense." She shook her head disapprovingly. "You always think the worst of me, Sylvia. I know you. You're always trying to solve some sort of mystery. I didn't want to bother you."

"Well, I'm not trying to solve a mystery this time," I said with firm resolve, mostly to convince myself. "I'm trying to keep my nose out of this investigation."

"Why? Because it's my neck on the line this time?" She sat back and crossed her arms with a shrewd expression on her face, but the hurt in her voice was too obvious to miss. "Must be I'm not worthy of your time or skills."

"Now who's the one thinking the worst?" I pointed out. "It was hard enough to remain objective when Mitch and Granny were suspects, but you're my mother." I looked deep into her eyes and tried to express what I never seemed to be able to say. "It would kill me if anything happened to you."

"Me too." She spoke with a quiet voice as her walls came down for a second and I saw a flash of genuine worry, but then she opened her purse and pulled out some cash and set the money on the bill. "Look at the time. I have a million errands to run, and I'm sure you must have something to do?"

I glanced at my watch and sucked in air through my teeth. "Oh, shoot, I'm late. Jo and Zoe are going to kill me."

"Joanne and Zoe?" My mother's ears perked up, and her face puckered in confusion. "I thought you didn't know what they were up to?"

"Oh," I responded, realizing what I'd just said. "I forgot. We're just making plans for Jo's baby shower, that's all." I couldn't very well tell my mother the three of us were going to snoop around the inn and try to uncover the meaning of Peirce's reading. She would be the first person to tell on us. I hadn't thought her feelings might be hurt in not being included in planning a baby shower, which honestly, we hadn't even talked about yet. But I could tell from the expression on her face that she was indeed disappointed.

"Oh, well, if that's all, then I'll let you get to it." She stood in one swift motion. "Say hi to the girls for me."

"Mother, I—"

"You're busy." She cut me off. "I get it. No one needs me in the way these days. Like I said, I have a million things of my own to do anyway. We'll talk later, darling." She turned and left before I could say anything more and headed across the street to the library, probably to the legal section to brush up on cases similar to her own.

I picked up my fringed knapsack and left the café, deciding to find a way to make it up to her later. Right now I was late. Starting my bug, I had just pulled away from the curb when a flash of white caught my eye. I glanced at the door and did a double take as an unlikely trio entered the café together.

What on earth was the IRS man still doing in town and why wasn't Brice Benedict in jail and who was the bald guy with them?

***

"Where have you been?" Jo asked the second I stepped out of my car in front of Smokey Jo's.

She was dressed head to toe in a black warm-up suit meant for comfort and efficiency that had clearly seen better days. Jo had always had curves, yet she always looked fabulous. Today, not so much. The stress was obviously affecting her more than I realized.

I shrugged and answered her question. "Appeasing my mother, though I think I just made things worse."

"Story of your life." Jo snorted.

"No kidding." I scoffed.

"I'm sure you two will work it out," Zoe said, as she walked out the door and joined us. She was also dressed head to toe in black, but she still maintained a sense of style with her snug leggings, knee high boots, and heavy sweater.

Something was up.

"Why on earth are you two dressed all in black? We aren't cat burglars," I said. "We have permission to be there, you know."

"That's what I told her," Zoe pointed out, "but you know Jo. She's hard-headed even when she's not hormonal."

"*Jo* is standing right here," Joanne said. "And I'm not that hormonal, I'm just adventurous."

We both stared hard at her with doubtful expressions and raised eyebrows.

She laughed a little hysterical like, then said, "Okay, fine, it's the only thing I have that still fits." Her voice hitched. "All I know is it's either we all look like burnt marshmallows or I dissolve into a puddle of tears again. Take your pick."

Suddenly everything made sense.

"One burnt marshmallow coming up," I blurted quickly before she gave truth to her words. I couldn't get over how fast she was growing. Then again, we didn't call Cole Sasquatch for nothing. Opening my trunk, I reached in and pulled out Mitch's oversized sweatshirt. Thank goodness I hadn't cleaned out my bug in ages. Swapping my sweater coat for the puffy sweatshirt, I looked like a little kid playing dress up as it fell almost to my knees. "Will this work?"

Jo threw her arms around me in a bear hug, swallowing her tears as an answer.

"Okay, then, we'd better get going before Mrs. Theodore changes her mind." Zoe gave me a look that said, *Move it now before the floodgates open again.*

"Let's go," I agreed and we drove in Jo's SUV once more.

"She won't change her mind." Jo sounded more like her old self as she got us there in record time, thank goodness. "First, she'd be afraid we'd say something about her lover boy. And second, she's a believer in Sunny's abilities now. I'm betting she won't take a chance of missing out on any money Peirce might come into."

"I wonder what the *something from his past* is?" Zoe mused excitedly as we all climbed out of the vehicle. "Maybe a lottery ticket a long lost relative forgot about or some priceless antique that's been right under his nose all along."

"Anything is possible, I suppose. Only one way to find out." I headed toward the back yard of the inn.

"Where are we going?" Jo asked, hurrying to catch up with me.

"By the lake."

"Why? I thought the secret lay within the walls of the inn?" Zoe asked, sounding confused and a little breathless.

I stopped walking and faced them. "Remember when I went into a trance during the reading for Peirce, and I had a vision?"

They both nodded.

"I was in the body of a man. I remember feeling older with more aches and pains than the average person, and I felt as though I had been on a boat for a long time. Then suddenly I was standing right here." I walked over to the edge of the water. "There's a river that runs into this lake, and boats travel through here all the time. I'm sure they did years ago, too." I turned around and faced the inn. "This is the exact spot I was standing in my vision."

"Okay, but now what?" Jo asked, joining me to see what I saw.

"I'm not sure," I replied while crossing my arms and studying the grounds. "I guess we start by putting ourselves in this man's shoes, literally. What was he looking at? What did he see? Where did he go?"

"That's right, I remember now," Zoe said. "One minute you were here, and the next you were someplace else. Someplace cold and dark and musty with something yucky above your head."

"Yeah, and you heard a thumping or fluttering or something, right?" Jo said, getting into it.

"That's exactly right. So now we just have to figure out how he got from here to there, and who the heck he is, and how any of this leads to Peirce's fortune."

"I just remembered something else." Zoe's face paled. "When you were under, you mentioned feeling afraid and angry."

"You also said someone was after you," Jo chimed in. "That you had to hide and get away. Who do you think could have been after him and why?"

"I have no idea." I blew out a breath and suddenly got the feeling we were being watched. The same uneasy feeling I'd had the day of the wedding came back to me. My body tensed and grew alert as my eyes darted everywhere. "We may have bitten off more than we can chew with this one, ladies. Maybe this wasn't such a good idea." I glanced around but didn't see anything, yet undeniable chills raced up and down my spine.

"What's wrong?" Zoe grabbed my shoulders. "You look odd, like you've seen a ghost or something."

"Gotta say I'm getting a little creeped out, too." Jo's gaze followed mine, and I could feel the waves of tension roll off of her.

"Why? You two are scaring me." Zoe turned in a circle, looking everywhere.

"I don't know for sure. Just a feeling, I guess." I shook off the weird sensation. "It's probably nothing."

"Well, I don't see anything except the back of the inn, the deck, the beautiful grounds, some tables and chairs. Nothing out of the ordinary." Zoe waved to the maintenance man, Frank Lalone, as he came out of a shed on the far corner of the property.

He paused and gave us a funny look, then smiled and waved back.

She giggled. "Did you see the look on his face? He must think we've gone a little crazy with what we're wearing."

I couldn't help the bubble of laughter that slipped out of my throat to join hers. We needed this before we all freaked out. Jo nailed us both with a warning look, but then burst into laughter as she joined us. Just like that the tension was broken.

"Come on you nutcases, let's go before he calls the fashion police." Jo hooked both of our arms, and we all started walking.

"Don't worry, hon," Zoe said. "We'll go shopping tomorrow."

"I'll even join you," I added reluctantly, my mother's words of not being a very good friend haunting me. "And you know how much I hate shopping. Deal?"

"Deal." Jo squeezed us both. "I love you guys."

"Awww, me too." Zoe smiled.

"Ditto," I said, "but remember when I said the creepy feeling we just had was probably nothing?" I pulled them both to a stop and looked them each in the eye. "*That* is definitely something." I pointed to the tall bush by the back deck of the inn. Something or someone was clearly behind it, and suddenly the tension was back.

Jo picked up a stick from the ground and Zoe grabbed a rock while I formed my hands into fists and tried to remember the self-defense Mitch had taught me as I led the way slowly toward the bush. It stilled right as we drew close, and I held up my hand for the girls to halt. I mouthed, *On the count of three*, then raised my fingers up in a one, two, three motion and jumped behind the bush on three.

"Hiyah!" I yelled with my hands held in a karate position.

Jack Shepard the groundskeeper jumped a foot, the rake falling from his fingers. He was a large man with a ponytail and beard, looking more like a frightened little boy at the moment. He flushed red and then frowned, once more looking like the big tough guy he was, even though he'd clearly just proven he was a teddy bear and not some monster.

Whoops. "I'm so sorry. I didn't mean to scare you," I said.

He straightened his ponytail and smoothed his beard as he picked up the rake. "No worries, I wasn't scared at all." After clearing his throat, he continued, "Um, can I help you with something, ladies?"

"We saw the bushes rustling and thought you were the one who needed help, bro." Jo winked.

"Thanks, but I'm fine. Just pulling some weeds. I lost a good ten years," he admitted and offered us a small smile, "but it's all good. I don't need any help."

"But obviously you three do," said a familiar voice from behind us that was scarier than any monster could ever be. "What in the world do you have on?"

We all whorled around to face the music.

"Mother, what are you doing here?" I stared at her in shock.

"I could ask you the same thing." Her smile was stiff and tight. "Planning a baby shower? I think not. How about you tell me what you're *really* doing, and then I'll decide what I'm going to do about it."

Chapter 11

"I am in so much trouble when Mitch finds out." I walked every inch of the inn, searching for anything that might trigger a vision as to what happened in the past that could possibly help Divine Inspiration in the present.

"Well, he's certainly not going to find out from me," my mother said, adding dryly, "unless you try to shut me out again."

"Awww, we weren't shutting you out, Vivian." Jo placed her arm around my mother and gave her a squeeze. "You know I would never plan a baby shower without you. Sunny was just trying to protect you."

My mother patted Jo's hand and shot me a smug look. "I'm a lawyer. I think I know how to protect myself. You all have permission to be here and this quest doesn't have anything to do with the case. It has to do with the mystery of Peirce's reading, so there's no reason why I can't be involved. Not that I think we're going to find anything, mind you." She scoffed, never willing to admit she believed in my abilities in the slightest way.

"We don't know for sure it has nothing to do with the murder." She didn't know that Linda had an affair and that maybe her husband had found out. "Not to mention you're a suspect in Mr. Theodore's murder. I highly doubt his widow is going to want your help with anything," I pointed out.

"From what I saw, she didn't seem too shaken up over his death. Besides, she won't even know I'm here since she's making herself scarce these days." My mother threw up her hands. "Look, I simply need something to do before I go out of my mind and give the authorities just cause to lock me up for real."

"Whatever," I said, "but don't say I didn't tell you it was a bad idea when something goes horribly wrong, which it undoubtedly will."

She ignored my warning as her gaze traveled over the three of us. "What is with the black attire? Are you supposed to be Ladies in Black, or something?"

"Or something," Zoe said. "Don't ask. Just be ready tomorrow morning, and we'll pick you up. We're going shopping."

"Oh, yay." My mother clapped her hands.

Oh, great. I groaned.

"You okay?" Jo asked.

"Just peachy," I replied in an overly cheery voice while avoiding my mother's gaze. "Okay, we're not getting anywhere by walking around aimlessly." I changed the subject. "I've touched a bunch of objects, but I'm not picking anything up from the past."

"That's probably because this house has been refurbished over the years. Anything ancient is long gone," Sally Clark the housekeeper said, eying me sharply. She wiped a smudge off a vase I had just set down. It was clear she didn't like me. I wasn't sure if it was because she was protective over her boss, Linda Theodore, or if there was something more to it.

"Hey, what about floor plans?" Jo snapped her fingers. "I'm sure Mr. Theodore kept good records. He must have the original plans somewhere, right?"

Ms. Clark shrugged. "I wouldn't know anything about that. You would need to talk to the maintenance man, Frank Lalone. Now if you'll excuse me, some of us have real work to do." She eyed several more objects I had smudged and added, "or should I say *redo*." Sending me one last hard look, she stalked away at a brisk pace, tension in her every step.

"What on earth did you do to that woman, darling?" My mother eyed me curiously. She had the most uncanny way of saying *darling* and making it sound like she was on my side, yet making me feel guilty as sin. A person could be innocent, yet she would make them believe they were guilty by the end. It's what made her such a great lawyer.

A great mother, not so much.

"I have no idea," I responded on a heavy sigh.

"Never mind her." Jo rubbed her hands together in excitement. "Let's go find Franky Boy and get this party started."

"Last we saw him he was by that shed out back." Zoe took charge and led the way outside.

Jack Shepard, the groundskeeper, held up his large hands and took a big step back when he saw us. His expression was one of mock fear, but the twitch of his lips peeking through his beard gave him away.

"Cute *and* a sense of humor," Jo said with a snicker. "There just might be hope for you yet, Big Guy."

My mother looked at him oddly, then at Jo sharply as we walked past the patio. I raised a brow, and Zoe pressed her lips together as she looked everywhere except at Jo.

Jo rolled her eyes at us all, her look saying: *You know I love my big guy, but I'm still mad and getting fat and in major need of an ego boost, so don't judge.*

None of us said a word.

"Mr. Lalone," I hollered when I saw him working on the generator.

The short, stocky man's head popped up. When he spotted the four of us, he stood fully and wiped his hands with a rag as he lumbered toward us at a surprisingly nimble gait. He came to a stop and smiled wide. "What can I do for you ladies?"

"Ms. Clark said you might have the original floor plans to the inn before it was remodeled," I said. "Any chance we can take a peek at those?"

His forehead puckered, and he rubbed his whisker-free jaw. "I suppose that would be okay, but what in the world for?"

"A project we're working on for Mrs. Theodore," Zoe chimed in.

He frowned.

"Don't worry, pops. We're not trying to take over your job." Jo's stomach growled and she rubbed it, looking just about out of patience.

He chuckled. "I'm not worried about that. Linda and I go way back and no one knows this place like I do."

"Then you shouldn't need the floor plans, now should you," my mother said pleasantly enough, but the hard-edged lawyer lay just beneath the surface ready to pounce if need be.

She really was something to behold when in action, I thought with reluctant pride.

"Well, I've never had a use for them, and I'm not sure where Mr. Theodore kept them. I have to finish the project I'm working on right now. Give me a day, and I'm sure I can dig something up for you."

"You do that." Vivian smiled a steely smile. "We'll be back tomorrow afternoon after we're finished shopping. Will that be a suitable amount of time?"

"That'll be just fine, Mrs. Meadows." He smiled back at her just as pleasantly, but I detected a level of steel of his own. "Though I have to say after everything that's happened, I'm surprised to see you here."

"You're not the only one," came a deep voice from behind us.

Oh, yeah. I was in so much trouble. We *all* were.

***

"I really don't see what the big deal is." My mother sat perched on the edge of a cold, vinyl sofa in Mitch's office in the police station that afternoon.

Jo, Zoe, and I sat beside her like four naughty children in a time-out. Mitch had insisted we follow him to the station for questioning, and to make matters worse, he'd called in reinforcements. Donald and Harry had left their fishing posts early, stopping by to pick up Granny and Fiona in the middle of their party planning. Cole had left work during the middle of overseeing a big construction job, and Sean had found someone to cover Smokey Jo's.

None of them looked happy.

"The big deal, Mrs. Meadows," Mitch said in full detective mode now, "is that no one, *especially* you, has any business anywhere near the crime scene of a murder investigation. Are you trying to get yourself convicted?"

"The CSI department is finished, from what I could tell." I stepped in and tried to help. So not working judging by the look on his face.

Detective Stone—boyfriend Mitch was *nowhere* to be found—shot me a glare. "I'll get to you later, Miss Meadows."

"Mitch, buddy, cut us some slack." Jo donned her best innocent look. "We were only trying to help Linda by figuring out her dearly departed Peirce's reading."

"Since when did you become on a first-name bases with the Theodores?" Cole looked as if he didn't even recognize her anymore.

"Since Linda hired me to do a job, Mr. West," Jo snapped, adding on a grumble, "At least someone wants me."

"Well, technically, she didn't actually hire you to do the job," Zoe chimed in, and then winced apologetically.

"I'm pretty sure she didn't hire you either, love," Sean added his two bits, earning him a scowl of his own.

"Look, I'm just trying to help. Maybe if I can figure out how and when Peirce is going to come into money, then Linda can keep the inn going. It's all she has left, and I just feel like it's the least I can do." I tried to plead my case.

"Might I remind you there's a killer on the loose?" my father boomed. "And frankly, Vivian, I'm surprised you would want anything to do with this."

She snapped her spine straight. "Since no one else has any time for me, what on earth did you expect me to do?"

"Oh, fiddle-dee-dee, that's the farthest thing from the truth," Granny Gert chimed in. "Fiona and I have spent all our time doing nothing but thinking about you. Who in the world do you think this party is for?"

"Then shouldn't I be a part of it?" my mother responded with an appalled tone. "Now that the wedding is over and I'm under suspicion, no one seems to want a single thing to do with me. I'm normally a strong woman, but this is tough, I tell you."

Granny and Fiona started fussing over my mother, reassuring her that they still believed in her. Meanwhile, Cole and Sean were alternating lecturing and apologizing to Jo and Zoe, who remained stoically miffed. I sighed, and Mitch grunted. Peeking at him from the corner of my eye, I could see his disapproval clear as day.

"What?" I finally said, unable to hide my exasperation.

"You promised to stay out of this case," he replied.

"What do you think I was trying to do?" I threw my hands up.

"With you, Tink, I never know."

"According to you, my readings aren't real, so technically this shouldn't affect your case in one way or another, right?" I crossed my arms over my chest.

"There's still a killer on the loose, Sunny. And if he or she had something against Peirce, they just might have something against Linda. I don't want you anywhere near that inn. And why in the name of all that's holy would you put your friends in danger?"

"Well, you see, that wasn't really my fault…"

"With you, Tink, it never is."

"Would you stop saying that?" I snapped, spreading my arms wide. "I can't control their actions."

"No, but you *can* control your own." He shoved his hands through his hair and then dropped them to his waist. "For once in your life quit being so stubborn and listen to someone else."

"You should talk. You're so hard-headed you won't let anyone help you. You don't have to be alone in this, Mitch."

"I'm the cop, you're not. Why can't you remember that?'

"I'm not trying to be a cop. I never was."

"Look, I don't want to argue, but you make it damned difficult. I can't worry about you and do my job." He blew out a breath, rubbing the back of his neck. "If you would just let me do my job, things would be so much easier."

"Agreed, but it goes both ways, Detective." I raised my chin. "You don't have to believe in what I do. In fact, I don't expect you ever will. But I do expect you to give me enough respect and consideration to allow me to do *my* job."

A knock sounded at the door and seconds later, Captain Walker poked his head inside. "Am I interrupting something?"

We all just stared at him, growing quiet and looking guilty. Granny finally gave him a wave, and fluttered her eyelashes, but even that was half-hearted at best.

Captain Walker raised a brow, and then looked at Mitch. "May I have a word, Detective Stone?"

"Of course." He headed for the door, looking over his should at the last second. "This isn't over, Tink."

"With you, Detective Grumpy Pants, it never is."

Chapter 12

The next morning I stood outside of our town Vet's office, waiting for Dr. Sherry Parker to let me in. She had agreed to meet me here before office hours since I was supposed to hook up with the girls for shopping soon. It was a dreary fall day, with a chilly breeze blowing the smell of wet leaves and decaying earth around. Normally I loved fall. The vibrant colors and crisp air making Divinity look beautiful. But the recent murder had put a damper on the season, reminding me that fall meant the death of so many things. After my argument with Mitch the day before, I was fearful my own Fate Line was at risk.

Would we always be at odds when it came to our careers?

The door opened and Sherry popped her head out, her wide smile cheering me up instantly. She might be my cat's doctor, but we had become more than that over the past year. We had become friends.

"Sorry to keep you waiting." Her brown ponytail swung about as she moved. "I had a minor problem with my own pooch. Took me forever to get out of the house." Her eyes were such a warm brown, kind and full of compassion. It was no wonder she was so well-liked by all the pet owners in Divinity.

"I hope everything's okay," I said, genuinely concerned because I knew how much animals meant to her.

She held the door open and waved me inside. "Oh, he's fine. He's just getting old. Now this one I can never quite tell what's up with." She gestured to Morty as I set him on the exam table.

I chuckled. "You and me both."

Morty didn't like many people, but he had developed a soft spot for Sherry. She normally used homemade treats and toys unique to each of her regular animals she treated. With Morty, she had been at a loss as to how to get through to him since he didn't seem to eat or play for her. Until one day she found out by accident that he was partial to the massage therapy she used for certain pets. Since then that had become their thing.

"What seems to be the problem with Sir Morty?" She rubbed him down until he purred louder and louder, softening like putty in her hands.

I couldn't help but grin from ear-to-ear every time I saw him become the consistency of Jell-O as she massaged him with a firm but gentle touch. His black eyes seemed to glow through the slits his half-closed eyelids had formed. He was such an independent, arrogant, proud cat, it was quite amusing to see his limbs wobbly. When he caught my expression, I swore he could read my mind. He stood straight, stretched, then hopped out of her embrace and walked to the end of the table.

My jaw fell open, and it took me a minute to recover. "Nothing, apparently," I said, unable to register what my eyes were seeing.

"Pardon me?" Sherry blinked, looking confused.

"Well, he's been acting stranger than usual lately. First he kept rubbing at his eye and digging in the dirt, and then he's been limping for an entire day like there was something wrong with his leg. Now he's walking like he's half his age. I guess I just don't get it." The wedding was over, Mitch had lived with me for a while now, there was nothing new that had happened. So what was causing this crazy behavior?

"Hmmm." Sherry examined him. "His eye looks fine, and he seems to be walking great. Maybe he just wanted to see his favorite vet and get a free massage." She wagged her eyebrows at me and wrinkled her nose at him.

"Maybe," I said, studying him suspiciously.

"I wouldn't worry too much. He seems fit as a fiddle to me, but by all means bring him back anytime. I'll let you in on a little secret." She leaned over and said in a mock whisper, "I think up excuses to see him, too. Why don't I finish giving him a therapeutic massage, and I'll run him home for you when I'm finished."

My jaw fell open. "Seriously?" She nodded vigorously, so I continued, "That would be fantastic. Thank you so much."

"No problem. Now get on out of here. You've got some shopping to do. While you're at it, please get your granny some new material. Morty's bowties are completely out of season." She tsked in a perfect imitation of Granny Gert.

We both laughed, and after saying our goodbyes, I headed to the fashion district to meet my mother, Jo, and Zoe. The more I thought about it, I came to a conclusion. As much as Morty loved his massage therapy, I realized this wasn't the first time Morty had acted strange. And whenever he started acting strange, it usually meant one thing. He was trying to tell me something.

The real mystery was figuring out what.

***

Jo was in much better spirits that afternoon with her cute new outfits that were chic and flattering yet had room for her to grow. I had to admit my mother's taste was impeccable, and Zoe looked like a fashion model. Where Jo was va-va-voom and sassy, Zoe was oh-so-chic and classy. I felt like Plain Jane tagging along after them, being no help whatsoever.

"You guys ready to go?" I asked. "I'd say we've given Mr. Lalone enough time to find those old floor plans."

"Actually your grandmother and Fiona have asked for my help in planning the Fall Harvest party," my mother said, sounding happy.

"That's great, Mom." I squeezed her hand.

"I knew they couldn't get along without me." She stood and grabbed her purse. "It's been fun, ladies. Please do try and stay out of trouble." Her gaze settled on me for a moment, and then she left.

"I have to say I'm relieved I won't have to worry about her getting into it with Linda or anyone else. The last thing she needs is to mess up her case." I rubbed my hands together in anticipation. "You guys ready?"

Jo and Zoe's gaze met in a meaningful way.

"Um, well, I hate to do this to you but I have an afternoon tea party to host at Smokey Jo's for the Mystery Mavens Book Club," Zoe said.

"Oh, okay, no problem." I turned to Jo with questioning eyes.

"Sorry, Sonny, but there's no way I'm saddling her with Sean alone, given the problems they're having. You understand, right?"

I shrugged. "Sure. No worries." I donned a smile, trying to reassure them as best I could. "This is my job, not yours. You both have your own jobs. I totally get that. I'll fill you in if I find anything."

We said our goodbyes, and I headed to the inn in the same dreary mood I'd started the day with. It had stopped raining, but the clouds still shrouded Divinity, blocking out the warmth of the sun. I passed by the housekeeper who was arguing with the groundskeeper over the bushes out front. Inside, I passed by the cook who was preparing another tray for Linda and looking in a foul mood. It seemed the weather was affecting everyone today.

"Ah, just the man I came to see," I said as I spotted the maintenance man coming out of Peirce's office.

"Perfect timing." He held a large rolled up set of floor plans that looked ancient in his hands. "I found the old floor plans. Not an easy task, let me tell you. They weren't in the regular filing cabinet with the others. I had to do some digging, but I found them in an old cabinet in the back that never gets used."

"Well, thank you, Mr. Lalone. I greatly appreciate it." I took the plans from him and shook his hand.

"You're welcome." He eyed me curiously. "Let me know if I can be of any more help. I can show you around if you want."

"Thank you again, but I'm all set." I could tell he was dying to know what I needed the floor plans for, but how could I tell them when I didn't even know myself. No, until I figured this out, it was probably best I kept things quiet.

I walked away, wandering into the empty living room. Finally, blessedly alone. Spreading the plans out on the table, I studied them. Pulling out the new set of floor plans that I still had, I compared them side-by-side. I was no architect, but it was easy enough to see a couple of bedrooms and one bathroom had been added. I squinted, looking closer for something I was missing. That was when I noticed what looked to be a basement. Something about that room drew me to it in a strong way.

Just then Sally Clark entered the room, paused a beat when she saw me, and then frowned as she started to head back the other way.

"Don't mind me. I'm all set in here." I stood and gathered up my maps. As I started to leave, I faced her for a moment. "Have I done something to offend you, Ms. Clark?"

"Mrs. Theodore has been through enough, I should think. First, those scary phone calls, then losing her dear husband, and now in jeopardy of losing the inn. The last thing she needs is someone nosing around, casting suspicion on her."

"I'm not trying to put her through any more grief, I promise you. I'm actually trying to help her. If I can find out how Mr. Theodore was supposed to come into his fortune, I just might be able to help Mrs. Theodore save her livelihood. I feel as though I owe that to him, to them both."

She studied me for a long moment and then nodded once, sharply. "Before the murder, there were rumors going around that there would be layoffs for many of us. Then when we heard about Mr. Theodore's life insurance, we had hope. But now that Mrs. Theodore has a buyer, we'll probably be laid off anyway." Sally shook her head sadly.

"Wait, she has a buyer?" I asked, surprised. "But I just talked to her the other day, and she was on board with letting me try to help."

"Let's be realistic, Miss Meadows. Your plan is a longshot at best. I don't blame Mrs. Theodore. She really has no choice, short of a miracle. The buyer sought her out. She'd be a fool to turn it down."

I headed for the hallway.

"Where are you going?"

"To find her miracle."

Minutes later, I entered the kitchen. "Ah, there you are, Mr. Desjardins." The French cook looked up from his recipe book with a startled expression on his face. I tended to do that to people as of late, I realized. I took a breath and forced myself to relax. "Does this house happen to have a basement?"

"No," he said pensively, "no basement." Then he paused before adding, "But it does have a root cellar. Why?"

"Just looking for a miracle." I searched through the kitchen until I found the door leading to the cellar, then I jogged down the stairs with enthusiasm.

"You won't find anything down there but canned goods, potatoes and turnips. You want a miracle come back to my kitchen at dinner time. Then I show you a miracle," he said from the top of the stairs with his thick, charming, French accent.

I just shook my head with a grin and started looking around. He was right. All I saw were lots and lots of food items on many shelves. I was probably down there for a good hour when I grabbed onto a particularly old shelf at the back of the cellar. A strange sensation came over me, and I was transported back in time. Standing in this very spot, I knew I had been here before. The proof was in the same shelves which were many years newer with less food stored on them. My body ached once more, and I gasped for breath.

They were coming. They would find me soon. I had to keep moving before it was too late. I had to move *it* before they discovered what I had. I had to...

I let out an ear-piercing scream as I heard a crack and felt blood spurt. Pain shot through my skull, and I fell to the dirt floor in a limp heap and everything went black.

"Miss Meadows, are you all right?" Pierre asked from above me sometime later. Behind him stood Jack, Frank, Sally, and Linda.

I grabbed my head as I slowly sat up. "I think so," I wheezed. "Someone hit me from behind."

They all looked at each other with puzzled expressions.

"Who?" Pierre asked. "I was in the kitchen the whole time. No one but you came down here."

"I'm telling you, my head is bleeding like crazy and feels like it's going to fall off. Please, someone, grab me a towel."

Jack knelt down beside me and looked at my pupils. "Hmmm, no concussion that I can see."

"I'm not crazy." I winced at the still lingering pain.

"You're also not bleeding." He felt my head and showed me his dry hand. "You also don't have a bump."

It suddenly dawned on me what had happened. "Help me up, would you?"

Jack helped me to my wobbly feet, eyeing me with concern.

"I might not have been literally hit or have a bump," I looked them each in the eye, knowing I was going to sound crazy as I finished with, "but *he* was and he did."

"He?" Sally asked.

"The person in my vision."

"You sure she doesn't have a concussion?" Frank eyed me warily.

"Positive." Jack rechecked my pupils.

"Well, she sure isn't acting okay," Linda said. "What are you talking about, Miss Meadows?"

"Your miracle."

"My what?"

"Your miracle." I shook my head and winced again. "Your way to save the inn. And it's right through here." I pointed to a shelf full of goods.

"There's nothing there but food." Pierre scratched his head.

"Look behind the food," I said. "Behind the plywood."

Linda sighed. "This had better be worth damaging my root cellar." She gestured for Pierre and Jack to move the food shelf and then for Frank to take down the plywood. The men responded immediately, and I couldn't help wonder if one of them could be her mystery lover. They all seemed to adore her, including Sally.

I pushed that thought aside as the plywood was fully removed. "Viola," I said, pointing triumphantly over their gasps to an ancient hidden door that led to a secret tunnel. I rubbed my phantom aching head. "Someone went to a lot of trouble to hide this passageway. I'm betting what's inside will *definitely* be worth your while."

Chapter 13

"It's so cold in here," Sally Clark said from behind me.

"And creepy," Linda Theodore added from beside her.

"You ladies really didn't have to come along." I led the way through the damp, dark, secret tunnel. Of course because the entire town of Divinity was old-fashioned, the inn catered to that charm with authentic oil lamps. I felt like I'd been swept back in time. Tripping over a tree root poking up through the ground, I realized this was the same path the man in my vision must have traveled.

"Easy now," Jack Shepard said from behind Sally and Linda. "We wouldn't want you to hurt yourself, phantomlike or otherwise."

"I'm okay, but thanks." Jo was right. He *was* cute. A little rough around the edges, but endearingly charming, which made me wonder if he was Lover Boy once more.

"You take care, there, Miss Meadows," Frank Lalone added from behind Jack. "I can fix a lot of things, but not broken bones. Your granny would tan my hide if I let anything bad happen to you."

"Awww thanks, Mr. Lalone. That's sweet." And so was he. Maybe Linda was into cuddly, sweet handy-men instead of big, rugged, jolly green giants.

"I still say this is silly. I can give you all the miracle you need in my kitchen if you just believe," Pierre Desjardins added his two cents, looking as dashing and debonair as ever.

"Silly or not, Mr. Desjardins, I owe it to both Mr. and Mrs. Theodore to finish this thing." I forged on ahead, but that didn't stop my brain from recognizing there was a mysterious quality to Pierre that was undeniably intriguing. Linda had been surrounded by interesting people and a husband who virtually ignored her. She was a young, beautiful woman whose husband didn't appreciate her. Right or wrong didn't matter. I was beginning to *get* it.

"Oh, we're not stopping now," Linda said. "If I truly do find my miracle, I can save this godforsaken place. It doesn't matter if I want it, the fact is I *need* it. And I'm not heartless enough not to know that you all need it as well."

"Whoa, what's that?" I yelled and ducked at the same time, covering my head as a wild fluttering sounded above me.

"Is it spiders?" Frank said. "I hate spiders."

"Or snakes." Pierre shuddered. "I don't do snakes."

"Most likely bats." Jack's alert gaze searched the dark nooks and crannies of the tunnel with wariness.

"Bats?" Sally shrieked.

"I don't see anything except dirt and roots and stone." Linda looked around impatiently, obviously not afraid of any rodents or winged creatures.

"Has to be water nearby," Frank said. "I can smell the mustiness."

"You're a regular genius, you are," Pierre chimed in with an eye roll. "We all know there's water around these parts. Why there's a river that feeds into the lake right in our very own backyard."

"We're close," I said, in part because it was the truth and in part to shut them all up. "When I read Mr. Theodore's palm, I was transported to this very spot. I was in an old man's body. Someone who was no stranger to a boat. He had trouble breathing and this place underground didn't help matters any. I remember hearing fluttering. I'm thinking that was the bats we just saw."

"Do you remember anything else?" Jack asked innocently enough, but I could see the blazing curiosity in his eyes. I could see it in all of their eyes.

"Well." I rubbed an ache in my leg. "I heard a thumping noise. I wasn't sure what it was at first, but now I'm fairly certain it was a wooden leg. Our mystery man walked with a limp and talk about phantom pain." I shuddered.

"Okay, so now what?" Linda stared at me eagerly.

"I'm not really sure."

She let out an explosive breath like a deflating balloon, followed by a not-so-silent curse.

"Maybe we should head back." Sally's gaze darted around apprehensively.

I glanced at my watch and realized it was nearly dinner time. "Maybe you're right." Mitch was going to skin me alive if I worried him again.

"No!" Linda raised her voice. "I mean, we've come this far."

"That we have, milady," Pierre said.

"As you wish," Frank chimed in.

"After you," Jack added.

"Well, okay, then," I said, not having much choice.

I kept us moving a bit further. I had no idea how long we had been walking, but it felt like forever. I was about to stop and turn around before a certain detective locked me up for good, when a whisper ran through my mind for me to stop. I obeyed, and everyone bounced off my back.

"Sorry," someone mumbled.

"Pardon me," someone else said.

"My bad," yet another comment came.

"This is it," I replied.

"What is it?" Linda asked.

"This is the spot where we dig." I turned to face them. "I'm sure of it."

"Dig you say?" Sally looked appalled and then winced in disgust at her clean fingernails and apron.

The men didn't hesitate. Everyone started using whatever they had on them to start digging. Everyone except Linda. She sat back and watched like the Queen Bee. Fifteen minutes went by with no luck when I spotted an odd looking rock in the side wall. While they kept on digging, I started working on removing the rock. It didn't quite fit in the hole naturally, as if it didn't belong there. Like someone had placed it there. I'd almost given up hope on resurrecting it, when suddenly it wiggled free.

This time I gasped.

Everyone's head popped up, and they all stood to join me in my discovery. We peeked inside, hoping to find a stash of money, but instead only saw a single piece of paper.

"What's that?" Sally asked.

"It looks like a note," Linda said.

"Maybe it's a love letter." Jack winked.

"Or a confession," Pierre gave his two cents.

"Or a suicide note," Frank added.

"Only one way to find out." I reached inside. Slowly pulling the piece of paper out of its hiding place, I opened the folds and smiled wide. "It's not a note, or letter, or confession," I said with excitement.

"Then what, pray tell, is it?" Linda demanded. "Is it my miracle; where's my money?"

I stared her in the eye with pure satisfaction. "It might not be your money just yet, but it's the next best thing. It's a treasure map."

***

"I want to call a truce," Mitch said later that night while we were curled up on the couch, sitting by a warm fire in our living room.

I still loved the sound of that. *Our* living room. I adored the Victorian theme with the heavily upholstered overstuffed chairs and sofa, sporting uniquely shaped and curved backs that sat atop oriental rugs that covered the hard wood floors. Damasks, silks, and velvets covered all the surfaces available and heavy fabric draperies in deep reds, greens, gold and rich browns dressed the stained glass windows.

Granny Gert kept them pulled back and secured with heavy cording and tassels, putting the lace underling on display in such a beautiful fashion. The house had come fully furnished. It was Granny Gert who made it shine.

Mitch normally spent his free time in the garage since that was where he had set up his workbench and put his stamp on our home. He knew with Morty he had to tread lightly in making any changes, so when I came home and found him in the living room, I was surprised. He had asked me to join him the second I walked through the door. Not hounding me as to where I was or yelling at me. Just a civilized request that I couldn't deny him. I had dropped my purse and joined him, no questions asked.

Morty had been watching him like a panther when I had walked into the room. He narrowed his dark eyes as if to say, *I've got my eye on you, Stone. One wrong move, and I'll turn you into cat food.* Then he stretched, shot me a bored look, and walked out of the room as if he had much more important things to do than hang with uneventful old us.

"This is nice." I snuggled up beside my favorite detective with my head on his shoulder and legs thrown across his, which were propped up on the coffee table.

He tucked the blankets more securely around us. "What is?"

"You and me together, not arguing, and Morty leaving us alone for once."

"Agreed." He sighed and rubbed my back. "Why is it the only time we argue is when a case is involved or your cat is eying me for dinner?"

Because you're stubborn and I'm stubborn and that's half of what makes us work, I wanted to say. "I don't know, but maybe if we worked together instead of keeping secrets, we would avoid a lot of squabbles and get results sooner," I said instead. Hey, a girl could hope. "And maybe you could try a bit harder with Morty," I added as an afterthought.

Mitch waited a beat as if mulling over something of great importance. "Okay."

"Okay?" I peeked up at him, my blond brows shooting up beneath my pale spikey hairline. "Okay we can work together, or okay you'll try harder with Morty?"

"Yeah," he kissed my nose, "okay to both."

"I'm so glad you said that." I bit my bottom lip and jumped to my knees excitedly, kissing him all over his face.

His hands grabbed my hips to keep me from tumbling to the floor as his eyes sprang wide and then narrowed suspiciously. "Am I going to regret this already?"

I pointed at him. "Truce, remember?" I hopped off the couch with purpose.

"Unfortunately." He scrubbed a hand over his whiskered jaw.

I grabbed my satchel and joined him back on the couch once more. "Look what I found today." I pulled out the treasure map.

He frowned. "What is that?"

"Mrs. Theodore's miracle."

"Come again?"

I waved my hands in front of me. "Her treasure map. Whatever. It's the miracle that's going to save her inn."

"Treasure map, miracle, saving the inn … what are you talking about, Tink? You're giving me a headache."

"Peirce's reading."

"Ah, I'm guessing this has to do with the fortune he's supposed to come into, right? Now my head is pounding."

"Yes," I answered, ignoring his sarcasm. "Morty had been acting really strange—" Mitch smirked, and I smacked him. "—

stranger than usual, anyway. When I was raking, he popped up, looking like he was wearing a leaf eye patch. And then he kept limping as if he had a bum leg. I know Morty. The little scallywag was trying to give me a hint, and sure enough, the clues led to this." I handed Mitch the map.

"And where exactly did you find this map?" He studied the ancient piece of paper closely.

"In a secret tunnel hidden behind a shelf in the root cellar of the inn," I said so matter-of-factly, Mitch actually laughed.

"Just like that?" He shook his head at me in wonder.

"Not exactly. First I got clonked on the head, but only phantomlike, so no worries." I rubbed my still aching scalp. "Didn't stop it from hurting something fierce, though." His ink black eyebrow crept higher, so I hurriedly continued. "I was completely safe, mind you. Linda and her entire staff accompanied me."

"Through an ancient tunnel that hasn't been occupied in decades I'm guessing. Yeah, that sounds perfectly safe."

"Exactly." I gave him a look that said, *Truce, remember?* "Anyway, it's missing a corner of the map that has the final location for where the treasure is buried, but I'm certain if I work at it enough, I can find it."

"Using your psychic abilities, of course." His expression remained neutral. *Smart man.*

"Um, yes." I nodded.

"Anything else?" He sounded exhausted.

"Well, no." I kissed his cheek, then my lips parted as I thought of something else. "Oh, wait, yes."

"I can't wait." He grinned, his face looking almost pained.

"Mrs. Theodore was having an affair while Peirce was still alive, but I'm not sure with whom yet."

"Doesn't really surprise me. Could explain the life-insurance policy. Maybe they planned to off him and collect on the money together, not counting on Peirce being broke and the IRS taking it all."

"Maybe, or she could be telling the truth when she says she was afraid for his life from the people who had been threatening him before he died and didn't want to get saddled with his debt. The thugs we now know about."

"The thugs that will soon find out about this treasure along with the rest of the people around town and beyond." Mitch pointed out as if I hadn't already thought of that.

"Small town living, I know." I snorted, then sat up. "Hey, you just made me realize that something else I predicted is about to come true."

"Yeah, what's that?" He drew his brows together in curiosity.

"Divine Inspiration is about to be put on the map once news of this ancient treasure spreads. It doesn't even matter if we find the money. People will fill the inn just to check out the historic find. Maybe my efforts will end up saving the inn after all. Linda has a buyer, you know." I wrung my hands together.

"So I heard. No one knows who, though. The buyer wishes to remain anonymous." Mitch frowned.

"Hmmm, I didn't know that." I sat back and studied him closely. We'd been down this road before. Every time he said he would open up to me and share info, he never did. "What about you? What did Captain Walker call you out of your office for yesterday?"

Mitch looked like he was about to clam up. I sent him a look that said he was on thin ice if he planned to break our truce already, especially after all we had been through and after all I had just shared with him.

He sighed long and deep, surprising me by saying, "We had a break in the case as we went over the guest list from Jo and Cole's wedding."

I sat up straight. "Like what?"

"Well, we compiled a list of everyone who was there at the reception, or was involved with setting up the reception, and did a thorough background check on them all. For one, the man who set up the tent works for the tent company."

"Okay, I would assume that."

"I know, but what you wouldn't assume is that his name is Ron Durkin. As in Ron and Amy, the future Mrs. Durkin. The couple who lost out to Jo and Cole on having their wedding at the inn on that very day."

"Are you serious?"

"Very."

"Anything else?"

"Actually yes. Theresa McFarland was also there."

I felt like I'd been sucker punched. "But she wasn't on the guest list."

"She obviously crashed the wedding."

"But why? Jo fired her as her wedding planner before she hired Zoe. I mean, I can't blame her. The woman called Jo fat. Not a very smart thing to do, especially at Pump Up the Volume Hair Salon and Spa. Tracy and Raoulle are nothing if not loyal, and they adore Jo. Of course they were going to tell her."

"And in a town this small, one mistake can ruin a person's reputation. Everyone adores Jo."

"So what does this all mean?" I wished I could read his complicated mind.

"That maybe we're looking in the wrong direction for a motive."

"I don't understand?"

"Maybe the killer didn't have something against Peirce. Maybe they set out to ruin Jo and Cole's day. In fact, maybe the target hadn't been Theodore in the first place. Now do you see why I worry? I need you to be safe, Sunny. You and all the people we're close to." He cupped my cheek with his large palm, and I melted into it.

I nodded, coming to the only answer. "Then there's only one solution."

"I'm not gonna like this, am I?"

"Probably not, but you are going to agree to it. I need to do my job and you need to do yours, so why don't we do what we do best and work together. Deal?"

"You're right. I don't like it. But I'm too damned tired to fight anymore. You've got a deal, partner."

"Good." I bit back a grin over his use of the word partner. He'd come such a long way since the days when we first started working together, though he'd never admit it. "We start in the morning. But first," I wagged my eyebrows at him, "how about dessert?"

"Now, *that's* something I'd like very much." He tackled me on the couch and took a bite, making me squeal with delight.

Chapter 14

Papas Restaurant was a Greek restaurant with an ancient Athens theme and marble statues everywhere. My mother hated it, of course, but it was one of my favorite places. Jo, Zoe, and I often had lunch here.

"I can't get over how much you can see." I held Jo's 3D ultrasound image in my hand as if it were precious cargo. "The color's amazing, and the baby looks so big already."

"I know, right?" Zoe chimed in, holding her hand out eagerly. "I'm going to be an auntie."

I laughed and handed the picture to her a bit reluctantly, secretly wishing I could be an auntie, too.

"Technically a second cousin," Jo corrected, but the glowing grin remained fixed on her face.

"But more like an aunt than any of your siblings, and you know it, Cuz," Zoe said excitedly.

"True." Jo winked at her and then smiled softly at me as if reading my mind. "You both are."

"So I take it things are going better between you and Cole?" I asked, careful not to upset her.

Jo's smile only dimmed a little. "We're fine. He still thinks he's cursed, but at least he's not asking to annul the wedding anymore. And he is scared to death but admittedly excited about the baby. I let him back in our bedroom, but rest assured, I haven't totally let him off the hook just yet."

"That's good that you're fine now, and I'm sure he'll get over his worries in time. You two are meant for each other." I looked at Zoe. "And how about you and Sean?"

"I have to admit he's wearing me down. I still don't know if I can totally trust that he wants to be with just me and no other women, but I did agree to go out on a date with him. But enough about us. Did you find anything at the inn?"

I nodded and waited a beat, relishing in their looks of anticipation for a moment before finally saying, "We found a treasure map."

"Get out!" Jo gaped at me. "Like a real life treasure map with pirates and X marks the spot and everything?"

I nodded. "Well, I'm assuming there's an X to mark the spot. The map's corner is ripped off with the final destination on it, so I'm not exactly sure how we're ever going to find it unless I can pull a reading off it."

"Wait … who's we?" Zoe tilted her head with curiosity blazing in her gray eyes.

"Linda, Sally, Jack, Frank, and Pierre."

"Since when did you become on a first name basis with Cruella and her band of misfits?" Jo snorted.

"Since getting hit on the head—sort of—and finding a hidden door and exploring a secret passageway."

"Okay, backup, sister." Jo crossed her arms and settled in. "Start over and don't leave anything out.

I told them everything that had happened in great detail through our entire meal and even dessert.

"I'm taking it the map is the secret that was hiding within the walls of the inn." Zoe dabbed a napkin at the corners of her mouth.

"Exactly. The map is the key to Peirce's fortune, but even if we don't find it, the historical find of the map alone as well as the ancient hidden tunnel will put Divine Inspiration on the map just like my vision predicted."

"It's almost better if the treasure isn't found," Jo said. "I bet the rumor of it alone will bring people from all over to the inn. Maybe Linda won't have to sell now."

"That's what I'm thinking," I said. "If she's innocent, that is. She's not completely out from under suspicion in the death of her husband. And we still don't know who she was having an affair with, but I have my suspicions."

"Oh, hey, there's Wendy Statham." Zoe stood up and waved, trying to get the woman's attention.

"Who?" I asked.

"The cake lady," Jo responded, watching Zoe walk over to talk to the woman. "Zoe is helping Granny and Fiona plan the Fall Harvest party for Vivian."

"Ah," I said. "Speaking of party planners, I have something to tell you."

Jo frowned, her attention back on me now. "Why so serious? You look concerned, or constipated, which is something I know lots about these days." She smirked.

"Funny." I shook my head, then looked her in the eye until her smirk disappeared. "I don't want you to be afraid."

"Now that you've said that, how can I not be?" Jo wrung her hands together. "What the heck is wrong? Did you have a vision about the baby?" She dropped her hand and covered her belly. She was going to make such a great mother.

"Nothing's wrong with your baby," I quickly reassured her, but at her doubtful look, I admitted, "Okay, well, maybe a little something's wrong, but I promise it has nothing to do with the baby. Mitch thinks that maybe the killer wasn't someone with a grudge against Peirce or Linda. Maybe the killer had something against you and Cole."

Jo wrinkled up her face. "Why would you think that?"

"Well, you did fire Theresa McFarland as your wedding planner," I pointed out as gently as I could.

"After she called me fat," Jo snapped. "She had it coming."

"I know, but I also know something you might not."

"Like what?" She eyed me with confusion.

"She crashed your reception."

Jo gasped. "Are you kidding me? I didn't even see her."

"She was on the police list of people who were there. I'm sure she kept a low profile. She probably just wanted to see Zoe fail."

"Or she made sure my day was a disaster." Jo's jaw hardened. "I can't help it I ruined her reputation. People like me."

"She made her own bed," I agreed. "But I'm just not sure she would kill someone to get even."

Jo pushed the last of her dessert plate away, a true indication she was upset. Jo didn't push *any* food away these days. "What are you going to do about it?"

"Actually Mitch was going to talk to her today."

"I'm surprised you let him go without you."

"I already had plans with you and Zoe. I wasn't about to bail on seeing your first sonogram."

"Spoken like a true best friend, but..."

"You know me too well." I laughed. "But that doesn't mean I don't plan to do a little investigating of my own."

"There's more?" Jo actually looked sick.

"Unfortunately yes. You know Ron Durkin and his fiancé Amy?"

"You know I do. They're the couple who lost out on having their wedding at the inn the same day we were. I can't help it Peirce chose me. I refer people to the inn all the time when they eat at Smokey Jo's. He owed me a favor."

"He probably also felt he owed Ron something, so he hired his tent company to put up your wedding tent. Ron was on the police list. He's the boss. He doesn't set up tents, yet he did yours."

"Yeah, he helped set it up all right. Set it up to fall." Jo ground her teeth. "You won't have to put them away in prison if they had anything to do with ruining my wedding. I'll put them six feet under when I kill them both myself."

***

Later that afternoon I headed to Mini Central Park with its old fashioned street lamps, park benches, gazebo, and swan pond. Granny and Fiona and my mother were all there, overseeing the preparations for the Fall Harvest Party which was due to take place in two days. The sun was shining bright, the fall colors of brilliant reds and yellows and golds and various shades of orange on display in gorgeous fashion.

The gazebo was set up for the DJ to use and a big tent was being constructed near the swan pond. Fred and Ginger— Divinity's resident swans—were protesting people so close to their nesting place, even though their babies were grown and getting ready to leave the nest any day now.

"There's my Sunshine," Granny Gert said, throwing her arms around me in a big hug, squeezing me hard. She had on a warm sweater coat over her polyester pantsuit and of course her tried-and-true apron. She'd brought apple and oatmeal cookies for the crew setting up the scene. "Care for a cookie, dear?" She held out a plate and grinned at me endearingly, her snappy brown eyes standing out beneath the clear plastic rain cap she had secured to her head. There wasn't a chance of rain today, but Granny wouldn't risk the wind messing up her perfectly set, snow white hair.

"Oh, Sunny, it's so nice to see you." Fiona hugged me, patting my back. "You're looking darling."

"You too," I replied, taking in her fashionable cotton pantsuit and trendy cut and color. "Looks like renewing your vows agreed with you."

"It's about time you got here to help," my mother chimed in from beside her. "And taking a break already, no less."

"It's nice to see you, too, Mother." I smiled.

"How's the treasure hunting?" She said casually as if she didn't give a hoot, but I could tell she was dying of curiosity. It didn't surprise me that she'd heard already. Not much got by my mother.

"Unfortunately, we're at a dead end, but I still have the map. Hopefully something will come to me to clue us in on the whereabouts of the treasure. In the meantime, I'm helping Mitch with your case."

"Ah, so *now* you care."

Just then Morty appeared by my side from out of nowhere, wearing a flannel bowtie. Granny's idea of helping him ward off the chill. My mother shrieked, jumping back a step, and I could have sworn I heard hissing laughter.

I scooped Morty up, giving him a stern disapproving look, and then met my mother's eyes with an apologetic look of my own. "Sorry," I muttered and steered the subject back on track. "I've always cared, Mother. I was simply trying to keep the peace with my boyfriend, but now he's agreed to work with me. In fact, that's why I'm here. Do you know if Ron Durkin is here?"

She refused to make eye contact with Morty as she searched the area. "Ah yes, I thought I saw him earlier. He's right there by the tent, overseeing his crew." She narrowed her eyes. "Why?"

"Oh, I just need to speak to him for a moment, is all. Have fun with the party preparations." I walked away before she could grill me further.

My father and Harry were talking to the DJ, Jason Shank. He was being a good sport about being stuck in town. So was Wendy Statham the Cake Lady. I was glad Zoe had talked Granny into using them both for her party so at least they could make a little of their money back that they were undoubtedly losing from missing out on parties in the city.

"Mr. Durkin." I held out my hand. He was a middle-aged, attractive man with a successful business and an equally attractive fiancé. I still couldn't see him risking it all by committing murder, but I had to be sure.

He shook my hand with curiosity in his eyes. "And you are?"

"Sunshine Meadows, but you can call me Sunny."

His eyes showed recognition and genuine warmth. "Your grandmother is a very sweet lady. She speaks of you all the time."

I matched him with a warm smile of my own. "She is pretty special."

"I'm sorry to hear about the suspicion surrounding your mother. I'm sure it will all work out."

He seemed so sincere, my doubt about his guilt was growing. "I know it will," I responded, "because I know she's innocent. I'm pretty certain the guilty party had something to do with Peirce Theodore, his wife, or the bride and groom—Jo and Cole West."

Ron's face hardened so quickly, he transformed into a completely different person, making me reassess my first impression of him. "That wouldn't surprise me one bit."

"Would it surprise you that Jo is also my best friend?"

He narrowed his eyes in suspicion. "What exactly did you want to see me about, Miss Meadows?"

Morty jumped down and wandered off toward the tent. Instead of answering, I followed Morty's lead and walked over to inspect the tent his crew had just installed. "I see you didn't raise this tent yourself like you did the one for The West Wedding. I'm curious, Mr. Durkin, why is that?"

"I'm not shorthanded today like I was for the wedding." He looked at me incredulously. "What are you getting at?"

"I'm just curious why a tent you had a hand in setting up fell down?"

"Accidents happen, Miss Meadows. Everyone knows that. We had to push our wedding back a whole month. I might not like the Wests for stealing the reception sight my fiancé and I had booked first, but I certainly wouldn't resort to murder for revenge."

"Did I mention I work with the police?" I said, and he paled. "What everyone *doesn't* know, Mr. Durkin, is that the reception tent falling down was no accident." I stared in his eyes. "The ropes on that tent were deliberately cut three quarters of the way, knowing the storm would take care of the rest. And not only that, but the reports came back confirming they were cut with the same knife used to stab Peirce Theodore to death."

Chapter 15

"I thought I would find you out here," I said later that night as I wandered out to the garage in my sea-foam green yoga pants, orange tie-dye T-shirt, and brown leather flip flops. What could I say? I tended to hold onto summer as long as I could.

Mitch had transformed the space, making it his own over the past couple of months. When he'd agreed to move in, he'd gotten out of the lease for his apartment and had moved his things to my house. His style was contemporary while mine was Victorian, but I was hopeful we could find a way to make it work. I had told him he could move his things inside, but Morty had made it clear that wasn't going to happen.

So Mitch had taken over the garage, and I had gladly let him. I wanted him to feel like my house was his home. Whatever it took to accomplish that, I was all for it. He'd built a workbench to tinker with things in the back, installed indoor/outdoor carpeting throughout the rest, moved his couch, chair and a couple tables inside, and even added a TV, a mini-fridge, and a portable heater. Everything else he'd either donated to the needy or given away to friends, including his bed. I had to admit I was relieved. The last thing I wanted was for him to spend the night out here.

"Just working on my bike," he said in a crouched position while tightening some bolts on his Harley.

He wore his old, charcoal gray NYPD sweatpants with a snug black short sleeve T-shirt that revealed the play of his muscles as he moved. He never failed to make my heart beat faster just from the sight of him. He glanced up at me and then at my bare feet, his lips twitching slightly. He knew I hated shoes and fought donning them for as long as possible.

"Still cold outside?" he asked.

"Chilly, but it's nice and cozy in here." I held my hands over his space heater, kicked off my flip flops, and put one foot on top of the other as I stood in front of the heat, trying to get warm.

He dropped his wrench, wiped his hands, and stood, then went to his fridge and pulled out two longnecks. Walking over to me, he smiled slowly, looking worn out as he handed the bottle to me. "Beer?"

"Sure." I took the bottle from him and sipped. "How are you?"

"I'm okay." He took a big drink, then pulled me down onto his lap as he sat on the couch and crossed his feet on the coffee table. "But I'm feeling better now that you're here." He gave me a soft kiss, chasing away any chill I might have felt. He tasted like chocolate chip cookies and tangy beer and something unique Mitch. "How about you?" he asked, looking concerned. "You look tired."

I snuggled into him, curling my legs up and leaning against his chest. "It was a long day for sure," I responded, as he wrapped his arm around me and rested his palm on my hip. "But you make every day better." I rested my hand on his chest.

"Lunch was good, though. I can't get over the technology these days. You should have seen the 3D sonogram Jo had of the baby. It was amazing."

"I bet," he said with a slight smile. "Babies are pretty amazing, but I admit they scare the hell out of me."

"Me too," I agreed, and once again wondered if he even wanted children. I still didn't know if I did, either. We would have to discuss this before I proposed, but I didn't want to ruin the mood we were in right now. It felt too good being in his arms.

I laid my head on his shoulder and looked up at him as I traced his cheekbones with my fingertips. Moving on to his forehead and down his nose, I didn't stop until I ran my finger along his jaw and traced his scar. He made a noise that sounded like Morty when he purred. Tipping back his head, he rested it on the couch and closed his eyes. I bit back a smile, kept my fingers moving, and started talking again.

"After lunch with the girls, I went to the park to see if I could help out with the Fall Harvest Party. Granny and Fiona were in the thick of it. I'm actually shocked there haven't been any disasters yet. Of course both the police and fire chief were on hand, so the Dynamic Duo were on their best behavior. My mother was her usual lovely self, and of course Morty just had to show up to terrorize her." Mitch chuckled and I couldn't help giggle a little, but then I bit my lip, knowing he wouldn't like this next part of my story. "Um, did I tell you Granny is using Ron Durkin's company for the tent? And, well, he was there."

Mitch's eyes popped open on full alert, his head snapping up and his gaze nailing me suspiciously. "I'm guessing you knew that, and that's why you went to *help*. Did you talk to him?"

"Of course." I smiled pleasantly.

He scowled. "I thought we were going to do that together?"

"And I thought we were going to talk to the party planner together, as well?" I blinked at him in an innocent fashion.

"I'm not the one who had lunch plans." He pinned me with a knowing look.

"And I'm not going to pass up an opportunity when it presents itself." I ran my fingertip over his Adam's apple and down his chest.

He caught my hand, then threaded his fingers through mine as he grunted, and finally he gave up the fight. "So what did he say, anyway?"

"Well, he says he was only helping to set up the tent at the wedding reception because he was short-handed that day. He claims he has no clue how the ropes were cut three-quarters of the way with the same knife that was used in the killing."

"I figured he would deny any knowledge of wrongdoing." Mitch shrugged, and absently rubbed my back with his large palm, looking pensive. "He's not stupid, not to mention his company's reputation is on the line."

"I agree, but I have to say I believe him." I ran my thumb over his as I thought about my conversation with Ron Durkin. "He genuinely seemed surprised about the ropes being deliberately cut." I looked up at Mitch again. "How about you? What did Theresa McFarland have to say?"

"Pretty much what you would expect. She admits to crashing the party, but she claims she just wanted to see Zoe fail as the wedding planner." Mitch chuckled sarcastically. "I guess calling Jo fat damaged Theresa's reputation more than she realized." Mitch shook his head. "What did she expect? She's lived in this town long enough to know this is Joanne Burnham we're talking about."

"Joanne West now," I said with a wink.

"Jo is Jo, it doesn't really matter what her last name is. McFarland should have known that. Apparently no one will hire her to plan *any* party now. She's not a happy camper," he sighed, "but I don't think she's a killer, either."

I frowned, and my stomach twisted into painful knots. "I have to say I'm getting worried, Mitch. What if we don't find someone who looks guiltier than my mother? She can't go to jail. That would ruin my father and devastate Granny Gert."

"And you," my smart detective said softly, touching the tip of my nose. "I know you two have your differences, but I also know you both love each other."

I fought back tears and swallowed the lump in my throat. When I could finally speak, I said, "You're right. It would kill me."

"I'm not going to sugar coat things. I can't promise your mother going to prison won't happen, but I *can* promise you won't go through this alone." He stared deep into my eyes with his intense dark gaze. "You have me, and I'm not going anywhere, baby. We'll figure this out, you have to have faith."

"I do, I just need to find a way to take my mind off of things." I bit my bottom lip and stared at his mouth, letting my fear, my frustration, my affection, my desire—everything I was feeling—show as clear as the water in Inspiration Lake.

"You took the words right out of my mouth," he growled, and then proceeded to distract the breath right out of me.

***

"Granny Gert, you look fabulous," Raoulle down at Pump up the Volume Hair Salon and Spa said on Friday morning.

The spa was a contradiction with its eighties theme big hair day style like Tracy the owner still wore, with cans of Final Net hair spray to boot. Yet the place oozed comfort and class like a modern day oasis, painted with relaxing blues and greens, complimenting Raoulle's style.

Trays of cucumber water and lemon water and finger sandwiches were being passed around. Soothing sounds of nature played in the background. Therapeutic smells enticed the senses. And trays full of modern entertainment magazines covered coffee tables and end tables, while guests who were waiting sat in overstuffed comfy furniture.

I smiled at Raoulle in appreciation, and he shot me a conspiratorial wink. He had a way of making all the ladies feel special, but he especially took a shine to my grandmother.

"Boys oh day, do you really think so?" Granny patted her set and styled hair to perfection, looking at her reflection both left and right.

"Honey, I know so. I have clients who pay big money to make their hair shine like your snowy white do. That's God-given, right there, and anyone who knows anything about hair knows you can't imitate God-given color."

"And anyone who knows anything about hair knows color is only half the battle," Fiona said in the next chair over, admiring her perfectly colored red hair and chic, modern cut. "We all know you're the star around here."

"Don't you worry, Miss Fiona." Raoulle fussed over her as well. "You're just as stunning. You lovely ladies are going to be the envy of the Fall Harvest Party."

"Raoulle, *honey*, you wouldn't be trying to get more of a tip out of these two *lovely* ladies, would you?" Jo asked from a chair next to Fiona. He was taking care of all three women at once.

Raoulle let out a gasp worthy of Broadway. "Why, Mrs. West. I don't know what you're talking about." He squinted his eyes and studied her closely, then let a beaming smile spread across his face. "And might I say you are simply glowing. Your skin tone is amazing. What's your secret?"

Jo's face flushed, and she was unable to stop the goofy grin from spreading across her glowing cheeks. "Oh, healthy eating, I reckin'. Guess we all can't be bandits forever. Gotta grow up someday, right?" She trilled out a giggle.

Reckin'? Bandits? Giggling? Oh, my. My jaw fell open, and I gaped at her, feeling like I was on an episode of *Smokey Jo and the Bandit* gone horribly wrong.

"Oh, he's good," Zoe said, just shaking her head.

"He's something, all right," I responded. Tracy the salon owner had already finished with Zoe and me an hour ago. She'd done a great job, but she was all about efficiency. Raoulle, on the other hand, was all about the money.

"Hey, how did your latest fad work out? Did you ever get anyone to buy your idea for those Puffed Up Jeans?" Raoulle asked Granny.

"No." She pouted. "I thought for sure they would bite. I mean so many jeans are too tight they make you look wrinkled because they suck the air right out of you. We pump air into air mattresses so why not jeans? Puffed Up Jeans would have taken years off a woman's face, making her look smooth as a baby's bottom."

"Well I can tell you right now, they might take years off your face, but I'm thinking the extra air might add pounds onto your nether regions. Last I checked babies' bottoms were plump. As much as I want you to succeed with one of your ideas, doll face, I know for a fact all of my clients would take the wrinkles over the pounds every time."

"Oh fiddle dee dee, that's what *they* said. And I say that's what wrong with the world today. Whatever happened to models like Marilynn Monroe? And look at the women in paintings from years ago. They were all full-figured, wrinkle-free, beauties. We need more of that in this crazy world we live in."

"Here here, Granny. Ain't that the truth? There's a difference between rolls and curves," Jo said on a snort, and I could tell she was thinking of Theresa McFarland's unfortunate comment. "I'd toast you if I could," she added.

"Any other news?" Fiona asked, obviously eager to change the subject since she was like my mother ... one of those *other* clients who would take wrinkles over pounds, and for once, I was glad of her interference.

"Well, Lulubelle was in here this morning." Raoulle glanced around as though what he had to say was top secret.

Granny, Fiona, and Jo leaned in while Zoe and I rolled our eyes.

Raoulle continued. "She said poor Linda Theodore is having a rough time of it. She doesn't want to sell, but she might have to. Except now there's some crazy rumor about some treasure hunting going on. It's all the buzz. Mark my words, people are going to hear about that and come running. People do crazy things when money's involved."

I hadn't thought about small town gossip and how fast rumors spread. The last thing Divinity needed was a bunch of treasure hunters storming the town, wreaking more havoc than there already was with the murder investigation going on. My stomach churned. I had a bad feeling about this, and that was never a good thing.

"Oh, the poor dear," Granny said with a sympathetic tsk, bringing me back to the conversation at hand.

"I just can't imagine losing your husband," Fiona said.

Zoe and I locked eyes, knowing Linda wasn't that broken up about losing her husband because she had a secret lover. But we also knew that was something no one else knew except Joanne, and we hoped to keep it that way. It just irked me that everyone pitied the *poor* widow when she might possibly still be the killer.

"And finding out your husband's accountant lost all your money," Jo said, joining in, obviously still under Raoulle's spell. What was she doing spilling secrets willy nilly, especially while the investigation was still going on? My mother's future was on the line.

"That's just terrible." Fiona sounded shocked.

"Oh, my, I should bake her some cookies," Granny added.

"I agree it's a downright shame," Raoulle said. "The last thing the poor dear needs is that tax guy poking around the inn. She already lost the life insurance she took out on Peirce. What more does this blood sucker want from her?"

I bit back a gasp over how much Raoulle knew about the case. It shouldn't surprise me that in a town as small as Divinity, gossip spread like wild fire, yet the speed of the gossip spreading still did shock me. Although, he did just help me and not even realize it. What exactly *did* the tax guy want with Linda? I'd have to find out. In the meantime, I needed to put a cork in Smokey Jo the Bandit's mouth.

"Maybe he—" Jo started to say.

"Was trying to help her sort out this whole mess." Zoe cut her off and shot me a look that said, *No worries, I've got your back, and yes, she's done lost her mind.*

"Well, whatever he wanted, I'm sure the police will figure it out," I chimed in, shooting a *Shut up now!* look at Jo.

She jerked as if the I'm-having-a-baby-and-can't-think-straight goggles had finally, blessedly, thankfully been lifted.

"Everyone looks great, Raoulle," Zoe chimed in. "I think we're done here, Sunny, don't you?"

"Absolutely." I knew exactly what I was going to do with the rest of my day. I was going to pay a certain accountant a little visit. Presuming I could find him, that is. He'd been laying low lately, but I was a resourceful psychic. How hard could it be?

Chapter 16

Okay, so it was harder to find Brice than I thought. It didn't matter that Divinity was a small town, and being psychic was no help when I didn't have anything of Brice's to read. So basically I had driven all over the place, trying to catch sight of him without much luck: he wasn't at work, he wasn't at home, he wasn't around town. I'd checked the library, the grocery store, the hardware store, the auto body shop, I'd even checked the hospital. It was foggy and dreary and just plain spooky out today.

Not a very good omen in my book.

I remembered him acting afraid and preferring jail to dealing with the thugs who had roughed up Peirce because of the bad investment. Where would I go if I were afraid and needing help and wanting to be safe from bad guys? I knew he hadn't gone to the police because Mitch would have told me. Going on instinct and a hunch, I took a shot. It was a long shot, but at this point, I didn't have anything to lose.

Moments later, I pulled my bug into Sacred Heart Church and cut the engine. Sacred Heart was a small quaint church with rows of pristine white pews and gorgeous stained-glass windows gracing the sidewalls, and Father Moody was the resident priest. I was catholic and I had actually been confirmed, I just never seemed to have time to go anymore. Granny always went, and my mother forced me to when she was in town, but willingly going on my own terrified me. I always felt like I was being judged somehow.

It was Friday afternoon. Church wasn't in session, but it was always open for those needing a place to pray or someone to talk to or simply a safe haven. I walked through the doors and paused for a moment in the lobby. A nervous giggle slipped out when I realized I was waiting for a lightning bolt to strike me dead or the roof to collapse or something. I took a deep breath, knowing I was being silly.

Making my way inside, I glanced around. No one was there, but then I saw a solitary figure in the middle pew with his head bent in prayer. I crept forward and let out a sigh of relief when I recognized the man.

Brice Benedict.

Finally, something was going my way. I might not go to church very much, but I did know a thing about common decency and respect. I waited for him to finish whatever prayer he had been reciting and lift his head. Only then did I make my way to his pew and quietly slide onto the bench beside him.

He turned to look at me and jerked, seeming startled. "M-Miss Meadows, you're the last person I expected to see here."

Darn gossip mongers, I thought.

The resident Mad Hatter church going ladies still thought I was the devil's spawn just because I was psychic, though they loved my parents. Probably because they pitied them for having a fortune-teller like me as their only child, since they were such prominent, upstanding citizens. Needless to say my parents loved the attention. Me, not so much, especially coming from hypocrites like them who went to church all the time yet lived their daily lives in an unchristian like manner. It made me crazy, but I wasn't here to dwell on that. I was here to get to the truth.

"You and me both, Mr. Benedict," I replied honestly. "But trust me, I have enough sins of my own to confess."

"Who says I'm confessing sins?" He pushed his glasses up his beak-like nose and squirmed in the pew.

"No one. I'm just assuming you're in here because you have a lot on your mind." I patted his hand. "Or you're hiding out from the bad guys," I added sympathetically.

"Maybe a little of both," he admitted, looking too exhausted to keep up the charade. He also looked like he didn't have a friend in the world, which was something I could relate to. Things were great now in the *friend* department, but not long ago I knew exactly how he felt. I could empathize, and something told me he could sense that.

"How did you get out of jail so quickly, if you don't mind my asking?" I studied his face to gauge his reaction.

"I got out on bail," he said matter-of-factly.

"Oh, wow, I heard it was set pretty steep. You must have had a lot of money saved." That would explain the expensive items in his office. Because the deal he had made with Peirce Theodore's money had gone south, so there was no way he could have made money off of that. Which made me wonder again how he had such nice things. Maybe he had a rich relative who had left him some money.

As if reading my mind, he said, "I can see those wheels in your brain turning, Miss Meadows. You're nothing if not thorough, I'll give you that." He smiled a smile of admiration, if I wasn't mistaken. "I had an anonymous benefactor who posted my bail. Let's just leave it at that, shall we?"

"I'd rather not, but I'm pretty certain you're not going to tell me who it was. Does it have something to do with the thugs from the shady deal you were involved in with Mr. Theodore's money?" At his shocked expression, I explained, "I *am* dating Detective Stone, and I *am* a consultant to the Divinity Police Department. There's not much about this case that I don't already know." I looked at him with genuine concern. For him. For Linda. For us all. "Are you afraid they will come after you now that Peirce is dead?"

"I plead the fifth, for your protection as well as my own, but I *will* say your powers of observation are uncanny." And that was all I needed to hear to know the truth. The thugs were still after money, still out there, and still very much a threat to many people of Divinity. Whoever ran them obviously had Brice in their pocket. Poor man. I truly believed he was a good guy who had made a bad decision but now was stuck with no way out.

Then again, maybe there was a way. "If you would just talk to the police, I know they would help. They could put you someplace safe for your testimony, I promise." I hoped he could hear the sincerity in my voice.

"I'll think about it," he finally responded. "I just don't want to put anyone else in harm's way. I really did like Peirce Theodore, and I would give anything to make things right for his widow."

"Is that what you were doing with that tax guy and the bald man at the café the other day? Trying to make things right?"

He nodded. "I was talking to the IRS man—whose name is Drew Cummings—trying to find a way to help Linda save the inn. I know she lost her life-insurance policy, and I feel just awful about it. The man who was with us is a buyer—whose name I shall withhold as he wishes to remain anonymous for personal reasons until the deal is final. The important point is that he is interested in buying Divine Inspiration, even with the recent murder tainting its image. That's hard to come by these days. I'm just trying to help her out any way I can."

"Me too." I thought of Peirce's reading.

"I heard about the treasure map." Brice's comment had a funny tone to it.

I looked at him surprised, wondering if Raoulle's prediction was about to come true. "You did? Gotta love small towns."

"Yes, well, I'm not the only one who heard." His face took on an anxious look. "Don't be surprised if a lot of outsiders start showing up, wanting a piece of the action. Linda won't be hurting for buyers then."

"Is that what you're worried about? That your buyer will be angry if she stalls the sale of the inn? Or that the thugs will show up and more murders will happen?"

"Like I said your powers of observation are uncanny." He met my gaze, and I couldn't quite read the look in his eyes. "I hope you're prepared for the consequences of what you started."

***

Saturday afternoon I still couldn't stop thinking about what Brice had said. Was I prepared for the consequences of my actions? I'd had no idea when I set out to help Linda save the inn that we would find a treasure map and what that might mean for our conservative, old-fashioned town. I glanced around at the crowd who had shown up for the Fall Harvest Party in Mini Central Park. It was double the size we had expected.

Tons of outsiders had ascended upon the town, as predicted.

Granny and Fiona were in a tizzy, worrying about having enough food. While my mother's face was puckered like a prune with disapproval. This party was supposed to be about her and helping with the predicament she was in, not about some silly treasure, as she had put it. At least the weather had held out, thank goodness, with the sun shining bright and the temperatures just warm enough to make the event pleasant. So far Morty was on his best behavior, but he was so unpredictable, no one ever knew what he had up his sleeve—or under his bowtie, as the case may be.

Crockpots of chili sat steaming on the table, with bowls of shredded cheese and sour cream nearby. Loaves of warm Italian bread were sliced in baskets with napkins over the tops, and several antipasto salads were ready to be dished. And of course the cake was the centerpiece, as it should be.

It was a masterpiece.

It was a replica of a courtroom with a man on trial. The pews of spectators were packed, the jury full, the judge front and center, and my mother standing tall and proud in action. The detail was amazing. Cake Lady, Wendy Statham, had done a fabulous job once again. At least she would get more business after being stuck in our town. And the music was perfect. Jason

Shank the DJ seemed to know exactly what his audience wanted, not to mention he was funny and entertaining. He was already a huge success back in the city, but winning my mother over was truly an accomplishment that would book him plenty of additional gigs.

My mother took the microphone and cleared her throat. "I want to thank everyone who was involved in planning this party. The cake looks incredible, which doesn't surprise me." She glanced at Wendy. "Cake Masters has a fabulous reputation, and you can bet I will tell all of my friends about this."

Wendy was a middle-aged woman with shoulder-length blond hair pulled back in a ponytail. She smiled and tipped her head in appreciation. Granny was a big fan and kept trying to get her to stay in Divinity so they could open a cake cookie shop together. I had to hand it to Wendy over being a good sport in putting up with the Dynamic Duo as well as my mother. The woman was a saint.

"And much to my shock, the music is surprisingly entertaining," my mother went on with her usual back-handed compliments. "I will surely recommend your DJ services if any of my friends are ever in the need of a non-band or orchestra entertainer."

Jason was about my age and looked to be used to tough customers. He bowed at the waist gallantly and then blew my mother a kiss. My mother blinked rapidly and flushed, Granny and Fiona giggled, and Jason shot them a wink.

Turning the focus off of him and her heated cheeks, my mother continued speaking. "Granny Gert and Fiona Atwater did a wonderful job with the food."

Granny and Fiona curtsied and waved to the audience as they twittered about, fussing over the dishes.

"And, well, my daughter is here," my mother continued. "And that's something in and of itself."

I smirked at her. She had no idea just how much I was doing in trying to save her from life behind bars. I waved at the audience and did a little twirl, not quite knowing what else to do. Jo and Zoe joined my side immediately, and I shot them grateful smiles.

"So please don't worry about me, people. I will be just fine." My mother smoothed her burgundy jacket over her matching skirt. "I hope everyone enjoys the food, and welcome to all the newcomers in Divinity. You picked a perfect time to visit our lovely town."

Our? I all but choked on the thought.

"Easy there." Jo whacked me on the back. "You don't want to give your mother anything else to frown about."

"No kidding." I took a deep breath. "Is it happy hour yet?"

"Not quite," Zoe said. "But Ron Durkin and his fiancé are here, and they look pretty happy. Not exactly what I would expect from people who are guilty."

"I know," Jo responded. "They certainly don't look like a couple set on vengeance. And I have to say the tent looks sound."

"I'm telling you, I believe him when he says he doesn't know how the tent at your reception got cut. I think someone's looking for easy targets to blame," I said.

"Don't get too excited," Zoe added. "I saw Theresa McFarland here. We still don't know what she was up to at Jo's reception."

"True," I chimed in. "We'll have to keep an eye on her for sure. In the meantime, did you see how many out-of-towners are here?"

"Yeah, and it has me concerned." Jo rubbed her stomach. "They've been swarming Linda Theodore all day like vultures. What do you think they want?"

"A piece of the action, I'm sure." Zoe stared out at the crowd with wariness. "It's kind of unnerving."

"That's the thing," I said. "Linda and her crew and I searched for hours, but we didn't find anything. Without that missing piece of the map, I'm not sure how we will ever find the treasure."

"You haven't been able to pull a single reading from the map?" Jo asked with a curious expression on her face. "I thought for sure you would."

"Not yet," I answered. "I'm thinking I would need something from the man who created the map in order to get a reading off of it. And since he's been dead for a very long time, I doubt anyone around here has anything of his."

"Well, keep trying, please," Zoe said. "I know our original goal was to help Linda, and the mysteriousness of a long lost treasure will definitely pick up business for her, but I don't think our town will be back to normal until that treasure is found. And I for one like my normal boring life."

"I am so with you, sister," Jo said. "I have about had it with drama."

"I agree. I can't promise anything, girls, but I will see what I can do." I hugged them both and looked beyond them, focusing in on the scene before me with dread. "Oh, no."

"What now?" Jo asked.

"Morty," was all I had to say.

"Oh, my," Zoe responded.

"Let's go," I ground out, and we all headed over to the cake table as quickly as we could. But it wasn't quite quick enough.

My mother was just about to cut the cake when Morty appeared in front of her. I could see by his stance he was about to pounce. That little stinker was determined to terrorize my mother, no matter how much I scolded him to play nice in the sandbox. I had just about reached him when he looked over his shoulder at me, and if I didn't know better, I would swear he gave me a cat-who-ate-the-canary grin.

"Noooooo," I shouted, but it was too late.

Morty pounced, landing smack dab in the middle of the cake and bit the head off the fondant replica of my mother. He gave her an intense look as she gasped, and then he darted off into the woods.

My mother stared at her headless body. His paw prints were all over several people in attendance, and the cake was pretty much ruined. She let out a squeal, and then collapsed to the ground in a heap.

All heck broke loose.

Doc Wilcox ran over to her, conversations raised, people ran helter skelter, the police jumped into action, and I chased after the guilty culprit. When I caught up to him, it wasn't going to be pretty. He thought he ruled the roost, and most of the time he did, but today he had crossed the line, big-time.

The question was, what kind of punishment did one give to an immortal cat?

Chapter 17

Sunday morning at the Divinity Hotel Granny Gert and Fiona were moaning something fierce, sounding miserable. Morty was MIA, the little rascal. He probably knew if he showed his face, he would be in the dog house for sure. We were trying for a big breakfast while Fiona and Harry were still in town, but that wasn't happening. My mother refused to step foot in my house, anywhere near Morty the Monster, so we'd opted for the hotel. But Fiona and Granny were so sick, that the thought of breakfast turned their stomachs even more.

"What do you think is wrong with them?" Mitch looked concerned and so adorably helpless.

Harry and my father just stared, scratching their jaws.

"I would almost guess it had to be food poisoning from the look of it." My father tilted his head sideways and studied them in their bent over agonized forms.

"But no one else got sick from the food," Harry reasoned.

"Maybe it was just the food at their table that got tainted," my father replied.

"Then why didn't Vivian get sick?" Harry asked, analyzing them as if he were still a judge.

"You know how picky she is," my father pointed out. "She doesn't eat half the things that are put out, while Granny Gert feels the need to sample everything."

"That's true," I said, "but I'm still worried."

"As we all should be," my mother chimed in. "And I'm standing right here, by the way. I can hear everything you say."

"Nothing was meant to be a secret, darling." My father kissed her cheek.

"Just stating the facts, dear." Harry patted her back.

"Come on, Mitch." I grabbed his hand. "Let's take the Not-So-Dynamic Duo to Doc Wilcox."

"Your wish is my command." He tagged along, letting me lead the way.

Ten minutes later, we were in Doc Wilcox's office.

"I don't usually keep Sunday hours, you know," Dr. Wilcox said, his sandy blond hair looking like a perfect Ken doll, his face clean shaven, and his build as fit as ever.

"I know, and I appreciate you opening your office for me," I responded. "So how is Nurse Doolittle?" Tina was a slightly chubby, rosy-cheeked brunette with curly hair who had been head-over-heels for him since forever. After going above and beyond the call of duty to help him, he had finally opened his eyes to the longtime crush she'd had on him. Ever since then, they had been inseparable.

"She's great," he said. "In fact, we're engaged now. So you're one of the first to know." He actually seemed happy, especially after losing his long-time crush—our former librarian—to an unfortunate murder not long ago. She hadn't returned his feelings, which was another blow. I was glad he had Tina to help him pick up the pieces.

"Awww, I'm so happy for you, Doc. I mean that sincerely."
I smiled.

"And that's why I opened my shop today. We've been
through a lot over this past year." He nodded. "I haven't
forgotten the good word you put in for me at the police station
when I had my own little mishap."

"My pleasure." I tipped my head in salute.

"So, Doc, what do you think the problem is?" Mitch asked.
"Could it be food poisoning? We all know Granny Gert can't
see that well, hence the failing of her road test so many times.
Maybe she used food beyond its expiration date."

"Good Lord, I hadn't thought of that," I mused out loud.
"She truly is blind as a bat. I'm still terrified every time she
takes her caddy for a spin."

"Little Miss Sunshine, I am sitting right here," Granny
Gert said weakly. "And my food is never spoiled."

"So am I sitting right here," Fiona chimed in on a whine.
"Gerty wasn't the only one who pulled this party off, and I can
see just fine."

"*See* yes," Granny said, "but you can't cook worth a lick.
Maybe you put the wrong ingredients in my food."

"Then the whole darn lot of them would have been sick,
you numbskull. If you haven't noticed, we are the only two in
agony."

They started to squabble, their old high school rivalry
never completely forgotten, even though they truly were friends
now. I was beginning to wonder if maybe frenemies was a more
appropriate word.

My mother chimed in, "Oh, can it, you two. We've all had
about enough of your shenanigans. You guys didn't have ten

years scared off your life when that evil cat tried to put me in an early grave."

"I'm sorry about that, Mother." I hoped my sincerity came through in my tone. "I don't know what got into Morty. He's never done anything like that before."

"Well, then, he must really hate me," she said on a sniffle. "He bit my head clean off. Do you know what it's like to see a replica of yourself without a head? Why, I just might faint from simply thinking about it. I have nightmares, you know."

"I know, and I truly do apologize. As soon as he shows his feline head again, I will let him know exactly how I feel about what he did. You have my word on that."

She just harrumphed. Apparently my word didn't mean much to her. Then again I often questioned if anything about me meant much to her. I sometimes caught fleeting glimpses of affection, but she certainly wouldn't win any Mother-of-the-Year awards.

Doc Wilcox got a call and excused himself. Moments later, he returned. "I don't think Granny's eye sight or Fiona's cooking skills are the problem," he said gravely, holding a piece of paper that had come through his fax.

"Then what is?" Mitch asked, and all of us stopped making any noise, tuning in to the doctor's every word.

"Granny Gert and Fiona were poisoned. And I'm not talking about food poisoning, I'm talking about antifreeze. Not enough to kill them, but just enough to make them violently sick. Small amounts are hard to detect. If given enough over time, it would do the trick for sure, though."

"Oh my heavens to Betsy." Granny Gert fanned her face.

My mother took her hand, and my father squeezed her shoulder in a unified show of support. Family was family, and we all loved each other no matter what.

"I don't want to die," Fiona wailed.

Harry rushed to her side.

"Who would want to kill Granny and Fiona?" I asked, still trying to process what we had just discovered and make sense of it all.

"I don't think the culprit was after the Dynamic Duo," Mitch said. "If I had to guess, I would wager they were after Vivian, or trying to set her up again. Lucky for you, she's such a picky eater, but one thing is clear. The killer obviously has unfinished business."

And this time my mother fainted for real.

***

Later Sunday afternoon Mitch and I went for a walk through the park. The sky was overcast, the air still as death, the temperature cold. Not the best day for a walk, but Mitch had insisted we get out, even though I was the outdoor, walk-in-the-park kind of person. Not him. But needing the escape, I'd gladly agreed.

Granny and Fiona were resting comfortably at my house with Harry watching over them, while my father had taken a distraught Vivian back to their hotel. Everything from the party had been taken down and hauled away as if nothing had taken place just one short day before. I tightened my hand around Mitch's, having waves of uneasiness roll over me time and again.

"What's wrong?" he asked, sensing my mood.

"I don't know." I looked around, spotting people I knew and many I didn't. "I just keep having this strong feeling that someone is watching us."

Mitch might not fully believe in my abilities, but he had learned to trust my gut. "It's probably nothing, but I'm glad you're staying alert. I don't trust all these strangers in town now that I know our killer still has an agenda."

"Me either. I don't like it one bit, and for once I regret giving a reading." Mitch smirked, and I nudged his arm with mine. "What I'm saying is that I never should have tried to decipher the meaning of Peirce's reading. If I had left well enough alone, we wouldn't have all of these new people in town. I fear no good is going to come from all this treasure hunting."

"That map would have been found eventually. Linda isn't Peirce. She probably would have rearranged the root cellar and found that secret passageway at some point. Or if she sold the inn, the new owner would have. It was only a matter of time."

"I would have preferred later rather than sooner, instead of during a murder investigation involving my mother."

"Agreed, so now we just have to make the best of it by trying to figure this case out before things get even crazier."

We sat in the gazebo and stared at where the food had been. I curled my legs up under me, finally donning socks and sneakers with a pair of jeans and a sweater. I might be confused, but at least I was warm.

"I still can't believe someone poisoned Granny and Fiona's plates. I just don't understand why." I shook my head.

"Your mother was an easy target to take the fall for Peirce's murder, given their arguments and her threats." Mitch scrubbed a hand through his thick dark hair. He had on a pair of jeans as well with a T-shirt and his leather jacket. "Maybe the killer thinks your mother knows something and is worried about being discovered, so they want to keep making her look guilty. She was sitting right beside Granny and Fiona, so she had easy access to their plates if she felt like tampering with them."

"Ron Durkin is also an easy target in wanting revenge on Cole. The same with Theresa McFarland in wanting to get back at Jo. So how come they aren't still being made targets by the killer?"

"Maybe because one of them *is* the killer," Mitch speculated. "Or maybe because framing your mother is more believable."

"Maybe," I mused. "Ron and Amy just don't seem the type, but something about Theresa seems off to me."

"Me too," he said. "You're getting good, Tink." He winked, and I warmed with pleasure over his compliment. "That's why I brought you here this afternoon," he went on. "I've been watching Theresa for a while now. She likes to jog in the park every day around this time. I had a hunch we would run into her right about now." He glanced at his watch, and sure enough, a few minutes later she rounded the bend and jogged straight for us. "Just like clockwork," he said with satisfaction.

"Theresa McFarland," I hollered. "Can we have a word with you?"

Mitch raised a brow with me. I gave him a look that said, *Relax, I've got this.* He had just said I was getting good. Now he needed to start letting me prove that.

Theresa eyed us warily, glanced at her watch, took her pulse and then joined us with a frown. "I've already talked to the police." She looked at Mitch dryly. "I really don't see the need to talk anymore."

"I know you talked to Detective Stone, but you didn't talk to me," I said carefully. "Unless you have something to hide."

She hesitated only for a second, but I noticed. "You've got five minutes." She sat down under the gazebo across from us.

"Fair enough," I responded.

Mitch leaned back and crossed his arms, letting me take the lead.

"I heard you crashed the West wedding reception," I started the conversation. The wind picked up, swirling leaves around our feet. I looked at the darkening sky and wondered if the still air a moment ago had been a calm before a storm.

"Which the police already know," she pointed out, taking a swig of water from a bottle attached to her running belt.

"Do they also know you cut the ropes on the tent, trying to make Ron Durkin look guilty?"

She spit her water out everywhere and sputtered, "I did no such thing." Then she wiped her mouth with the sleeve of her dry-fit running shirt.

"Ah, but you could have. You were angry at Joanne for firing you. Maybe you were trying to make the tent fall and ruin her day."

"She didn't just fire me, she destroyed my reputation. I heard Ron wasn't happy with Cole either after he stole his venue. Ever think maybe Ron cut his own tent? If I were going to ruin her party, I can think of better ways than that."

"Like tampering with the punch?"

Theresa didn't have to say anything. Her guilty expression said it all.

"I saw you at the Fall Harvest Party. Did you have a good time?" I asked, and Mitch's other brow raised to join his first. Ignoring him, I focused on Theresa.

"What are you getting at?"

"Divinity's a small town, Ms. McFarland." I leaned forward and narrowed my eyes. "I'm sure you heard Granny and Fiona were poisoned."

"Are you implying I had something to do with that?" she asked with an incredulous tone and an expression that said I was out of my ever-loving-mind.

"I don't know, did you?" I pressed on.

"No, I most certainly did not." She set her jaw. "I was at the Fall Harvest Party, hoping to land some new clients. I still have to make a living, you know. As far as the punch at the West reception, I didn't poison it, that's for certain. I simply poured vinegar into it. That was all, I can promise you that."

I shuddered, remember the large sip I had taken just before the cutting of the cake. "That was plenty," I said. "You're running out of excuses, Ms. McFarland."

"And you're out of time." She checked her watch and stood. "I hope we're finished here. Don't you have a treasure to find or something? I suggest you focus on that and your real job instead of trying to play cop which is obviously out of your league." She hoisted her chin a notch and then jogged off in the direction she'd come.

"Vinegar in the punch?" Mitch shook his head on a wince. "What has this town come to?"

"Not sure." I sighed. "And I'm also not sure she's the one who killed Peirce. She's right. We are literally running out of time."

"Don't give up," Mitch said, stroking his hand over my short cropped hair and then massaging the back of my neck with his wide palm. "We haven't ruled out Ron Durkin or Theresa McFarland completely," he went on. "They both had access as well as motive with a grudge against Jo and Cole. We also still haven't ruled out Linda Theodore or Brice Benedict, either. They certainly had access and motive for wanting Peirce dead."

"And my mother had access and motive as well. She most of all despised Peirce Theodore. Everyone knows that. But I know she isn't capable of murder, yet she is the one who was standing over his corpse when the tent was raised."

"True, but like we said, she sure makes for a great scapegoat in taking the fall. It's almost too easy, and any savvy investigator can see that. A jury will too, if it comes to that."

Once again I had that creepy feeling of being watched. "We should probably head back." I looked around as the first fat raindrop fell.

"You getting that feeling again?" I could feel him studying me.

"How'd you know?" I peeked up at him.

His gaze was heavy-lidded, his dark eyes as full of passion as ever. "There isn't much I don't know about you, Tink."

A thrill shot through me. I had to wonder if it would always be this way between us. I secretly hoped so. We stood up and started to walk out of the gazebo, when a hiss sounded.

Mitch jumped out of his skin and reached for his gun, while I crossed my arms and tapped my foot.

Unbelievable.

"Morty Meadows, you'd better come out from behind those bars right this minute," I ground out and stabbed a finger in his direction. "You've caused quite enough trouble, mister. It's time you answered for it."

I stared at a guilty Morty who was hiding behind the slats of the gazebo, staring at me in his usual intense way, which looked even more intimidating than normal. Probably because he knew he was in big trouble. The slats were wood not metal but he still looked like he was behind bars, which is exactly where I was going to put him if he didn't start behaving.

Mitch holstered his weapon and took a deep breath. "That cat is going to be the death of me yet."

Morty just blinked at me, not afraid in the least, and then he ran off again.

I hollered after him, "The leash law isn't just for dogs, you know. You'd better be home when I get there."

"Do you think he will listen?" Mitch asked in a tone that was clear he hoped not.

"Oh, he'll listen. He knows when he's pushed me too far, and enough's enough. It's time he accept his punishment."

"Like going to live with your mother?" Mitch asked hopefully.

"Or you out in the garage." I gave him a pointed look that warned him to behave or he would be in the doghouse right along with my cat.

He held up his hands and backed off. "Just a suggestion."

Speaking of dogs… "No, I have a better idea." I grinned, warming up to the idea. "Granny Gert is going to dog sit Biff for Jo and Cole to give them time alone just as soon as she's feeling better, and I think Morty would make the perfect assistant, don't you?"

Mitch winced. "I can actually say I pity the fool."

Chapter 18

Tuesday morning I decided to pay Linda Theodore a visit at the inn. There was a reason so many strangers were in town, and it was basically all my fault. So I decided to see if she needed my help.

Morty had shown up as I expected by Sunday night. Monday had been a day of rest for Granny while I took care of her for a change, but by today she was fit as a fiddle and insisting on dog sitting Biff so Jo and Cole could get "back on track" as she put it. Morty was none-too-happy when I'd left.

Granny had put a striped black and white bowtie on him, and he'd defiantly allowed her, letting me know I'd pretty much put him in jail anyway by confining him to a day with Granny Gert dressing him up and Biff being, well, Biff. But Morty had taken his punishment like the truly aristocratic feline that he was. King of the beasts, or at least king over Biff who had acted much more like the jester from the moment Jo had dropped him off.

I couldn't help but giggle just thinking about it, except now wasn't the time for amusement. I wiped the smile from my face as I pulled my bug into the parking lot of Divine Inspiration. The parking lot was full of cars and people milled about every inch of the grounds at the inn. I cut the engine and climbed out, locking my car behind me. That was something I hadn't done since moving away from the city.

Jack Shepard the groundskeeper did not look amused when he spotted me. I raised my hands up in an *I'm-sorry* gesture, but he just shook his head and wandered off to talk to a swarm of people who were tearing up the lawn. His lawn.

Frank Lalone was gesturing animatedly to a group of people who were trying to take his tools. I caught a few snippets of the argument which had to do with directions and digging and scent dogs, oh my.

I quickly made my way inside, happy to escape their wrath. My happiness evaporated when Ms. Clark spotted me.

"Do you see those vultures?" she hissed, waving her feather duster around madly. "They've already broken three vases in their haste to get to the root cellar and explore. I like to see the inn full, mind you, but this is insane. They are going to ruin the place. And after Mr. Theodore worked so hard to make it a classy, elegant, place of peace and serenity for those guests who wanted a relaxing, tranquil place to rest. This is anything but relaxing. It's downright chaotic, I tell you."

"I know, and I'm so sorry," I said.

"Saying you're sorry isn't enough. Those are just words. What I want to know is what are you going to do about it?"

I took a breath. "I'm going to try to fix it. But first I need to see Mrs. Theodore. Do you know where she is?"

"In Mr. Theodore's office, though I suppose it's hers now." Sally pointed the way with a thrust of her feather duster, and then let out a yelp over a crash down the hall. "They're animals, I tell you. Animals." She hustled off after the culprits, feather duster pointed like a sword, slicing the air with every step. I felt sorry for anyone in her path.

I headed toward Peirce's office and passed Pierre Desjardins chasing someone out of his kitchen with a frying pan. Ducking behind the corner, I escaped without him seeing me. The last thing I wanted was another confrontation right now. Good Lord what had I started? When the coast was clear, I continued on my way.

I had almost made it to the office, when I heard raised voices coming from within. Something told me not to reveal myself, so I hesitated, and then hid just outside of the door behind a large potted tree.

"What do you mean you don't want to sell now?" Came an angry male voice from inside. "A deal is a deal."

"A deal isn't a deal until both parties sign on the dotted line," Linda said. "I'm sorry, but I have to think about my future."

"You have no future." A bang sounded as if someone had slammed their fist on the desk or against the wall. I was about to step inside the room, but his words gave me pause. "You've lost everything, including your life insurance policy. Where's the future in that? You need me, and you know it."

"H-How did you know about the life insurance policy?" She sounded surprised and a little afraid.

"I know everything, sweetheart. I also know you knew about the whole thing. That's why you took the life insurance policy out on your dearly departed in the first place."

Whole thing? What was he talking about? I wondered.

She gasped. "I-I didn't do anything wrong. You can't prove anything."

"Tell that to the judge," he growled.

"I want you to leave now."

"This isn't over. Not by a longshot, Linda."

The door flew open, and I crouched down low. The bald man I'd seen at the café came storming out, leaving me wondering what exactly Linda had known about. And who the heck was this anonymous buyer? But one thing was crystal clear...

Baldy had known the Theodores.

I heard Linda sniffling inside and I was about to go in, but the sound of footsteps approaching down the hall made me stop. Someone was coming. I ducked down low once more. The person passed by while my head was buried so I didn't have a chance to see their face. The door closed behind them. Standing back up, I leaned in to listen.

"Are you okay, my love?" came a male voice from inside that sounded familiar.

I sucked in a breath. I knew without a shadow of a doubt Linda's lover was inside. Biting my lip, I listened harder.

"No," she sobbed. "That man's a monster. He won't take no for an answer on selling the inn. Now that all of these treasure hunters are here, business is booming. I don't need to sell. I can live off the inn's income."

"Are you certain we can't find the treasure for ourselves? Then we can leave town like we planned and live off our riches."

"We've looked everywhere. I really had faith in Miss Meadows. I mean she knew all about us. But she hasn't been able to find the treasure. Or she knows where it is and wants to keep it for herself, which is why we can't rely on that. I don't trust her. I don't trust anyone but you. You were right in suggesting I take out the life insurance policy on Peirce."

"A lot of good that does us now. It's gone, and so is the treasure, apparently. So what are we going to do?"

"Not sell the inn."

"Why? He seems desperate to buy this place. If we get enough money for it, we can move on. Start over."

"He *is* desperate. He would do anything to buy this inn, but he won't give us enough money for it now. He's only doing this to keep my silence. He's forcing me to sell because he found out I only took out that life insurance policy because I was pretty sure someone was going to kill my husband. He knows I know about what went down."

"Mon Dieu, we're screwed."

And suddenly I knew who lover boy was. I would know that accent anywhere. Linda Theodore was having an affair with her French cook Pierre Desjardins. But more importantly what went down with Baldy? One way or another, I needed to find out.

I crept down the hall and made my way to Pierre's kitchen, knowing he might be a while with Linda. At least no strangers bothered me in there. After he'd chased the last one out with the frying pan, word must have spread that his kitchen was off limits, which meant the secret passageway was as well. Probably why people had shovels outside. They must be looking for another way into the tunnels. Poor Jack and Frank must be having fits about now.

A tray of fruit and cheese and crackers sat untouched, and my stomach growled. Maybe Pierre wouldn't notice if I had just a little. Before I knew what happened, the entire tray was gone.

What could I say, I was starving. I looked around desperately for more and quickly grabbed a random knife and sliced and diced, replacing what I had just consumed.

Pierre entered the room, looking frustrated and angry just as I set the knife in the sink. I let out a sigh of relief. His expression changed to surprise when he spotted me, but his look quickly darkened as he stared down at the counter. My relief was short lived moments later.

"Mon Dieu!" He gaped at my creation. "What have you done? Where is my plate of perfection? That was for Mrs. Theodore." His features hardened. "No one touches my utensils or cooks in my kitchen without my say so."

"I am so sorry," I started to say, but I could see from his expression, he didn't like mere words any more than Ms. Clark did. "I know it was wrong, but I was starving. Look," I pointed, "I fixed it. I made more."

"You made a mess," he growled, and something in his eyes told me he was much more dangerous than I had originally thought. "Maybe someone needs to *fix* you." He took a step toward me, his frame more solid than I had realized. I had definitely caught him at a bad time, and now he was taking out his pent up frustration on me. He looked intimidating with his dark slicked back hair and angry brown eyes boring into me.

I took a step back near the sink where the knife I had just used lay within easy grasp. Raising my chin a notch, I knew I had to do something quick. "You like to fix people, don't you?" I said. "Kind of like when you tried to fix Mrs. Theodore by convincing her to take out a life insurance policy on her husband. Funny how he died a short time later."

Pierre jerked to a stop, clearly thrown off balance, but then he quickly recovered. "I don't know what you're talking about." His face returned to the masked, expressionless one I was used to. I suspected that was all an act and this hot-headed man was the real Pierre Desjardins.

"I'm fully aware of the affair you were having with Mrs. Theodore, Mr. Desjardins. I heard you in her office just a short time ago."

His face paled slightly but then filled with the color of beets. "You can't prove anything. I am a passionate man, Miss Meadows. Mrs. Theodore is my employer. I am simply looking out for her well-being."

"By killing her husband in hopes of raking in the insurance money?"

"I did *not* kill her husband!" He slammed his fist down on the counter, the veins in his neck throbbing.

"You're right. You *are* a passionate man." I pressed on, knowing I was close to getting him to spill the beans. "Passion can make a person do all sorts of things they normally wouldn't. Bet you didn't count on her losing it all to the IRS, did you? Tell me, Pierre, what went down that Linda knew about? Why is she so afraid?"

He surged forward before I knew what was happening. I reached in the sink and wrapped my fingers around the knife, but he stopped one inch from my face, his hands bracketing either side of me, fencing me in. All I could think about was Mitch and how upset this would make him.

"You think you know so much, *Sunny*," the cook ground out through his teeth. "You're passionate in your quest to know the truth, and you're right. Passion can get you into trouble,

Sunny. Passion can make you afraid. Are you afraid now, *Sunny?* Do you plan to use that knife you're holding on me? Are *you* capable of killing someone?" He reached out and squeezed my hand until the knife cut into my finger just enough to draw blood and make me wince.

I swallowed hard, trying not to show my fear. Maybe I had provoked him too much, pushed him too far. I wasn't passionate so much as impulsive, which was way more dangerous. I'd landed myself in many scrapes because of it. This time was no exception. In fact, this time was one of the worst I could recall at the moment.

I opened my mouth to speak, when the door flew open.

"We have a problem outside." Jack stepped through the opening and stopped short. "Do *you* have a problem in here?" His voice changed from one of frazzled to one of angry disapproval as he looked between Pierre and myself.

Pierre stepped back, his usual mask firmly in place as he replied without missing a beat. "Not at all. I was showing Miss Meadows how to use a paring knife. As you can see by the mess she made on my counter, she has no clue what she's doing. Someone needs to steer her right before she hurts herself."

"Is that right, Miss Meadows?" Jack asked me, his jaw tight and eyes locked on mine. "Are you sure you're okay? I'm glad Pierre was here to help." He stared Pierre down from his tall height, his impressive frame indicating he meant business. "Women and children should be cherished. I hate when I see anything bad happening to them. It does funny things to me. Makes me go a little crazy. Don't you feel the same way?"

Pierre cleared his throat. "Of course."

I set the knife down slowly and ripped off a paper towel, giving my heart time to slow its racing pulse and my breathing a chance to even out before speaking. I smiled gratefully at Jack, avoiding Pierre's gaze. I didn't want him to know how much he had gotten to me. "I'm fine now. Thank you, Mr. Shepard. It's just a little cut, but Mr. Desjardins is right. I clearly have no place in the kitchen. Good day, gentlemen. I'll be leaving now, but rest assured," I finally made eye contact with Pierre, "I'll see you later."

"Anytime," Pierre fairly purred.

Jack just narrowed his eyes.

***

Later that afternoon when Mitch came home for lunch, I told him all about what I'd heard when I went to see Linda. He asked about the Band-Aid on my finger, so I told him I did it in the kitchen. It wasn't a lie, it did happen in a kitchen. Just not *this* kitchen. I couldn't help if he assumed it happened while making his lunch. Granny Gert and Fiona were feeling much better. Fiona and Harry had left town, but Granny had worn herself out dog sitting Biff and coddling Morty, so I'd made her go rest while I took over the kitchen duties.

Mitch ran a hand over his whiskered face, eyeing the mess of a sandwich I'd made him. I almost thought he was going to push it away, but he lifted it and took a bite. Probably more to distract himself while he formulated how he wanted to respond to my story. He clearly was not happy once again that I had gone somewhere without him and put myself in danger.

"Seriously, Sunny?" was all he finally said.

"You had already gone to the station." I threw up my hands. "I only went to see if I could help Linda since I am the one who started this whole treasure hunting debacle. I couldn't control what happened after I got there. How could I possibly have predicted Baldy would show up?"

"I thought you were psychic?" He smirked.

"Funny." *Not!*

"Baldy who?" Mitch scratched his head, smartly moving on.

"The anonymous buyer." I waved my hands through the air. "That's not important. The point is, I can't run away every time a lead breaks just because you're not with me. At least I came right home to tell you about it."

"Well that's something." He grunted.

"I have an appointment with a client this afternoon for a reading, but maybe after dinner tonight we can go together to see Drew Cummings the IRS guy. He's the one who helped Brice and Baldy with Linda and the sale. Maybe he can shed some light on who Baldy really is. If we don't have a name, then how are we supposed to find out about what went down that Linda knew about?"

"If we can find him. I haven't seen him around town lately. Maybe he's finished with his audit. We could question Linda's lover, Pierre Desjardins," Mitch pointed out innocently, having no clue what had happened to me earlier.

I paused a minute, forcing myself to keep calm because Mitch knew me too well and was way too good of a detective. "I kind of already did that," I finally admitted sheepishly.

"Why am I not surprised?" He leveled his gaze on me. "Keep talking."

"Okay, so I didn't go straight home after eavesdropping. I hung out in Pierre's kitchen and waited for him, then I confronted him about Linda and what I'd heard. He played dumb and pleaded the fifth. I don't think we're going to get much out of him." I didn't bother to tell Mitch that Pierre threatened me. Mitch was already mad enough. If he thought for a moment that anyone had hurt me in any way, he would put his career in jeopardy and dole out justice himself. I shuddered to think of what his idea of justice would be.

Mitch turned into Detective Stone and studied me knowingly. "I'll let whatever it is you're not telling me pass ... for now. And as for Mr. Desjardins, you let me handle him. Something tells me he might respond to my powers of persuasion over yours. Let's just say mine are a bit more *powerful*. I'm thinking that's exactly what Mr. Pierre Desjardins needs right about now." Mitch curled his hand into a fist and his jaw tightened, telling me he knew exactly what went down and wouldn't rest until he "rectified" the situation.

Men! I just shook my head. "You'd better not be thinking of doing something stupid." I blinked, realizing I was starting to sound just like him and we weren't even married yet.

"Me? Never. Whatever would give you that idea," he threw my words back at me, and suddenly I knew what it was like to be in his shoes.

Chapter 19

"I can't believe Mitch did something so stupid." I sat at the bar in Smokey Jo's. "You should have seen his knuckles. They're swollen and bruised. I asked what happened, and he said straight to my face that he and Pierre had a conversation, and then they both fell down the stairs to the root cellar. Imagine that. Does he really think I'm that stupid?"

"Maybe that is what happened?" Jo avoided my eyes as she made drinks and slid them down the bar to the waitresses without missing a beat.

"Funny how after that Pierre confessed to having the affair and convincing Linda to take out the life insurance policy on her husband, but he swears they had nothing to do with the murder. He says he doesn't know what Linda knows or doesn't know. She doesn't tell him everything. I'm sure Mitch punched him, but he pleads the fifth. I can't believe he would risk his career by acting like a child."

"I can," Jo said easily and patted my bandaged finger with a knowing look and half smile. "It's because he loves you."

"It's stupid is what it is." I held up my finger. "This is only a small cut. Hardly worth getting into a fight over. Men are such hotheads. And he didn't even learn anything knew. We still have to find out the name of Baldy. He's off looking for the

IRS guy. I was too mad to join him. I don't like when he risks what's most important to him for me." I popped some beer nuts in my mouth and chewed vigorously.

"Honey, when are you going to learn," Jo said. "It's not his career that's most important to him. You are."

"And that cut wasn't just a small cut. It was a small cut made by a knife and put there by someone intending to do you harm," Zoe chimed in, glancing at Sean who was at the other end of the bar serving the evening crowd.

She took a moment to stare longingly at him in his low riding, snug fit jeans and tight green Irish t-shirt. He was his charming self with his blond curls, blue eyes, and deep dimples, but something was different. His body language said he was off limits. As if drawn to her, he glanced in our direction and she quickly looked away.

"Men kind of go crazy when it comes to protecting the things they care about." She blushed.

Jo and I both said at once, knowing he was out of earshot. "All right, what aren't you telling us."

"Nothing really." Zoe's face flushed brighter, and this time she avoided looking in his direction. "It's no big deal."

"Oh, no you don't," Jo said. "You had your first date with Sean, and I want to know how it went."

"Ditto," I chimed in on a mock whisper. Many locals filled the bar, but it wasn't packed like it would be on a weekend evening. "Spill it."

Zoe blew out a breath, trying not to squirm, until she finally gave in. "Okay, but you have to promise not to laugh."

Jo and I locked gazes and pressed our lips together, trying not to giggle already, but we both agreed.

"Well, the date was amazing," Zoe admitted with a dreamy sigh. "Sean was different than how I ever thought he would be. He took me to dinner, and then we went for an evening stroll through the park, and then we ended up back at his place. I thought for sure he would pour on the lines and make a move on me like he always does, but this time was different. This time he just wanted to talk."

Jo let out a snicker, then coughed to cover it. "That's nice. Continue, please."

I bit back a grin, secretly proud of Sean for taking my advice to heart.

"We had dessert and wine which I'm really starting to love by the way, and then we talked for hours. He finally kissed me. It started out pretty chaste, but then it gently progressed into something so much more. I never knew I could feel that way. Suddenly I found myself getting carried away, and, and, oh God it's too embarrassing to say."

"I knew he was too much man for you." Jo set down her towel and untied her apron. "I'll kill him for—"

Zoe grabbed her hand. "You've got it all wrong and that's the embarrassing part. He wasn't too much man for me. I was too much woman for him."

"Excuse me?" I spit my beer out everywhere, earning us a few curious glances. I tapped my throat as if I had choked but was okay now until everyone went back to ignoring us. Thank goodness because I had to find out the rest of this story.

"What she said," Jo echoed me, while cleaning up my mess.

"He was the perfect gentleman," Zoe explained. "I couldn't stop myself from making the moves on him. I practically threw myself at him. Okay, so there was no practically about it. I did throw myself at him, big time. But he fought me off. I was so upset, thinking I was finally willing to give myself to him, but now he didn't want me."

"I'll kill him just the same for hurting you," Jo said on a growl, but waited a beat before marching over to him.

"No need. He ran after me, scooped me up and, ignoring my crying protests, he brought me all the way back to his place. Then he sat me down and talked to me. Really talked to me. He told me how much he wanted me, which I could pretty much see anyway, and that he would give anything to make love to me. But that he wanted what we had to be about so much more than sex."

Jo and I stared over at Sean as if aliens had taken over his body.

"He said he's never felt this way before about any woman, and then he vowed to remain abstinent until he knew I felt the same way about him, no matter how long it took," Zoe continued. "And then he held me in his arms for the rest of the night. Just held me, and nothing more. That's how I know men do crazy things to protect what they cherish." She shook her head, still in awe.

Jo and I remained speechless, not a giggle to be heard.

"Well, say something," Zoe said.

"This *is* Sean we're talking about, right?" Jo asked.

"I know. Like I said," Zoe repeated, "crazy."

"I told you so," I finally said, and only then did I let out a small laugh of joy. "I knew you would be the luckiest woman on earth once you let him in." I met Sean's curious gaze, and I shot him a thumbs-up. He just raised a brow while wearing a goofy grin, still looking confused but undeniably happy as he went back to serving customers. I looked into Zoe's eyes. "Yup, he's a goner. He loves you, Zoe. He really, truly does."

"Awww, you're gonna make me cry." Jo sniffled. "That's the sweetest, most romantic thing I've ever heard. Now do you believe he's a good guy?"

"He's a great guy." Zoe blushed brighter this time. "And he's all mine."

"Speaking of great guys," Jo said as Cole came out of the kitchen, carrying a big case of liquor and setting it behind the bar.

"Not great. Just smart enough not to lose the best thing that's ever happened to me because of some stupid fear." He slowly walked toward her, cupped her cheeks, and leaned down to kiss her tenderly on the lips. When he raised his head, she had tears in her eyes. He brushed them away with his thumbs and pulled her into his arms, resting his chin on top of her head. "I'm not gonna let fear win this time, baby, I can promise you that."

"I take it your date went well earlier," I said, misty eyed myself.

"You could say that. We owe Granny Gert in a big way." Jo hugged her man tight before letting go of him. "Let me get back to work, you big lug." She patted his chest, her face happy and beaming.

"Don't work too hard, Mama." He grabbed her hand and kissed it before picking up a big crate of dirty glasses and heading back into the kitchen.

"Mama." Jo sighed. "Sweet, sexy *and* he cleans. I'd say I've got a winner."

"For sure," Zoe added. "Now we just have to work on Sunny."

"Oh, no you don't." I held up my hands. "You guys had your time to be mad. Now it's my turn."

"What are you going to do?" Jo asked.

"I don't know, but you can be certain I'm going to make it memorable."

***

Later that night, I lay in bed tossing and turning. So much for punishing Mitch. I was the one being punished. He hadn't come home, and he wasn't answering his phone. I was starting to get worried. Yes I was mad that he'd gotten in a fight and jeopardized his career, but that didn't mean I didn't want him to come home. I feared he was sleeping in his man cave instead of our bed, but when I went to check, he wasn't there. I even called the station, but they said he wasn't there, either.

We were a couple. I didn't expect him to ask me for permission to go places, but I did expect him to check in with me if he was going to be late or simply not going to come home at all. It was common courtesy not to leave someone who cares about you wondering if you were even alive. He had just recently gotten mad at me for doing the same thing the night I first questioned Linda Theodore.

That's why I was terrified something was wrong.

Granny Gert's car was in the shop, so she borrowed my bug to go to her monthly Sewing Sister's meeting. She wasn't back yet, so I was home alone. Morty was still angry with me, so he had made himself scarce. So I'd turned off all the lights and headed upstairs early to read in bed. I couldn't focus on reading, so I tried to sleep. That wasn't working either.

Finally I heard a noise downstairs. Mitch must be home. I propped myself on my pillow and opened my book to make it look like I hadn't been worried at all. When I realized I was holding the book upside down, I gave up and decided to pretend like I had fallen asleep. I closed my eyes, and laid there waiting. And waiting. And waiting.

What on earth was he doing down there?

I sat up and listened hard, but I didn't hear anything. Frowning, I threw off the covers and pulled on a robe over my Tweety Bird PJ bottoms and tank top. Deciding to go investigate, I wandered downstairs and turned on the lights. The house was eerily quiet all of a sudden. Where had he gone?

"Mitch? Are you home?" I walked into the living room and looked around. The hum of silence was deafening.

No answer.

"Granny Gert? Is that you?" I wandered into the kitchen next, and a creepy feeling slithered up my spine.

Still nothing.

"Hello, anyone here? This isn't funny." I heard a shuffle coming from my office and ground my teeth, heading in that direction. I never did like Hide and Seek. In fact, I wasn't big on games of any kind.

I had almost reached my destination when something jumped out in front of me. I screamed a high pitched shrill that could probably shatter my Victorian china.

Morty hissed.

"Oh my gosh, Morty Meadows!" I stabbed my finger at him. He'd appeared out of nowhere, blocking my path in the hallway, not looking frazzled in the least by my scream. In fact he didn't seem to be looking at me at all. "You scared the life right out of me," I snapped. "Why I ought to … owwww!"

A shooting pain sliced through the back of my head, and I crumpled to the ground. The last thing I remembered was Morty drawing back his lips and the biggest razor sharp fangs I'd ever seen flashing just seconds before he pounced at something behind me.

***

"Sunny? Can you hear me?" Mitch's deep voice came from somewhere above me, laced with concern.

He smelled great and his touch was warm and I missed him. I didn't like it when we argued. All I wanted to do was snuggle into him, but then I realized my head was pounding something fierce.

"You're here?" I struggled to sit up.

"Don't move, Tink. You've got a nasty bump on the back of your head." He adjusted an ice pack over my skull, his hands trying to be gentle.

"What happened?" I opened my eyes and then slammed them shut. The pain was unbearable.

"Here, take these." He pressed a couple of pain pills into my palm and slipped a straw between my lips.

I did as he suggested without question because I was in agony. Finally, I cracked my eyelids just a hair until my eyes adjusted to the lights. When I could finally open them all the way, I asked again, "Mitch, please tell me what happened?"

"I don't know," he said honestly. "One minute I was helping Granny Gert, and the next Morty appeared out of nowhere. He had blood on his paw, and he let out the most heart-wrenching meow I've ever heard." Mitch stroked my cheek with his palm. "I've never been so scared in my life." His Adam's apple bobbed up and down. "I knew that something bad had happened to you. I just knew. Morty and I might be at odds about a lot of things, but one thing is clear." His gaze bore into mine so intensely, I sucked in a breath as he said in a voice filled with more emotion than I'd ever heard him reveal, "We both love you unconditionally."

And there it was. The words I had craved to hear for so long now.

I placed my hand over his and held on tight, and my heart burst with joy. "I love you, too, Mitch."

He struggled with his feelings and lost the battle as a single tear slipped out and rolled down his cheek. "Don't you ever scare me like that again, Tink. I can't lose you, too."

I knew he was referring to his sister and ex-fiancé. "Come here," I whispered. He lowered his head and I kissed him gently, pouring everything I felt into an act meant to show him just how much he meant to me too.

He laid down beside me on the floor.

"I can get up," I said.

"Not a chance," he replied with a don't-argue-with-me tone. "Not until Doc Wilcox gets here and says it's okay. Until then, I'll keep you company." He tweaked my nose and kissed me again.

"You're still not off the hook, you know."

"I know," he responded sheepishly and glanced at his bruised knuckles, then slipped his arm carefully beneath my head. I rolled over to snuggle him, throwing my leg over his, and he wrapped his arms around me then stroked my back.

"I wasn't referring to that, though you're not off the hook for that, either." I peeked up at him. "I was referring to tonight. I have been trying to reach you since forever, but you didn't answer your phone. You weren't in the garage or at the office. You recently yelled at me for making you worry, yet you did the same thing. Where were you?"

"I'm sorry about that. At first, I was working. I tried to locate the IRS guy, Drew Cummings, but he's nowhere to be found. I'm pretty sure he must have left town, which doesn't add up if he was in the middle of an audit. Then a bit of an emergency came up." He paused for a moment. "I wanted to call you, but Granny wouldn't let me."

"Emergency? Granny Gert?" My stomach bottomed out, and I groaned. "What happened?"

"Well, when I was getting nowhere with the case, I was about to head home, but then I got a call."

"From Granny?"

He nodded.

It had taken Granny Gert five times to pass her road test, and even then she'd only passed with a little *help*. People stayed off the roads when she took her Cadillac for a spin around Divinity. There was a reason her car was in the shop.

I swallowed, knowing I wasn't going to like his response to my next question. "This has to do with my baby, doesn't it?"

He groaned as if dreading telling me, and then finally blurted, "She kind of, sort of, put your Bug in a ditch after leaving her Sewing Sisters meeting."

I whimpered. What else could possibly go wrong tonight, and more importantly what had I done to deserve it? "I wondered why she wasn't home yet," I whined, "but I was afraid to find out the answer."

Mitch patted my back. "It'll be okay, I promise. We were at Big Don's when Morty made his miraculous appearance."

"Well, that explains a lot. How bad is the damage?"

"Don says it won't take more than a week to fix."

"Good Lord, I don't even want to know what this will cost me."

"Not a penny. You know Granny. She's got more money hidden than probably the whole treasure everyone's seeking. She said not to worry about a thing. Speaking of treasures, you're not going to like something else I have to tell you."

"There's more?" I groaned.

"The thief wasn't after money or jewelry or electronics. It's apparent the culprit came here for something very specific. And with all the cars gone, they obviously thought no one was home. You're very lucky you were knocked unconscious and not killed. Money can make the sanest person do insane things they normally never would."

"What do you mean?"

"Your treasure map's gone."

Chapter 20

Wednesday morning I was housebound without a car, ordered to rest. Not to mention I was in no mood to socialize since my treasure map had been stolen. A lot of good it would do the guilty culprit since a crucial piece of the map had been cut off. Besides, my head still ached horrendously. Doc Wilcox said I had a mild concussion.

Mitch took a sick day, but he was driving me nuts with watching my every move, so I sent him out to his workshop to tinker. It was bad enough I had to deal with Granny Gert and Morty both hovering over me, refusing to leave my sight. So when the doorbell rang, I eagerly answered it.

Baldy.

I blinked, but didn't panic. He was mysterious, yes, but alarm bells weren't going off in my head, which was a good thing, and Morty—aka my lethal guard cat—paid no attention to him, which put my mind somewhat at ease. My brain couldn't handle any more trauma at the moment.

I stepped back and said, "Please, come in, Mr....?"

"Ronald Winters, Miss Meadows. I'm new in town. Nice to meet you." He stepped through the door, pulled off his driving gloves, and held out his hand.

I shook his hand, studying him closely. "Welcome to Divinity. Are you here for the treasure hunting like everyone else?"

"Oh, no, no. That's not my sort of thing." He dusted off his overcoat. "I'm passing through on a bit of business, is all, and I heard about your establishment. I must say it intrigued me."

"Intrigue is good," I said, thinking, *You're pretty intriguing yourself.* "What can I do for you, Mr. Winters?"

"I heard about your accident. Small town." His expression looked grim. "That must have been terrifying. I hope you're okay."

"I'm stronger than I look," I said by way of an answer, lest my reading of him be off, which wouldn't be shocking given the present state of my brain.

"Do you take walk-ins?" He peeked past me, glancing around my house, making me realize whoever broke in last night could have been anyone. "I was hoping you might have room for me in your schedule."

"I've never had a walk-in, but yes, I suppose I could fit you in. I actually had a few cancellations today because of the attack." I leveled him with my own version of an intimidating stare, just in case he was formulating any funny ideas. Not to mention Mitch was out in his shop. One scream and this guy would be toast. "Let's just say the people of Divinity are very protective of me."

"Oh, well, if you think it might be too much for you, I can come back." He turned and started to open the door.

"Honestly, no." I gave up all pretenses because they took too much energy. "At this point, I could use the distraction."

"Wonderful." He let go of the doorknob and turned back around, looking as if he'd known I would say that all along. "Where would you like me?"

There was more to Baldy than what first met the eye. I could tell he was used to manipulating people and getting his way. He also didn't seem like the type to have his fortune read. He wanted something. I just had to figure out what.

"Normally I do all my readings in my sanctuary," I replied, "but since that was trashed last night, let's move out into the living room."

"After you." He gestured for me to lead the way.

I headed into my living room and sat on the couch, motioning for him to sit beside me. Once he did so, I took his hands. He raised a brow at me but didn't object. He looked to be in his forties, clean shaven with no hair, but his eyebrows were salt and pepper. I couldn't get a vibe off of him as to whether or not he was a believer or a skeptic.

"Normally I can tell by holding your hands what type of fortune-telling tool will work best on you, but since my other tools were damaged during the break-in, I will stick with palm reading. Is that okay?"

He shrugged. "Fine with me."

I turned his palms over and began to study them.

"Did the police catch the person who broke in?" he asked with a casual tone.

"No, they must have worn gloves and whoever it was knew how to cover their tracks. So far no DNA has been found." I chose his right palm which looked to be his dominant hand.

"I never would have known you had a break-in." I could feel him examine the room. "Everything looks untouched."

I stared up at him. "The thief only seemed interested in my office."

"That's terrible." He looked at me innocently, but there was nothing innocent about his eyes. "I hope you didn't have too much stolen."

"I'll be fine." I sat up and really looked at him. After a moment, I asked, "Why so interested, Mr. Winters?"

"Just curious and concerned, of course." He tried for a reassuring smile, but it wasn't working for him.

"Why?" I narrowed my eyes. "You don't even know me."

"I would be concerned about anyone who lives in Divinity having someone break in and attack them, Miss Meadows."

"How come? You don't live here."

"Who says I won't someday? One never knows what the future might bring." His eyes took on a sparkle. "Unless they're psychic like you, I suppose." Did he believe I could predict his future, or was he afraid I would discover something and try to shut me up?

Nothing ventured, nothing gained, I thought, and plunged ahead. "And I suppose you'll live here when you buy the inn."

His eyes widened for a moment, and he looked like he was going to act as if he didn't know what I was talking about. But he seemed shrewd enough to know when someone was bluffing or telling the truth. I was onto him, and he knew it.

"That information was supposed to be confidential," he finally responded. "Who told you?"

Realizing I was treading on thin ice, I explained, "Like you said, I *am* psychic, after all, but this really was just an educated guess. I saw you in the café with Brice Benedict and Drew Cummings. I know Mrs. Theodore was thinking about selling the inn because of her financial dilemma and Mr. Benedict was trying to make up for wronging her husband, so I put two and two together. Mr. Benedict said Mr. Cummings was helping him, though I'm really not exactly sure why."

"Lucky guess then," was apparently all Mr. Winters was going to offer. He glanced at his watch. "On second thought, Miss Meadows, I'm going to reschedule. I just remembered there's something I have to do."

"I'll walk you to the door," I said.

"No need. You just rest. I can see myself out." He stood and left with purpose in his every stride.

I sat there confused, wondering what had just happened. Was it something I said? Then I realized he'd left his gloves on the couch. Morty appeared at my feet, jumped on my lap and put his paw on my chest. Mitch had said when Morty had shown up to warn him I was hurt, he was covered in blood. But the next time I saw Morty, there wasn't a speck on his pristine white fur as usual.

I rubbed him behind the ears, and he let me. "I never said thank you, did I, buddy?" I kissed his brow, and he rubbed his head under my chin for a moment. Then he hopped off my lap, stared at the gloves and scratched them, leaving deep grooves along the leather. "Morty!" I set him on the floor. "That was very naughty."

He just blinked at me and walked away.

I sighed, and then frowned. Scratches. The thief who had broken into my house had worn gloves, and Morty had lunged at him. Maybe he was trying to tell me with the scratch marks that Winters was the thief? He had been awful curious about what happened, and he hadn't liked the fact that I knew he was the anonymous buyer. Good thing I hadn't told him everything I'd found out. Like I knew Linda was afraid of him and he knew about something that had gone down. I wished now more than ever that I'd had a chance to read Ronald.

Glancing at the gloves one more time, it dawned on me that maybe it wasn't too late. Taking a few deep breaths to relax, focus, and ground myself, I picked up Ronald Winters' gloves and slipped them on. Closing my eyes, I concentrated. Everything grew dark in my mind's eye, and my world spiraled into tunnel vision.

I saw Ronald Winters years ago as a boy. He was throwing a baseball to a boy about his own age. I could feel the bond between them. They were best friends. They went everywhere together. I saw them on the baseball field at school, at the playground in Mini Central Park, swimming in the river in the woods that led to the lake.

Suddenly they were older in high school. I saw them on the varsity baseball team. It was clear Ronald was the athlete of the two. Then I saw he was the smarter of the two and had even won Student Council President. Ronald was also popular with the girls, but through it all, he remained true to his best friend. Always there for him. Always looking out for him.

Always loyal.

They even went to the same college in New York City. Still best friends. Still doing everything together. And when they graduated, Ron introduced his friend to the woman the friend would eventually marry. Ron was in the wedding and never lost touch even though he moved away for a time, climbing up the ladder of various businesses, honing his skills and becoming ruthless. While his friend never moved away, never accomplished much, and finally took over his family business.

When the time was right, Ron moved back to Divinity. He hooked up with his friend again, the man he had spent his life looking out for and helping. He partnered up with his friend, helping him to turn his family business into a big success. But the friend had changed. He didn't want to share the glory since he finally had something better than Ron. It didn't matter that Ronald was responsible for taking the business to the next level. The friend had found a loophole in the contract and forced Ron out of the company.

Rage.

That one word described how I was feeling at the moment. My body shook with vibration and hatred that Ronald had felt over the betrayal of someone he had loved. He had loved him as a friend, then as a brother, then as a romantic soul mate, even though he knew the feelings weren't reciprocated. Ronald Winters was devastated because the love of his life had broken his heart and stabbed him in the back, ruining everything beyond repair.

And that person was Peirce Theodore.

***

"Sunny, are you okay?" Mitch came running into the house, barreling into the living room and jarring me from my reading.

"Put that thing away," I said, gesturing to his drawn gun.

He holstered his weapon. "I just saw Baldy," he grimaced over starting to sound like me, "or whatever his name's car taking off out of the driveway in a hurry." Mitch shoved a hand through his hair, looking frazzled. "My mind has been so preoccupied with solving this case, I didn't even know he was here. He didn't hurt you, did he?" He frowned when he noticed my hands. "Why do you have those gloves on?"

I pulled the gloves off and set them down. "First of all, I'm fine. Second, Ronald Winters is intimidating, I'll give you that, but I'm not sure he's our killer."

"Who?"

"Baldy's name is Ronald Winters. He showed up and asked for a reading, but I could tell he didn't really take my abilities seriously. He was simply probing me to see what happened in my office. I think he wanted to know what the thief took. Or maybe he's the thief. I'm not really sure."

"You should have called me in here." Mitch started inspecting me all over. "What if he attacked you again?"

"He didn't." I stilled Mitch's hands and made him sit beside me. "I'm fine, really. I knew you were right outside, and Granny was upstairs, and Morty would have let me know if I was in danger."

Mitch blew out a breath and scrubbed his hands over his face. "Okay. So back to the gloves. Why were you wearing them?"

"To see if I could get a reading."

"And did you?" he asked without missing a beat, no sarcasm in sight, just pure honest interest in what I had to say.

It was times like these that made me smile on the inside. We had been through enough things together that Mitch couldn't explain and stopped trying to. He might not outwardly admit he believed in my abilities, yet he always wanted to hear what they were and always followed up on them. A true non-believer wouldn't do that, and that was enough for me.

"Yes, actually. That's what you interrupted when you came running in. I saw Ron as a child all the way through adulthood. I was hoping to see right up to the present, but I doubt I would be able to recreate the reading and keep going now."

"What did you find out?"

"That Ronald Winters was Peirce Theodore's best friend since childhood and all through college. He even fixed him up with Linda. And he was the one who took Divine Inspiration to a whole new level. They were partners for a while. Ronald loved Peirce in all ways possible, that's why he's so angry now."

"What happened?"

"Peirce betrayed him. He fired him, tried to ruin him, and ran him out of town. While Ron had always loved Peirce in a romantic way, Peirce didn't return his affection. He only liked him as a friend, but even that faded over time. I think Peirce resented Ron. He was jealous of him and vowed to one day be the one on top. What I don't get is why Linda Theodore would agree to sell the inn to Ronald Winters, knowing all that."

"That was exactly my question. Maybe it's time we find out."

"We," I said with a smile. "I like the sound of that."

"Did I say we?" Mitch blinked.

"You sure did, and I'm holding you to it."

"I was afraid you were going to say that." He groaned.

Chapter 21

On Thursday morning, Mitch and I went to talk to Linda Theodore. He'd agreed to let me tag along, as promised, but not until the next day. Doc had said one full day of rest, Doctor's orders, and Detective Stone was all about following orders, most of the time. When it came to my well-being...

All of the time.

Divine Inspiration Inn was still crawling with people looking for the treasure like ants swarming a picnic basket, searching for a crumb. Leaves were falling in droves now, the grass growing dormant, and the water on the lake rippling. The rapids in the river down a ways in the woods must be churning something fierce with the way the wind had picked up.

I tightened my sweater coat and was glad I'd chosen leather riding boots and leggings instead of a long flowy skirt and strappy sandals. I sighed. Summer was officially over. Mitch locked the car, looking all business in his jeans, sport coat, and tie. He grabbed my hand and led the way inside.

We passed Frank Lalone who was walking with a limp as he worked on the lights of an outdoor pavilion. He looked like he'd been put through the ringer. Jack Shepard didn't look like he'd fared much better. His hand was bandaged but that didn't stop him from sharpening his garden tools. At least it looked like they had won the battle with the vultures since the guests seem to be giving them a wide berth.

When we stepped inside, things were just as busy. Everywhere you looked, people were having excited conversations while making animated gestures. Sally Clark did her duty and scurried about, keeping the place tip top and watching over the knickknacks like a hawk. I was impressed. Not a single person knocked anything over this time. Probably because of her feather duster ever at the ready.

We headed down the hall to Linda's office and passed by the kitchen on the way. Glancing inside, my gaze locked with Pierre's. His eye was swollen with purple and yellow bruises in various states of fading. For a moment, I saw a flash of resentment and anger directed at me, but when he spotted Detective Stone, he averted his gaze and started chopping celery at a furious pace.

"Those must have been some set of stairs." I looked up at Mitch and saw everything I needed to. He would do anything to protect me. I didn't particularly like fighting, but that hadn't been why I was angry. I understood he needed to make sure Pierre Desjardins never tried to hurt me again. What had frustrated me was the fact that in doing so, he'd put his career in jeopardy. What if Pierre lodged a complaint with Captain Walker? I knew how much being a police officer meant to Mitch, and I would do anything to protect that for him.

As if reading my mind, he responded, "They were." He flexed his fist. "Barely hurts anymore, but don't worry. I'll be more careful next time I go exploring."

"Next time?"

"Exploring can be fun but dangerous. I like exploring. It's a good workout. But have no fear. I only explore when I'm off duty, and what I do in my free time is my business." His gaze locked on Pierre's, but the chef refused to look at him even though Mitch had been speaking loud enough for him to hear.

This time I took Mitch's hand in mine and pulled him after me, far away from trouble. "I don't think you'll be having any more free time so long as I'm around. We have a murder to solve, Detective Stone."

"That we do, Miss Meadows."

Linda Theodore's office was closed. Mitch was about to knock when the door opened. Wendy Statham and Jason Shank walked out.

"You two sure do get around," Mitch said.

"Gotta make a living, Detective." Jason shrugged with a grin. "Do you know how many gigs I've lost out on, Dude? Not to mention my girlfriend misses me."

"I can only imagine," Mitch said. "Unfortunately, it can't be helped. Apologies to your girlfriend. There's still a killer on the loose, *Dude.*"

"Speaking of that, any idea when we can go home, Detective?" Wendy asked. "At this rate I'm not certain I'll have a job at the bakery much longer if I don't get back soon."

"Hopefully not much longer, Ms. Statham." He tipped his head. "Apologies to your family as well."

"My children are grown and my husband is away, so I don't mind. I'm more worried about my job than anything else."

"Blame it on my mother. I'm sure she can fix it. At least you're getting some work around here," I said sympathetically. "I'm curious. What does Mrs. Theodore want from you both?"

"She wants me to make a treasure themed cake, if you can believe it." Wendy smiled while shaking her head.

"And I'm spinning the tunes at the party." Jason winked.

"Party?" Mitch looked at me.

I shrugged. "When in Rome ... if you can't beat 'em, join 'em ... yadda yadda yadda. She's a business woman with an inn to save. I'm sure she's trying to capitalize on the craziness going on around here instead of fighting it."

"That's one word for it," Wendy said. "You two have a good day. If you'll excuse me, I have a cake to *try* to make. I'm not a miracle worker, but I always try to give people what they deserve. That poor woman deserves a lot after her husband was taken from her so senselessly." Wendy tsked.

"Amen to that," Jason said. He didn't come out and say it, but it was clear he—like the rest of the town—blamed that on my mother as well.

And I couldn't blame them. My mother had made herself look guilty in arguing with Peirce and threatening him and being just plain difficult. And I was beginning to worry that this time she'd gone too far and put herself in a situation she couldn't get out of.

"I'm sure you both will do a great job," I said.

"Granny Gert hooked me up with a fully stocked kitchen at her cooking class. She's a gem, that woman. Between her contacts and your mother's referrals, I might not need a job to go back to." She looked at her watch. "Guess I'd better get started. It's a good thing Mrs. Theodore is my only client at the moment. She wants this for tomorrow."

"Hey, wait up." Jason followed Wendy, no doubt networking her to death.

"Linda's husband's barely cold in the ground, and she's already having parties." Mitch shook his head and knocked on her door. "She sure doesn't act like any mourning widow I've ever seen."

A few minutes went by with no sound coming from the other side. I wondered if she was going to answer. Finally, she opened the door, stepping back with a surprised expression on her face.

"Detective Stone? Miss Meadows?" She eyed us warily. "Is there something I can help you with?"

"We would like a minute of your time, if that would be all right." Mitch stood tall, with shoulders straight and hands clasped behind his back. Feet spread shoulder-width apart, even I had to admit he looked intimidating.

"But I already answered both of your questions." Her gaze darted between the two of us, and then down the hall, making me wonder what or who she was looking for.

"Some new information has come to light." I spoke with an easy, friendly tone, trying to put her at ease. "May we come in?"

She stepped back and held the door open. Detective Stone walked inside and sat in a chair across from her desk. I took the seat beside him.

"Am I in trouble?" Linda sat in the chair behind her desk, straightening her calendar, rearranging her pens, fidgeting.

"That remains to be seen." Mitch pulled out a pad of paper and pen. He had a no-nonsense serious expression on his face, screaming interrogation time. The funny thing is he wasn't even trying for intimidating. That was just his nature, which was exactly why he needed me as a consultant, whether he wanted to admit it or not.

"Mrs. Theodore, we don't want to alarm you." I shot Mitch an I've-got-this look.

He just arched a brow, waited a beat, and then sat back.

"Ronald Winters paid me a visit yesterday," I continued.

Linda's jaw fell open as she inhaled deeply. "You know his name?"

"I know many things," I said with a calm, sympathetic tone before dropping a few bombs. "I know Pierre Desjardins is the man you're having an affair with." I held up my hand when she looked ready to deny it. "I also know he convinced you to take out the life insurance policy on your husband."

"And your husband just happened to die soon after," Detective Stone added, then nodded for me to keep going after I sent him a sharp look.

"Pierre didn't kill my husband and neither did I," Linda said vehemently.

"We're not saying you did," I quickly added.

"How do you know all this?" A deep V formed between her eyebrows. Her body language was once again defensive and on edge, thanks to Mitch.

I hesitated, taking a moment to think about my response. I didn't want to say I was eavesdropping outside her office, so I said instead, "I saw and heard things, giving me undisputable proof."

"Ohhh." Her eyes widened. I didn't lie, I just let her assume I meant I'd seen and heard things psychically, which was true in part.

"Mrs. Theodore." I gentled my tone. "If Ronald Winters was your husband's partner and they had a falling out, why on earth would you want to sell to him?"

Her shoulders wilted, and she looked defeated. "At first I didn't know Ron was the anonymous buyer. Mr. Benedict contacted me, apologizing profusely and saying he wanted to make up for everything he'd done. He said he'd gotten involved in something he never should have and couldn't find his way out. I was desperate, so I said yes. Until I found out who the buyer was. When I tried to get out of the deal, Ron wouldn't let me."

"If you hadn't signed yet, how could he stop you?" Mitch frowned.

Linda's face paled. "Ronald Winters is a very powerful man, capable of things you can't even imagine."

I reached across the desk and squeezed her hand. "If you tell us what you know, maybe we can help protect you."

She pulled her hand out from under mine and paused for a long moment, then seemed to make up her mind. "Ronald Winters is behind the bad deal Brice was involved in. He set the whole thing up."

My jaw fell open. "You're kidding?"

"Hardly," she ground out. "Brice is a fool. He had stars in his eyes and thought he could help Peirce and make some money for himself in the process. So he took the money and invested it without Peirce knowing. He knew my husband wouldn't go along with a deal that was questionable in any way, but he thought it sounded good. He just had no clue Ronald Winters was behind it all. Brice never dealt with him at first. He dealt with his partner."

"I'm guessing Ronald was looking to ruin your husband as payback." Mitch made some notes in his notebook.

Linda stared out the window. "We had all been so close once, but Peirce grew jealous of Ron's success. Of always being less than him. Peirce brought Ron into running the inn because he knew he could help him be successful, but then my husband forced him out just as soon as he could and never felt bad about it."

"Wow," was all I could say.

I'd had no idea Peirce could be that cold. Then again there were probably a lot of things about the people in my small town that would shock me. It made a person realize that you never really knew someone completely. I couldn't help but glance at Mitch, who looked at me curiously, but then Mrs. Theodore started speaking again.

"Ronald had been devastated." Linda looked down at her hands. "I felt bad, but what could I do? Peirce wouldn't listen to me." She looked at me. "I just had no idea how much it would change Ronald. He never got over it. I think he's been planning Peirce's ruin for a long time."

"Do you think Ronald Winters killed your husband?" Mitch asked.

"I don't know. There was a time I would argue that was impossible, but the man I've dealt with lately isn't the same man I once knew. He set up the shady deal, got Brice to go along with it, and then took everything from Peirce. Like I said, Brice had no clue Ronald was behind it all either. He'd always dealt with his Ronald's partner. Once the deal went south and Brice lost everything of Peirce's, Ronald came forward and revealed himself."

"Why didn't Brice go to the police?" I asked.

"He was afraid of Ronald. Ron made it clear that going to the police was a bad idea. He'd set the whole thing up on purpose so that Peirce would be vulnerable and would have no choice but to sell to him. Peirce refused, even though we were in trouble financially. Ron even had his *heavy hitter* partner rough him up, but Peirce still held out. I think he would rather die than sell to Ronald."

"That explains the threatening phone calls." Mitch jotted down more notes.

"Peirce tried to keep the whole thing a secret from me, but I'm no fool. I knew something was wrong. After my husband died, I tried to stop the insanity by agreeing to the deal. I finally got it out of Brice who the anonymous buyer was, but by then it was too late."

"What about Drew Cummings the IRS guy? Wasn't he helping Brice?" I asked. "Maybe he can help you, too."

Linda laughed harshly. "Drew Cummings? Oh, he'd like to help me, all right. Straight into an early grave."

Mitch's ears perked up. "What do you mean?"

"You don't get it, do you, Detective Stone?"

"I think I'm starting to. Drew Cummings isn't really IRS is he?"

"No." She looked us both in the eye, and I could see the very real fear she felt. It was the same fear Brice Benedict had shown. Finally, she answered, "He's Ronald Winters heavy hitting partner, and I don't think he's finished yet."

***

"I can't believe they did this to him," I said from Brice Benedict's hospital room later that afternoon.

"We can't prove it was Ronald Winters or Drew Cummings that did this," Mitch said, looking down at Brice who lay in an unconscious heap clinging to life.

"You know as well as I do that they are guilty." Anger surged through me on his behalf. "I told him we could help him. We could keep him safe."

"And I would have tried had he come to me, but he didn't, Sunny." Mitch squeezed my hand. "There's nothing we could have done."

"We can do something now." I turned to him. "We can stop them from doing this to anyone else."

"I have Detective Fuller looking for them now."

"I never should have told Winters that I saw him with Drew and Brice in the café and that Brice had later told me he was trying to help Linda out of her financial troubles with an anonymous buyer." I fought back tears, feeling terrible for my role in this mess. "I could see it in Ronald's eyes. He didn't believe that Brice had kept his secret and he probably wondered what else he'd told me. I'm sure that's what they were trying to beat out of him."

"Or stop him from saying anything more," Mitch pointed out.

"I should have told you everything so you could go after him yesterday. Instead I let you stay home and take care of me." I rubbed my throbbing temples. "Maybe we could have stopped this, Mitch."

"Sunny, listen to me." He took my shoulders and made me look at him. "People like that will find a way no matter what we do. Quit beating yourself up, okay?"

I nodded, but then my eyes sprang wide as I thought of something else. "What about Mrs. Theodore?"

"I've already put an officer at her place. Besides, Winters isn't stupid. He has to know we've discovered what happened to Benedict by now. He isn't likely to go anywhere near the inn anytime soon."

"We have to catch him, Mitch. If he's capable of this, then it stands to reason he's capable of murder."

"We'll get him. We always do." His phone rang and he looked at me as he answered. "Any news?" His lips flattened into a straight line as he listened. "Keep me posted if anything else turns up." He hung up.

"Well?"

"That was Fuller." Mitch scrubbed a hand over his face and then through his hair. "Winters and Cummings both skipped town this morning."

My heart sank. "What are we going to do?"

He thought about that for a moment, and then said with resolve, "Not give up hope. I have connections in other towns." He started to pace. "Hell, I have connections in other states. I'll make some calls. We'll find them."

"What am I supposed to do?"

"Your job." He looked me straight in the eye and said words I never thought I would hear. "See if you can get a read on Winters."

"Yes sir, partner." I smiled slowly, and he just shook his head, but the corner of one lip tipped up ever so slightly.

Finally, after almost a year, he was beginning to take me seriously. "What am I looking for?"

"I don't really know," he said honestly. "Just let me know if you find anything at all. And Tink?"

"Yes?"

"Try not to make more of a mess than usual."

And he's back. "Aye aye, Detective Grumpy Pants."

Chapter 22

"What are you two doing here?" I asked Jo and Zoe Friday morning at Divine Inspiration after locking my car. They had pulled into the parking lot just seconds behind me.

I had figured if Ronald Winters and Peirce Theodore had grown up together, then chances were they had spent a lot of their time here at the inn since Divine Inspiration had been in Peirce's family for generations. It seemed as likely a place as any to get a reading. I had already tried the gloves with no success, not to mention, I wanted to prove to Mitch he was right in asking for my help. And still another part of me needed to check on Linda and make sure she was all right.

"Following you," Zoe said as if that was the most natural comment in the world.

"Your mother called," Jo added by way of explanation.

"Of course she called you two." I rolled my eyes.

"Because she was worried about you," Jo explained with a meaningful tone.

"Oh." That got my attention. She hadn't called to check up on them for once. She had called to check up on me. A warmth I couldn't deny spread through me.

"Your mother said Granny Gert told her you were here," Zoe clarified.

"Which still doesn't explain what you two are doing here." I crossed my arms over my chest and waited.

"I have the morning off." Jo shrugged.

"Me too." Zoe grinned.

"Did you really think we were going to let you have all the fun?" Jo snorted. "I've been dying to go treasure hunting ever since I first heard about the map."

"I'm not here to treasure hunt." I tried to bite back my frustration because I knew they just wanted to help, but this was too important to me. I needed to remain serious and focused and do my job. "I am here to work. I am trying to pick up something about Ronald Winters."

"Who?" Zoe and Jo asked simultaneously.

I took a moment to fill them both in on everything.

"Wow, that's crazy," Jo said.

"So you can both go home now and tell my mother I'm fine."

"Not a chance," Zoe said. "We're here, we're dressed appropriately this time, and we're ready for an adventure."

"And," Jo held up her hand before I could protest, "we're your friends. You guys were there for me when I had a temporary moment of insanity."

"And me when I nearly died of mortification," Zoe added.

"It's time we return the favor. Enough said." Jo swiped her hand through the air as if slamming down a gavel, ending the discussion.

"What favor, dying of mortification?" I asked, trying to be funny. "I've got that covered on a daily basis all by my little lonesome."

"Nice try," Zoe said.

"We're not going anywhere," Jo seconded.

The Amazon Twins stood with arms crossed and feet spread wide apart, in perfectly appropriate fall hiking gear. I couldn't move them if I tried.

"Okay." I eyed their outfits of sweaters, jeans, and boots. "Out of curiosity, how did you know to dress for the outdoors?"

"We already searched the entire inn, so I'm guessing we'll either end up in the secret tunnel or the woods. Either way, I'm all about comfort these days," Jo responded.

"I see you're wearing shoes now." Zoe pointed to my feet.

"I guess I'm all about accepting my fate these days," I replied. "Summer's over and there's a killer on the loose. Let's go see if we can do something about it."

"Sounds like a plan, Boss." Jo grinned.

"Forget Charlie's Angels. I feel like Indiana Jones just sent us on a mission." Zoe giggled.

Jo laughed, and I groaned, thinking of Mitch's last words to me. *Try not to make too much of a mess this time, Tink.*

If he only knew....

***

Hours later, after checking in with the police Mitch had placed at the inn for protection and making sure everyone was safe, we'd searched the grounds for clues with no luck. It didn't help that people were everywhere. Frank and Sally had their hands full, but there was one place I knew the guests weren't allowed. The tunnels.

"Come on." I peeked around the corner into the kitchen. "The coast is clear." Pierre was gone, probably somewhere with Linda.

I darted through his space, careful not to touch a thing. Jo and Zoe followed closely. With one last look around, I opened the door to the root cellar and motioned them through. They quickly made their way down the stairs. I had just stepped inside and closed the door, when I heard Pierre come back into the kitchen. I held a finger to my lips in a *shhhhh* gesture for Jo and Zoe to freeze. We heard some humming, slicing, dicing, and cooking. Sally came in and said something about the lunch crowd. Pierre cursed but finally complied.

"I think I have some in the root cellar," he said.

Oh, Lordy, I thought and swallowed hard, pulling on the door tight to hold it in place. Jo and Zoe stared at me with mouths agape and eyes wide. Pierre tried to open the door. I held it closed. He mumbled another curse and pulled harder. I used every ounce of my strength to keep it firmly shut.

"Mon Dieu, I think it's stuck. Stupid door," he muttered.

I heard him rub his hands together, and I knew he meant to heave all his strength into opening the door. I also knew if he succeeded, we were all mincemeat. He was stronger than I was. Suddenly I felt Jo and Zoe's hands grab hold of mine. I hadn't even heard them move. We all held on together as tight as we could. Pierre pulled with all his might, but the door remained closed. He banged his fist against it once, and then went off in search of Frank for some tools. At least that's what I thought I made out between the curses and French mixed in.

"We only have a few minutes," I said to the girls. "Let's go."

Zoe started to open the door, but I grabbed her hand.

"Not through there," I hissed.

"Then where?" Jo asked.

"Into the tunnels," I replied. "You guys wanted an adventure. Looks like you're going to get one."

We made our way down the stairs in record time and moved the shelf aside just enough to open the door to the secret passageway. We slipped through and then pulled the shelf back before closing the door. I held up my hand for them to freeze once more. We stood silently behind the door and waited.

Seconds later, we heard Pierre and Frank open the door to the root cellar with ease. Frank mumbled something about Pierre having no strength, and Pierre let loose a string of rambling French I was glad I couldn't understand, and said it had been jammed a moment ago. Frank informed him it wasn't now and then he left.

Pierre stormed down the stairs and grew quiet. For a moment I thought maybe he had figured it all out and was ready to open the door and chop us all up, especially when he said, "Aha, there you are." But then it sounded like he pulled something off the shelf and made his way back up the stairs and shut the door.

"Oh my gosh," Zoe said. "That was so exciting."

Jo frowned at her. "And you are such a greenhorn. We nearly died. That is *not* exciting. Right Sunny?"

I let out the breath I had been holding. "I have to agree with Jo on this one."

"Oh, come on," Zoe sputtered. "I'm sure you haven't been through anything this dangerous."

"You have no idea," was all I said, and then I motioned for them to follow me into the tunnel.

"Hey, I just thought of something," Jo said. "We're stuck in here, aren't we? I'm thinking we can't go back the way we came."

"I'm thinking you're right," Zoe said.

"I'm thinking this tunnel has to lead to somewhere," I said. "We searched it before but not all the way to the end. You game?"

"As long as I get back by the happy hour crowd, I'm good to go." Jo nodded once.

Zoe's head bobbed eagerly. "Do you even have to ask?"

I chuckled and motioned for them to follow me. "Let's go."

"But we can barely see anything right here by the door. We'll never be able to see once we're deep in the tunnel." Jo sounded nervous.

"Last time we searched the tunnels, we used an old-fashioned oil lamp." I looked around. "I'm sure it's still here."

We all took a moment to look. I found it next to the wall and pulled out the lighter I used for my candles and incense. I'd packed a few essentials in my fringed knapsack, except I hadn't packed a flashlight. The wick on the lamp was broken.

"I've got an idea," Zoe said. She pulled off her sweater and took off her tank top.

"And how exactly will stripping help us?" Jo asked. "Good grief, Sunny, we've created a monster."

"Funny." Zoe tugged her sweater back over her head. Ripping a board off a shelf by the door, she wrapped her tank top tightly around the wood. "Now pour oil over my shirt."

I did as she complied.

"Viola." She handed it to me. "A torch. Got a light?"

"You're a genius." I laughed and lit the torch, admitting it really did feel like we were on the set of an Indiana Jones movie.

"Why do you think she's my favorite cousin?" Jo chuckled.

"I knew there was a reason I liked her," I said, and we set out on our journey.

***

Hours later we came to a fork in the tunnels and stopped.

"What now?" Zoe sounded as if the appeal of an adventure had worn thin. "I'm tired of walking, and we haven't even found anything."

"Yeah, my feet hurt," Jo chimed in, "and I'm getting hungry. And cold." She rubbed her arms. "What if we never find our way out of here?" They sat down and waited, counting on me for guidance.

I sighed, feeling like a fraud, and then sat down at the fork to lean against the wall. A feeling of déjà vu swept over me. It wasn't strong, but it was enough. "Just hold on, now," I said. "Be still and give me a minute. I think I'm getting something."

They froze.

"I've been here before," I continued, excitement humming through my veins. "Or rather Ronald Winters has."

"What do you see?" Zoe sounded breathless.

I closed my eyes. "Two little boys. The same ones I saw when I read Ronald's gloves. It's him and Peirce." I opened my eyes and surged to my feet. "I know the way." I looked at them. "I seriously know the way. Come on."

"Where are we going?" Jo struggled to her feet with a groan, not sounding half as eager as Zoe.

"We're following them. The boys in my vision." I scurried down the tunnel. "I think they're showing us the way out."

"If I didn't thoroughly trust you, I would think you were cuckoo right now," Jo grumbled, but kept up with my pace like the trooper she was.

We headed to the right of the tunnel and kept walking. It went on for a while and around a bend, then it began to narrow.

"This is freaking me out. It's not that big." Zoe started to hyperventilate.

"It's fine." I handed her a mint leaf from my knapsack. "Chew on this. It will settle your stomach."

"What's in there?" Zoe asked. "Your magic bag of tricks?"

"Something like that." I laughed. "And don't worry. We're okay. The boys used to play in here all the time."

"The boys as in *children*," Jo said. "What if my big ole behind won't fit?"

"It will, and you're not that big yet." Jo's expression had me hastily adding, "Not that you will get big. I mean ... look, we're almost there," I sputtered.

It didn't take much longer when we finally came to the end. It looked like a rock had once covered the opening, but now a bunch of branches with pine needles did. We all started pushing the branches aside, until the opening was clear. I climbed out, and they followed me. We were in the woods. I had no idea where the tunnel had taken us, but we'd gone deep enough to be close to the river. I could hear the sound of rushing water in the distance.

"Where are we?" Zoe asked.

"I'm not sure." I faced them as I bit my bottom lip.

"What now?" Jo questioned.

"I lost the vision."

"Great, and I don't have cell service out here." Jo held her phone at various angles, attempting to find a signal.

"We've come this far, let's head toward the river," I pleaded. "Maybe I'll pick something up again."

"But what if we get lost?" Zoe said. "That tunnel is our only way back to the inn."

"And Pierre Desjardins," I pointed out. "Frankly, I'd rather take my chances with the lions, and tigers, and bears, oh my."

"Bears?" Zoe squeaked.

"Days are getting shorter, ladies." Jo looked around warily. "We'd better get going if we plan to get out of here before dark."

We started walking toward the river. It was a windy day again, but at least the sun was out. A lot of the leaves had fallen but the forest still had a thick canopy of branches and pine trees. The crisp sound of leaves and twigs and pine cones crunched beneath our hiking boots as we trekked through the woods.

"Maybe we should have left a trail," Zoe said.

"And brought a weapon," Jo added.

"Or stayed home," I admitted. "The guys are all going to have a fit, especially Mitch. I wanted to find something useful so badly to help with the case. I'm really sorry. I think I messed up badly this time."

"Nah," Jo said like a true friend, putting my needs before her own and reassuring me. "We'll be fine."

"How can you tell?" I said.

"Because we've got each other." Zoe looped her arm through mine, and Jo followed her lead.

I felt like Dorothy in the Wizard of Oz, and they were counting on me to get us home. Except there was no yellow brick road to follow or Wizard in sight. We were close to the river now. I could smell it in the air, feel the mist increase the humidity. The sound of rapids was getting louder, but so was another sound.

I stopped. "What's that?"

"What's what?" Zoe looked around.

"Don't you hear it?" I asked.

"No." Jo's face grimaced in confusion, and it was clear she was quickly losing patience in me and this whole *adventure*.

"Listen harder," I said.

They did as I instructed, and both their faces went pale.

"Bear?" Jo gulped.

"Maybe," I responded.

"But I thought they hibernated?" Zoe's voice wobbled.

"They do during the winter," I said.

"What do they do in the fall?" Zoe fairly shrieked.

"Fatten up," Jo wailed.

We all started screaming and running as fast as we could, which was probably the worst thing you could do if it really was a bear. Something grabbed me from behind, and I started kicking wildly, thinking this was the end. I had finally messed up so badly, I was going to die. Jo and Zoe turned around, ready to tackle the beast with me.

"I said calm down, Miss Meadows," Jack Shepard shouted into my ear.

Wait. Bears don't talk, I thought. When I stopped thrashing, he set me down. I whirled around and gaped at him, dumbfounded.

"You scared us half to death, Big Guy," Jo said.

"I'd say that makes us even." He tried for some humor to lighten the situation, then frowned and cleared his throat when it didn't work.

"What are you doing out here, Paul Bunyan?" Zoe asked.

"Pierre sent me to catch some fresh fish for dinner," he said. "These guests are killing us all." He held up his empty basket. "I haven't had any luck." He eyed us curiously. "I might ask you all the same thing. What are you ladies doing out here in the middle of the woods? It can be dangerous, you know."

"Trying to find the treasure like before," I answered, not wanting to tell him about Ronald and Pierre. That was official police business that not everyone needed to know about. I looked at the girls, and they picked up on my vibe.

"Any luck?" he asked.

"No more than you," Zoe said.

"I've got some time to kill, and frankly I'm in no hurry to get back to the inn's guests." He shrugged. "I could help if you want. You might need some muscle if you find it, and I know the way back."

"We want," Zoe said, excited once more.

"That sounds like a win-win situation to me," Jo said.

That sounded like we were back on track with Detective Grumpy Pants none the wiser. I held out my hand. "You've got a deal, Mr. Shepard."

Chapter 23

An hour later, we had walked up and down the river with no luck. The wind whipped leaves about, treetops swaying and bending, and the rapids were churning violently, forming foamy white caps.

"Sorry, guys, I'm still not picking anything up," I grumbled, quickly growing tired of our adventure myself. So much for helping Mitch solve this case.

"So, you're really psychic?" Jack came to a stop beside me as we stared out over the wild raging water. He had that doubtful yet hopeful yet wary mix of an expression that most people had when they talked to me about what I did for a living.

"Most of the time I'm psychic." I laughed. "Apparently not much today, though." Jo and Zoe sat a bit further away, leaning against a couple of trees to rest.

"How does that work, anyway?" He threw a rock out into the water.

I shrugged. "It's hard to explain. Sometimes things just come through. Images, feelings, visions. And other times I have to work at it. That's why I use my fortune-telling tools to help tap into my abilities. And yet there are times that if I hold something that belonged to someone, I can pick up a reading of them. That's been useful in helping the police find missing people, among other things."

"What happened with Mr. Theodore?" I could feel his genuine interest. Maybe he wasn't as much of a doubter as I first thought.

"Well, in his case, I used palm reading," I answered. "I saw things about his past and his future, but I was also transported into a vision. That's when I saw the old man on the boat and found out about the past being the link to putting the inn on the map. I had a vision again in the root cellar, and that's when we found the map. And earlier today I had a vision where I saw Mr. Theodore as a child with a friend. That's how I knew which way to go through the tunnels that brought us here."

"So what now?" He studied me so intensely, it was unnerving.

"Well, I lost the connection and haven't been able to pick it up." I sighed and held my palms up. "I'm afraid finding the treasure is a lost cause. It doesn't really matter anyway. Just the thought of a treasure has made the inn a success and put it on the map, so to speak. So for all intense purposes, my vision came true."

"But ... what about the map?" He ran a hand over his beard and shook his head, his ponytail swaying in time with his confusion and agitation.

I could see he was interested in finding the treasure, same as half the town, but he had to accept a lost cause when confronted with all the facts, didn't he?

"It's gone," I responded with a firm tone, hoping to get my point across. "It was taken during the break-in at my house. It was missing a crucial piece anyway." I glanced at the sky and realized it was getting late. "I know you're disappointed. We are too, but we should probably head back now before it gets dark."

A long silence filled the space between us.

"We're not going anywhere," he finally said. He stared out over the river, a muscle in his jaw pulsing.

I blinked. "Excuse me?"

"You're wrong, you know. Finding that treasure *is* important." He stared at me with eyes that looked like they were vacant, if not a little crazy. "It's everything."

"Why?" I didn't understand why this meant so much to him.

"Because I've searched for that treasure my entire life," he growled, sounding so much different form the mild-mannered groundskeeper I had come to know and actually like.

My pulse began to race. "But we only just found out about it." I took a discreet step back, instinctively knowing I needed some distance between us and that raging river.

"No, *you* only found out about it." He took a step toward me.

"Okay, but like I said, my map is gone and it was missing a piece anyway. There's nothing more I can do."

He pulled out my map and the missing section from his back pocket, holding them up before me. "You mean these?"

"You weren't out here fishing. You were treasure hunting." I stared at his bandaged hand and realization dawned. "You're the one who broke into my house. Morty did that to you, didn't he? That was *your* blood on his paw when he went to Detective Stone, wasn't it?"

"Well, well. The little lady really is psychic." He rubbed his bandaged palm. "That cat of yours is a demon."

You have no idea, I thought, but said, "It doesn't take a psychic to figure that out or to see that you're crazy if you think I'm going to help you." I tried to sound brave.

"Oh, I don't *think*, Miss Meadows." He pulled out a gun. "I know."

"Hey, whoa, wait a minute, Big Guy." Jo stood up slowly and joined us. "What's going on here?"

"We've found our thief," I said. "Jack is the one who broke into my house and hit me on the head and stole the map."

Jo and Zoe gasped.

"I don't like hurting women, but you left me with no choice, and I'm not a thief." He held his gun steady on the three of us. "That treasure is rightfully mine."

"I thought you were our savior," Zoe said with a disappointed tone. "And you're delusional if you think that treasure is yours. You worked for Mr. Theodore and that treasure belongs to him and now his widow."

"Wrong. I might have worked for Mr. Theodore, but that was only so I could find what belonged to my ancestors. I've heard stories about the treasure from the time I was a boy, and when I was old enough, the remaining piece of the map was entrusted to me. I am the last in the line of Shepards and won't go to my grave until I make this right." He held his head high and proud, with his beard tightly trimmed and his hair pulled back in a neat ponytail.

All he needed was an eye patch and an earring, and he'd look the part perfectly. Morty's eye-patch of a leaf, his digging in the dirt, and his walking with a limp suddenly made sense.

He'd known who Jack was all along, but I had been too blind to see it.

"I come from a long line of pirates, believe it or not," Jack continued. "My ancestor was running from other pirates and sought refuge with the Theodores, creating the map and burying the treasure. But the Theodores betrayed him, killing him and keeping the bounty for themselves. The Theodores are the real thieves here."

"I hate to break it to you, Captain Jack, but pirates by their very nature are thieves," Jo pointed out. "Savvy?"

"I've waited and searched for decades, only having this one piece of the map," he went on, ignoring her. "I had thought the rest was lost long ago. When you found the rest of the map," he gestured to me, "my hope to discover what was rightfully mine was renewed. I had to have the rest. In all honestly, that map belonged to me as well. So it was just and right that I take back what was mine."

"You really are crazy," Zoe whispered.

"I am not crazy!" Jack shouted, and we all jumped.

"Okay, okay," I held my hands, "take it easy. You're not crazy. Just a little upset, and rightfully so by the sounds of it." I glanced at the other two, hoping they caught my drift.

"Absolutely, I mean I would be upset, too, if I were you," Zoe added, thankfully leaving off the arrrgh I knew she wanted to growl. Jo was bad enough to deal with in a tense situation like this.

"So tell me, mate," Jo said. "If you have the whole map, then you must know where X marks the spot is, and all that jazz. Why do you need us?"

"Because there's nothing there." He looked at me. "I was hoping you would have one of your visions, but you haven't. As I said, I don't like hurting women, but I don't need any loose ends either. I'm thinking you three met an unfortunate demise in the rising river. Or maybe the wolves and bears got to you during the night."

"Honey, if I don't make it back by happy hour, you're gonna have to deal with something much scarier than a wolf or a bear," Jo said.

"Sasquatch," I seconded, nodding. "Trust me, you don't want to deal with her husband when he's all riled up."

"Then I suggest you don't *rile* me." Jack cocked his gun.

"What do you want me to do?" I asked calmly, sensing this teddy bear could turn into a grizzly if provoked.

"Come with me to the cave and see if you can find anything."

"And what if she can't?" Jo asked point blank.

He narrowed his eyes, looking scarier by the minute. "You better pray she does."

"Oh, yeah. He's beyond crazy. The man's downright delusional," Zoe muttered beneath her breath, but I heard her.

Thank God Captain Jack didn't.

***

Hours later we had searched everywhere in a cave at the base of a hill beside the river. Jack had dug countless holes with no luck. He was happy to be our muscle, so long as it served his purpose.

"Where is it?" he growled, growing more and more impatient as the day wore on, his obsession mounting because this was the closest he had come to realizing a lifelong dream. It wouldn't take much to push him over the edge.

"I-I'm trying," I said. "I can't seem to pick up anything in here."

"That's because you're a fraud." He thrust his shovel at me, his gun tucked into the back of his jeans within easy grasp.

I knew what Jo was thinking. If only she'd brought her pistol. She'd had her pistol permit for years, and was one of the best marksman at her gun club. I could see her fingers twitch, itching to get her hands on his weapon.

Sasquatch really was going to kill him if anything bad happened to her or their unborn cub.

I had to do something quick. "Maybe I've been approaching this all wrong," I said. "Maybe the person I need to read is you." I pointed to Jack. "You're related to the creator of the map, after all."

He stilled, and I could see his brain working overtime. Finally, he nodded. "You two." He pointed to Jo and Zoe. "Keep digging." He tossed his shovel at them and faced me. "This had better work."

"I'll try my best," I responded and then looked around.

The cave was deep and dark and cold. We had left our torch in the tunnel, but Jack was prepared. He had brought along matches and knew his way around starting a fire. He'd lit the fire pit he'd created the last time he'd been here, right after he'd stolen the map from me and had searched for the treasure on his own. Light and warmth had flooded the immediate area. Further out was a bit creepy and chilly, but it would keep my friends safe.

"Over here," I said, choosing a spot.

He sat where I told him to. "Now what?"

"Well, since I don't have any of my tools with me," because you ruined them all, I wanted to say, "I will have to read your palms."

"Whatever," he said, "just make sure it works."

"You'll have to unbandage your hand."

He did as I requested, and I bit back a gasp. Morty had done a number on him, even through the gloves he had worn when he'd broken into my house. Red scratches that looked bone deep had sliced across the back of his hand. The same hand that had hit me on the head, I realized. It looked like he needed stitches, but he probably didn't want to raise any red flags so he obviously hadn't gone. Morty was my real savior. My heart softened just thinking about him, but I had a job to do now.

Inhaling a deep breath, I told Jack to hold his hands out, and he complied. I took his hands in mine to study his palms, but I didn't have to. Immediately upon touching his hands, I was transported back in time.

"He's coming," I said again, picking up where Peirce's reading had left off. "I am once again in the body of the old man. I'm at the root cellar and then traveling through the tunnels, dodging bats and swiping away cobwebs, my wooden leg thumping along painfully. Finally I emerge where the girls and I did this morning. I feel frantic and exhausted, looking for a place to hide my bounty.

It feels like I have traveled for hours. I'm thirsty, and tired, and my leg hurts above the wooden peg I've been cursed with for many years. This life is harsh. I always knew it would catch up with me one day, but everything I do is for my family and the future Shepards so that they won't waste their lives searching for more. Searching for something more leads to an unsatisfied life where nothing is ever good enough.

I see the perfect spot. A cave in the side of a hill by the river. I will bury my treasure here and leave a map where my loved ones can find it. I make my way inside the cave and sit my weary body down and pull out parchment paper. Drawing out the treasure map, a sense of peace comes over me. But the peace is short-lived.

He's here.

I scramble to my feet. No, it's not fair. I didn't have enough time to finish my quest. He's found me. He knocks me to the ground, takes my treasure, and rips the map from my hands. I am so weak. I cannot fight back. With one final blow, I start to lose consciousness and know this is the end. I will die here, and my family will do without. I have failed them all. As the breath leaves my lungs for the last time, I stare at my enemy, my killer . . .

My brother."

"No!" Jack yanked his hands from mine.

I jerked back to the present, wiping away the tears that were streaming down my face. Every time I did a reading, I became the person in my vision, experiencing all of their emotions. Frustration, pain, and betrayal of the worst kind had been the last feelings Jack Shepard's ancestor had felt.

"I'm so sorry," was all I could say.

"You lie. It's all a lie." Jack surged to his feet, pain and anguish showering his face. "My ancestor's brother could not have stolen the treasure and killed him. It is written that he was so overcome with grief, he moved away and no one ever saw him again."

"It's true. He stole the treasure, killed his brother, buried the map and ripped off a piece of it as a clue to give you all as false hope. Then he ran off with the goods, never to be seen or heard from again. The Theodores didn't wrong your ancestor or you. Your ancestor's brother did. I felt it all. His pain, his anger, his sadness … in the worst betrayal imaginable, hence the life of a pirate. I really am so sorry."

"You're sorry, all right. You're going to be more than sorry by the time I'm done with you. How could you lie to me like that? You're no psychic. You're a sick and twisted fraud who prays on the emotions of the vulnerable. I won't let you win." He lunged at me, and I screamed for all I was worth, rolling to the side just in time.

"Not so fast, Captain Jack," Jo ground out and cocked his gun. She'd snuck up behind him while he was in an emotionally enraged state and distracted.

He had face-planted into a rock, then rolled over, looking startled. He reached for the back of his pants. "My gun."

"That's right, Coco Loco," Zoe said, holding the shovel like a weapon. "Now someone's finally starting to make some sense. I'm thinking you were right all along. You're not crazy, you're just stupid."

I joined the girls, standing three strong over him while he lay flat on his back, looking floored. "I'm sorry, Mr. Shepard, but you're the one who is wrong. You have been living a lie your entire life. Your ancestor risked everything to stop the next generation from throwing their lives away in wanting something more. And you, my friend, sadly did exactly that. You're no better than his brother."

"Women or not, I will kill you all," Jack ground out.

"Like you did Peirce Theodore?" Zoe stated.

"I have hated the Theodores my entire life, but I didn't kill Peirce."

"Save it for the judge," Jo said. "If you're still alive that is. If I miss happy hour, I'll kill you myself."

Chapter 24

"Thank you," my mother said with rare emotion lacing her voice as she hugged me—actually wrapped her arms around me and hugged me hard—the next morning at the Divinity Hotel.

"You're welcome." I hugged her back tightly, trying to show her what I never seemed to be able to say. After a moment of just standing there in an embrace and slowly rocking back and forth, we broke apart. "I didn't do it alone, of course."

"Well, of course not, darling. Everyone knows that. You couldn't have done anything without Joanne and Zoe's help. Those two are such gems. You'd do well to hang onto them." My mother brushed imaginary lint off her perfect suit coat, looking more like the mother I knew and admittedly loved.

I let out a little chuckle and just shook my head. I knew the truth about how she really felt, and that was enough. "Oh, don't you worry. They aren't going anywhere. Not to mention I have Mitch in my corner."

"Ah, yes, Detective Stone." My father stepped forward and shook his hand. "I'm counting on you to take care of our girl. We owe you a debt of gratitude for arresting that scoundrel. To think the groundskeeper almost got away with murder and sent my lovely Vivian to prison." He shuddered. "I fear this old heart wouldn't have been able to handle that."

"All I did was arrest him. Your daughter and her friends are the ones who brought him out of the woods, proving they are more than capable of taking care of themselves." Mitch squeezed my hand. "I'm very proud of her. In fact, I couldn't have solved this case without her help."

And this is why I love him, I thought. He always had my back. I smiled up at him, trying to show my gratitude, and he winked.

"What happens now?" Granny Gert asked, passing around a tray of celebratory cookies in red, white and blue, in the name of truth and justice for all. Or at least that is what she'd said with a *boys oh day* thrown in to boot.

"Now we head into the station and finish the paperwork to clear your daughter's name." Mitch looked at Vivian. "You, Mrs. Meadows, are a free woman."

My mother inhaled a discreet but noticeably deep breath, and my father slipped his arm around her, giving her a gentle squeeze of support. My father smiled at Chuck Webb in thanks for putting up with them. Chuck nodded to my father, ignored my mother, and crossed their name out of his register with obvious glee.

"There you two are," Mitch said as Wendy Statham and Jason Shank brought their things to the front desk to check out. "I just wanted to let you both know you're all set. I cleared it with the captain. You can leave town any time now, and I thank you both for your patience and cooperation during this investigation."

"No problem, dude," Jason said. "It wasn't so bad. I made some new contacts, and that's always a good thing." He nodded at Wendy. "Keep in touch." He picked up his suitcase, waved to the rest of us, and headed out the door.

"Are you sure we can't convince you to stay," Granny Gert said to Wendy. "Between your cakes and my cookies, we could rule this pop stand."

Wendy smiled fondly at Granny. "As tempting as that is, I need to get back to my life. I still have so much to do. But if I find out I don't have a job left back in the city, I just might take you up on your offer. Thank you so much for all your help in finding me a place to work while I was here." She hugged her.

"Don't you worry about your job," my mother said. "I know your boss well. And I will definitely be recommending you and Mr. Shank to everyone I know."

"I don't know what to say," Wendy said, emotion clogging her throat. "How will I ever pay you back?"

"I'm sure you'll find a way." My mother winked.

"I'll certainly try." Wendy nodded, waved to us all, and then left the hotel.

We grabbed our things and followed Mitch to the police station. The sooner my hunky detective cleared my mother's name, the sooner they would leave, the sooner we could get on with our lives...

The sooner I could propose.

***

Later that day I sat on the back enclosed sun porch with Mitch, watching the sun sink lower in the sky, reflecting various shades of red, gold, orange, and yellow. He'd built this addition soon after moving in, and it had become a favorite spot of ours. Morty refused to enter this area of the house, probably because he knew it belonged to Mitch, which was fine by me. I was just glad Mitch had begun to put his stamp on this place so he could start to feel like it was home. Soon the sun would set and night would be upon us. There wasn't a cloud in sight. I knew the stars would be sparkling bright in an inky sky.

The perfect setting to propose.

"What's on your mind?" Mitch slipped his arm around me as we rocked in the porch swing.

"Listen."

"I don't hear anything."

"That's the point. The sound of silence." I sighed dreamily. "It has never sounded so good."

"No Morty, no Granny, no drama ... I have to say I agree with you." He chuckled, and I snuggled into him.

"I know it hasn't been easy for you, giving up everything and moving in with me." I looked up at him and stared deeply into his dark, stormy eyes. "I hope you know how much it means to me. How much *you* mean to me."

"I do," he said.

It was a sign.

If I didn't jump in with both feet and propose now, I probably wouldn't get up the courage again. "You know I love you, right?"

He drew his brows together curiously, his lips tipping up slightly. "Yes." He lowered his head and kissed me softly. "I hope you know I love you, too."

"I do," I said.

"Good." He pulled me onto his lap and started tipping me back into the cushions. "Now that we've settled that, how about I show you just how much."

I rested my hands on his chest to halt him. "As much as I would love to take you up on that, there's something I want to ask you."

He groaned, pressing his forehead against mine. "You're killing me, Tink." He squeezed his eyes shut for a moment, and then sat back up. "Shoot," he said.

And just like that, with one simple word as the trigger, I was hit with a vision.

My parents had said their goodbyes and insisted on taking a cab to the airport. It had been easier to agree than to try to change their minds. I could see them sitting in the back seat of a cab, but I couldn't see the driver through the divider. They were talking to each other about their plans for the future, when my father paused and looked out the window.

He told the driver this was the wrong way to the airport. The driver ignored him and kept driving. My mother insisted the driver stop at once, but the driver refused. I could feel their fear as the driver kept going on an unknown route with an obvious agenda. Finally the cab pulled off onto an old dirt road into the woods. I recognized the area. It was out beyond the inn. The cab finally stopped, the driver got out, and pulled out a gun.

"No!" I yelled.

"Sunny." Mitch shook me gently, snapping me back to the present. He looked in my eyes with alarm. "What's wrong?"

"We have to go now." I stared at him with a haunted gaze.

"Where?"

"Back to the woods behind the inn," I said with certainty, jumping up and racing to the foyer and grabbing my coat.

"Why?" he asked, following my lead while grabbing his coat and badge and gun along the way.

I stopped at the door, took a shaky breath, and turned to him. "Because the killer's still out there. My parents are about to die, and I know who's going to pull the trigger."

***

I crept through the woods, trying not to make any noise, with Mitch hot on my heels. He'd only agreed to let me lead the way because I knew where I was going. The girls and I had come this way when we walked out of the woods, holding Jack at gunpoint. He'd led us to the old dirt road which was a direct path back to the inn.

We'd already passed the cab. The sun had nearly set, the amber glow of daylight still lighting the way, but soon it would be cold and dark. We needed to hurry to keep the advantage. A gut feeling made me veer off the path near the rapids. I swallowed, my throat going dry, thinking about my parents being executed and their bodies being dumped into the raging river. With the ragged rocks, there would be nothing left of them by the time they were found.

We heard voices.

I motioned for Mitch to keep quiet and I led the way to a group of trees. We hid behind them and peeked through the branches. Wendy Statham looked like a wild woman. Her blond hair hanging loose and tangled, her makeup streaked as if she'd been crying, and her eyes tinged with a wildness she couldn't hide. She held a handgun pointed directly at my mother. My parents were on their knees with their hands in the air.

"I don't understand." My mother sounded weak and vulnerable, which broke my heart. "I was going to recommend you. I thought we were friends."

"We're not friends," Wendy hissed. "I've hated you for so long now."

"You don't have to do this." My father used a rational tone, but I could see the fear in his eyes. "There's still time to change your mind. We'll get on our plane and leave town and not say anything about this to anyone. You have my word."

"And you have *my* word, you won't see another sunrise," Wendy growled.

"What did I ever do to you?" my mother asked.

"You ruined my life."

"How? I don't even know you."

"Ah, but you knew my husband."

"What are you talking about?" My mother shook her head in confusion. "I don't know anyone by the name of Statham."

"That's because he has a different name than I do." Wendy's face hardened. "My husband's name is Mike Herwood."

I could see my mother's skin pale even from this far away. Mitch was trying to get a clear shot of Wendy, but she kept moving and trees kept blocking his view.

"You put him away. Got him locked up for years," Wendy continued.

"He robbed a bank," my mother said carefully. "Legally I had no choice. It had nothing to do with you."

"It had everything to do with me!" Wendy shouted. "I had to raise four children by myself. Do you know what that's like? I had to change my name to my maiden name just to get a job.

No one wanted to hire the wife of a bank robber. You took my identity away from me. You took my husband. You took my future. I have worked myself to the bone in order to make ends meet."

It suddenly dawned on me. That's why Morty had jumped on the cake and bit the head off my mother, trying to clue me in that she was in danger from the guy on trial—or rather, his wife, aka Cake Lady. And then later when he'd peeked through the gazebo bars, looking like he was in jail. Once again he'd been trying to tell me something all along, and as usual I had missed the clues.

"Why kill Peirce Theodore?" my father said, drawing me back to the scene unfolding before me. "He didn't have anything to do with any of this."

"There are always casualties of war," Wendy said, looking even crazier in that she truly believed she was justified for doing everything she'd done. "I have waited years for the opportunity to kill your wife. When I heard Cake Masters was going to make the cake for the West wedding and that Vivian would be there, I volunteered to bring the cake myself."

"You can bet you won't have a job for sure now," my mother said while looking down her nose.

She would never learn, I thought, and mentally begged her with my eyes to just stop talking. It had been her mouth that got her into trouble in the first place.

"Wendy laughed. Do you think I care? It was never about the job. I planned on killing you while I was here and then skipping town. But another opportunity presented itself. I saw how much you despised Mr. Theodore. After you threatened him, it dawned on me that killing you would be too easy. You need to suffer like my husband has for the past fifteen years. I knew if I framed you for murder, you would go to prison for life. And you, Mr. Meadows, would know exactly how I feel."

"That's just crazy talk. The truth always comes out. You would be caught eventually. Maybe there's another way. A better way," my father tried to reason with her once more. "Maybe we can talk to a judge and get your husband out."

"Someone has to be punished for the years he's suffered, and I don't trust the justice system. I have learned over the years that if you want real justice, you have to take it for yourself. So I cut the tent, killed Peirce, and shoved Vivian over him. I didn't count on so many other people in this town looking guilty. I had to resort to things like when I poisoned Granny Gert and Fiona's food, hoping to cast even more blame on Vivian, showing more proof of how desperate she gets when jealous."

My mother gasped and then harrumphed.

"You made it clear you didn't like being left out, and you always think you can do a better job than others," Wendy went on. "Crazy Jack Shepard had to go and ruin it all with his obsession for finding the treasure. If it wasn't for that meddling daughter of yours, everything would have worked out perfectly. But no, she had to go and clear your name. I couldn't let you get off that easy. What would be the justice in that? So it's back to plan A: kill Vivian. Killing you, Mr. Meadows, is simply another casualty that can't be avoided."

Wendy raised her gun, aiming it at Vivian and cocking it. Her finger was on the trigger, ready to squeeze, when Mitch jumped into action. He finally got a clear shot and pulled the trigger. Wendy's arm jerked and she fell backwards, but not before her gun went off. My father screamed, *No*, and threw himself in front of my mother.

I ran over to my parents, while Mitch charged Wendy, but not quite fast enough.

"Hold it, Detective. Take another step and I will gladly make you another casualty," Wendy said, on her feet again with a bloody arm still firmly clutching her gun. "Now, drop your weapon and join the others."

Mitch's jaw clenched and unclenched, but he dropped his gun and slowly made his way over to us. My father was unconscious but still alive. The bullet went through his side, but his pulse was still strong, giving me hope. My mother sobbed quietly, stroking his head and telling him how much she loved him. I felt so helpless. In trying to help my mother clear her name, I had probably just gotten us all killed.

"I think I've had enough fun for one day," Wendy said. "Get up, Vivian."

My mother froze with fear.

"Take me instead," I blurted. "She will suffer more that way."

Mitch stared at me, his expression saying, *That's not going to happen, Tink*. But I didn't know what else to do. I had to do something.

Wendy seemed to think about that for a moment, but then she shook her head. "No, I want you all to know why I did this. Maybe then you will understand when you see what it feels like to lose someone you love."

"But your husband is still alive," my mother said.

"He might as well be dead," Wendy responded. "And it's all your fault. It's time you met your punishment so justice can finally be served. Now get up and come to me."

"Mom, no." I grabbed her arm, my throat working overtime. I might lose my father. I couldn't lose her, too.

She held my hand with a firm grip. "It's okay, Sunny." She called me by my chosen name instead of Sylvia, letting me know she had truly accepted me for who I was.

That only made my cry harder. "Mom, please," I whispered through my tears.

"I love you, too, darling. Take care of your father." My mother peeled my hand from hers and stood. She made her way over to Wendy, standing tall and brave before her. "Is this what you want? I hope you gain some satisfaction from ruining the lives of so many people."

"Justice will be served," Wendy said.

"You're right. Justice *will* be served when you meet your maker," my mother said, "and you will be damned for all eternity."

"Not before you," Wendy spat and raised her gun, pointing it directly at my mother's face.

My mother kept her eyes open and refused to look away from Wendy's gaze. I was so proud of her, not sure I could have done that. Wendy faltered for just a second. And a second was all that was needed.

Morty appeared out of nowhere, leaping from a tree like a glowing mass of scary vengeance as he attacked Wendy. She shrieked and dropped the gun, while my mother fell to the ground in an emotional, exhausted heap.

Mitch sprang into action, grabbing his gun and hers as he stood above her. "Thanks, pal, I'll take it from here," he said to Morty, and called the crime in on his cell phone.

Wendy cowered in fear. "Please, someone help me. Call off that demon," she begged. "He's not normal."

Morty's eyes were jet black and eerie as he drew back his lips, exposing his razor sharp fangs for one final hiss. Then he walked over to my mother who sat on the ground, shaking, her eyes looking dazed and in shock. He climbed onto her lap. Her eyes widened a fraction, and she was frozen with fear. Then he did the most remarkable thing. He licked her cheek. She sucked in a breath and blinked at him, then fainted dead away.

Hissing laughter filled the air as Morty disappeared into the woods once more.

Epilogue

One week later, things were finally settling down. My father had been released from the hospital and feeling much better. My parents had actually come to my house to say their goodbyes, and my mother didn't even flinch when Morty entered the room. Their gazes met and something passed between them. A silent thank you, maybe? I wasn't quite sure, but whatever it was, Morty seemed pleased and he left her alone, much to my shock. My parents even let Mitch and I drive them to the airport where we stayed and watched as their plane took off, taking them back to their lives in New York City.

Jo and Cole went on their honeymoon to Hawaii where she phoned home that she was having twins. It finally made sense why her tummy was growing so quickly. Cole was more terrified than ever, but he refused to leave her side. Meanwhile, Sean and Zoe were playing house as they watched over Biff and ran Smokey Jo's while the newlyweds were gone.

Brice Benedict was out of the hospital and still had to answer for unlawfully investing Peirce Theodore's money, but at least he was safe. Ronald Winters and his partner Scary Guy had been found and arrested for assault as well as a number of other charges. Jack Shepard was still in jail for robbery, assault, and kidnapping. He was having a psychiatric evaluation. Linda Theodore and Pierre Desjardins sold the inn for a substantial sum and ran away together. While Sally Clark and Frank Lalone decided to stay on with the new owners.

All was right in my world.

Mitch and I were back on the sun porch, relaxing in lounge wear, and enjoying our quiet, peaceful existence. It was time. I turned to him and said, "Do you remember when I said I wanted to ask you a question?"

"Yes." He nodded while staring intensely into my eyes. "In fact, there's something I've been meaning to ask you, too."

"Ladies first?" I asked, not wanting any more time to go by before I told him how I really felt.

"Sure." He looked as nervous as I was and relieved to have a moment before he had to pose his question.

I turned to face him on the porch swing and took his hands in mine, resisting the urge to read his Fate Line. And then I talked as fast as I could, spewing everything I wanted to say before I chickened out. "We've known each other for almost a year now. You've come to mean so much to me, Mitchell Stone. I love how you make me feel so special and protected and loved. And I couldn't love you more if I tried. I can't imagine my life without you. You're my rock. You're my everything. Please say you'll be my husband?"

His jaw fell open and he just stared at me. I was terrified he was going to say no. I pulled my hands from his, bit my bottom lip, and sat back on the couch. I couldn't look him in the eye, feeling like a fool.

He dropped to his knees on the floor in front of me and faced me. Tipping my chin up, he said, "Look at me, Tink."

I blinked back tears and did as he asked. "It's okay if you don't want to. I mean, I said no to you when you asked me. I never should have done that, by the way, because I have regretted it every day. I just wanted you to be sure you could handle loving me and all that goes along with that. It's all good, we can still live together. Just forget I ever said anything." I tried for a smile, but my wobbling lips wouldn't comply.

"No," he said.

My lips wobbled more furiously now. "I ruined everything, didn't I?"

"No, you didn't. I meant no I don't just want to simply live with you, baby. I was sure about marrying you when I asked you the first time, and I'm even more sure now." He pulled a ring from his pocket. "Why do you think I've been trying to get the courage up to ask you again? But like always, you manage to beat me to the punch." He chuckled. "Frankly, I wouldn't have it any other way. I can't live without you, either. I love you so damn much. *All* of you, including that crazy cat of yours."

"Are you serious?" I blinked furiously, and tears streamed down my cheeks now, but I didn't care. His words were music to my ears.

"I've never been more serious." He wiped the tears away with his thumbs, then opened the ring box. "Sunshine Meadows, will you do me the honor of becoming my wife?"

I grinned wide, pretending to ponder his question, then I said, "Well, Detective Grumpy Pants, I do believe I asked you first."

"Technically I did months ago, Tink." He arched a thick black brow.

"Tell you what. How about we compromise and answer together," I said.

"Deal. On three?" He started to count.

I shouted, "Yes!" and threw myself at him before he'd hit the number two. Laughing with pure joy, he managed to slip the ring on my finger and then wrap his strong arms around me and kiss me soundly on the lips until he had me saying yes to so much more. I had everything I ever wanted and felt like my life was just beginning.

Suddenly I tore my lips from his and sucked in a sharp breath. My life wasn't beginning. It was officially over.

"What's wrong?" he asked, concern creasing his forehead. "Another vision?"

I nodded and swallowed hard on a groan. "And this one's so much worse than the other one." My life wasn't perfect. It was about to get turned completely upside down.

"Who's in trouble? Should I get my gun?" He tensed, ready for flight.

"We are," I wailed. "We're in trouble, and yes, please shoot me now."

He relaxed a little and eyed me suspiciously. "How exactly are we in trouble?"

I looked at him with doom. "My parents are retiring."

"And how does that affect us?" he asked on a soft chuckle.

"Because they're coming to Divinity."

That made him grow sober. "Oh, how come? I thought they hated it here."

"I'm pretty sure the Amazon Twins must have told them I was going to propose to you."

"Or that I was going to propose to you," he said dryly. "I told them, too."

"No wonder they wouldn't answer my calls. They probably had bets on who would ask first. Just wait until I see them again. I'll—"

"Throttle them, I know. And I'll gladly help you, but can we get back to your parents please?"

"I clearly saw them in Divinity."

"Well maybe that just means they will visit us. Maybe they won't stay long, and then they'll travel. It won't be so bad."

"Oh, no. It will be worse than bad. They're not just coming to visit." I took a breath and said with dread, "Donald and Vivian Meadows are the proud new owners of Divine Inspiration. They are here to stay. Still want to marry me?"

The End

Coming Soon!
Hazard in the Horoscope (a Sunny Meadows Mystery) - NOVEL - September 2015

ABOUT THE AUTHOR

Photo by Kari Lee Townsend

National Bestselling Author, Agatha, RT Reviewers Choice & Golden Duck Award Nominee. Kari Lee Townsend lives in central New York with her very understanding husband, her three busy boys, and her oh-so-dramatic daughter. A former teacher with a master's in English education, she is a long-time lover of reading and writing. She is best known as the author of the Fortune Teller Mystery series but also writes women's fiction and romance (under the name Kari Lee Harmon), as well as children's fiction about tween superheroes. These days you'll find her at home happily writing her next novel and still trying to find out whodunit.

ALSO BY AUTHOR

Books by Kari Lee Harmon

Romances
DESTINY WEARS SPURS
PROJECT PRODUCE

Women's Fiction
Comfort Club Series:
SLEEPING IN THE MIDDLE

Lake House Treasures Series:
THE BEGINNING
AMBER
MEGHAN
BROOK
THE COLLECTION (Amber, Meghan, Brook)

Shorts Stories
LOVE LESSONS
SPURRED BY FATE

Merry Scrooge-mas Series:
NAUGHTY OR NICE
SLEIGH BELLS RING
JINGLE ALL THE WAY

Books by Kari Lee Townsend

Cozy Mysteries

A Fortune Teller Mystery:
TEMPEST IN THE TEA LEAVES
CORPSE IN THE CRYSTAL BALL
TROUBLE IN THE TAROT

A Sunny Meadows Mystery:
PERISH IN THE PALM

Soft-Boiled Mysteries
KICKING THE HABIT
PERIL FOR YOUR THOUGHTS

Short Story Mysteries
SHENANIGANS IN THE SHADOWS (a Sunny Meadows
Mystery)

Middle Grade
Digital Diva Series:
TALK TO THE HAND (Book 1)
RISE OF THE PHENOTEENS (Book 2)

RECIPES

Gran's Orange French Lace Cookies

2 cups blanched sliced almonds (thinly sliced)
1 cup all purpose-flour
1/3 cup light brown sugar
¼ lb (1 stick) unsalted butter
1/3 cup light corn syrup
2 tbsp frozen orange juice concentrate, (let soften)
1 tspn vanilla extract
1 tspns orange zest

~Preheat oven to 375 degrees. Line 2 cookie sheet pans with parchment paper. On a third and unlined cookie sheet, spread the almonds out evenly, toasting for 5-10 minutes. Be sure to turn the almonds once until lightly browned on both sides. Place 1 cup of the toasted almonds into a food processor and chop coarsely (saving the rest for later). Mix the chopped almonds and flour together and then set aside.

Mix butter, brown sugar, corn syrup, vanilla, orange juice concentrate, and orange zest in a sauce pan and bring to a boil on medium heat. Remove pan from heat and slowly whisk in your flour mixture until completely combined. Add in reserved toasted almonds.

Using a spoon, drop a 1 ½ inch wide spoonfuls of mixture onto the parchment lined cookie sheets. Space them 2 inches apart (fitting 8-10 cookies on each pan). Bake for 7-9 minutes (turning the cookie sheet to brown cookies evenly) until edges of cookies are golden brown. Let cool and enjoy!

Granny's Butterballs

1 ½ cups butter (Granny uses unsalted)
¼ tspn salt
¾ cup powdered sugar (½ cup extra to roll cookies in)
1 ½ cups ground pecans, almonds, or walnuts (Granny uses all three)
1 tspn almond extract
4 tspns vanilla extract
3 cups flour

~Preheat oven to 325 degrees. Cream butter with salt and powdered sugar. Beat with mixer until texture is fluffy. Add almond and vanilla extracts to mixture. Grind nuts using a food processor, or blender, or magic bullet. Add nuts to mixture. Add flour and mix well. Roll mixture into small balls and arrange on ungreased cookie sheets. Bake for 12 to 15 minutes. Roll balls in extra sugar when warm. Roll balls in more sugar after they cool. Enjoy!

Granny Chip Delight

1 cup chocolate chips
1 cup white chocolate chips
1 cup peanut butter chips (or whatever flavor chips you want)
1 can of Chinese noodles
1 jar of peanuts or nuts of your choice. Coconut is also delish.
    (Granny uses unsalted or omit if you have an allergy)

~Melt chips double-boiler style. Add the rest of the ingredients and mix well. Drop teaspoonfuls onto wax paper and let cool. Enjoy!

Gran's Viennese Iced Coffee

6 (1 ounce) shots of decaf or regular espresso
3 tbsp sugar
1 tspn pure vanilla extract
¼ cup of hot water
2 cups of ice
4 yummy scoops of vanilla or coffee flavored ice cream or
    frozen yogurt
Unsweetened cocoa powder

Combine the espresso, sugar, vanilla and hot water in a blender
and mix until the sugar dissolves. Add ice and mix on high until
mixture is smooth. Divide up in 4-6 short glasses.

Place ice cream or frozen yogurt into microwave for 15
seconds (until soft, not melted). Add one scoop of ice cream or
frozen yogurt to each glass and then sprinkle with cocoa
powder. Serve with a straw or spoon and enjoy!

Apple Pie Ala Gran

Golden Brown Foolproof Crust:

1 cup shortening (Granny likes butter flavored Crisco)
2 cups flour
1 tspn salt
1 tbspn vinegar
1/3 cup milk

~Preheat oven to 450 degrees. Mix flour with salt. Cut shortening into flour mixture. Pour vinegar into milk to make sour milk. Combine sour milk with flour mixture. Add a bit more flour to need into a ball. Cut into 2 balls (one for the bottom crust and one for the top). 1 pie = 2 crusts. Roll out bottom crust and press into pie pan.

Apple Pie Filling:

3 cups heaping apples (Granny likes Macintosh, sliced super thin)
1 cup sugar
1 tspn cinnamon
¼ tspn nutmeg
2 tbspns flour
1 tbspn butter (can use unsalted, but Granny uses salted butter for her pies)

~Place apples in a bowl. In a separate bowl combine sugar, flour, cinnamon, and nutmeg. Mix well and then pour over apple mixture. Pour pie filling into bottom crust. Break up butter and place on top of pie filling. Roll out top crust and place on top of pie, sealing the edges with a fork. Make slits in top of crust. Brush milk generously all over the top of crust. Bake on 450 degrees for 10 minutes, then lower temperature to 350 degrees and bake for another 50 minutes. Enjoy with vanilla ice cream or sharp cheddar cheese!

Granny's Banana Cakes

3 large bananas
¾ cup sugar
1 egg
½ tspn salt
1 tspn baking soda
1 tspn baking powder
1 ½ cup flour
½ cup oil
1 cup mini chocolate chips

~Preheat oven to 375 degrees. Mash the bananas, mix in the sugar, followed by the egg (slightly beaten), then the salt, soda, and powder. Next mix in the flour, stir in the oil, and stir in the chocolate chips. Nuts are also delish if desired. Bake for 20 minutes and enjoy!